THE LAST VALENTINE

A LABYRINTH OF LOVE LETTERS NOVEL

FELIX ALEXANDER

Book cover design by Burak Gökhan ÜLKER

Photograph is under copyright and all rights reserved.

Printed in the United States of America

FELIX ALEXANDER OFFICIAL WEBSITE
FELIX ALEXANDER ON FACEBOOK
FELIX ALEXANDER ON TWITTER
FELIX ALEXANDER ON INSTAGRAM
FELIX ALEXANDER'S BLOG ON WORDPRESS
FELIX ALEXANDER ON GOODREADS
FELIX ALEXANDER ON AUTHORS DATABASE
SUBSCRIBE NOW FOR NEW RELEASE NEWS
(YOUR EMAIL AND INFO WILL NOT BE SOLD TO THIRD PARTIES)

THE LAST VALENTINE

A LABYRINTH OF LOVE LETTERS NOVEL

Praise for Felix Alexander's
The Last Valentine

"The writing style of Felix Alexander has something special
that kept me reading the book."
~Navika, Szebrabooks Reviews/Germany

"I always thought the French and the Italians knew about the
intricacies of love. Now I know it is the Spanish too. Felix
Alexander is in love with love. There is no way to read his
words without falling in love with love!"
~Amazon Customer Reviews

"The Last Valentine is an ode to love and romance.
From the passionate one to the possessive one,
the obsessive one; the love born of patience and understanding,
the one that is everlasting,
the one that's meant to be and the one that's forbidden."
~Ashamtly Lopez, Jewel GeekyShelf Reviews

For my dad, Miguel Chavez-Garcia
"the greatest man I've ever known"

"After all this time?"

"Always," said Snape.

~J.K. Rowling,

Harry Potter

and the

Deathly Hallows

PROLOGUE

During the first spring after the turn of the century, Isaac rediscovered the torments of true love when a flash of memory returned and he disappeared from the world the night before he died.

The scent of amber lingered when Olivia first whispered: *the only true love is unrequited love*. Isaac noticed it again when he walked through the garden of the retirement community where he had been left by relatives, too busy to care for his needs. The war veteran and unheralded writer had lost his home, his love, and his memory. All that remained in the slowing beat of his fading heart was the desire to understand what those words meant. For love is not measured by a beginning and an end but rather by the depth of its sorrow and the height of its passion.

He vanished from the garden just before dawn, its fountains, ponds, and neatly trimmed pines elaborately sprawled to inspire peace. The majestic façade and stunning architecture were more reminiscent of a country club than a retirement community. The towers, arches, and wings of the metropolis—where the elderly go to be forgotten—faded behind him. The search for him ran well past midnight. Friends, staff, neighbors, and even the police embarked on a futile effort to find the lonely soul, whom they figured had wandered into purgatory suffering from the purest of pain.

By the time anyone had noticed he was missing, Isaac had walked through the streets of Patillas, Puerto Rico and ventured into the historic quarter to the south, known as Old Sienna, beneath overcast skies where fog and mist lingered like a heavy blanket. The Cathedral of Santa Maria towered over the church square, the last remnants of a forgotten era in a vacant quadrant where its misty cobbled streets had been abandoned in favor of the progressive city that had emerged around it.

When he reached Calle de Los Santos, he continued until he arrived at the archway formed by overhanging branches and stepped onto an old stone bridge. A stream ran peacefully beneath it with a stone shore covered in moss.

Isaac froze when he saw her. He felt as though he was seeing her for the first time and he watched as the young lady approached. Time stood still when he gazed into her almond-shaped, dark brown eyes and he wondered about the strange sensation swirling at his core. He didn't recognize her. But he knew he had seen her breath-taking beauty in a lifetime before. Her smile was warm and her movements graceful. Her presence calmed him and her scent reminded him of why he had come. Her long hair fell over her shoulders in gentle waves. She was untouchable in her floor-length red dress that revealed nothing intended to inspire lust with its A-line silhouette and long sleeves.

The brightness of dawn broke through the clouds and cast its golden glow of slanting light on the green leaves of early spring. Her soft and gentle voice broke the silence.

"I wondered if you would return."

He closed his eyes and fell into the ocean of time where his sweetest memory lay hidden like a sunken treasure. The memory of that day returned to him. The ghost of a forgotten love that haunted his heart and inspired his dreams. He had buried that secret, but it reemerged from the shadows of his soul to reveal the truth he had vowed to take with him to the grave.

1935

When the corpse of an unidentified man was found in a darkened alley, his eyes had already been eaten by alley cats before the rats emerged to gnaw at his skin. The details surrounding his death had not been revealed to the newspapers for fear of encouraging a copycat amidst the string of unsolved murders in Old Sienna.

This led to rumors about the middle-aged man's untimely death. They ranged from a drunken brawl and an unpaid gambling debt to a robbery gone wrong and a crime of passion. The latter seemed most likely because in a drunken tirade at La Cantina de Las Botellas an investigator let slip that the man had a love letter in his possession, which he had written to a woman whose identity remained unknown.

Given the contents of the letter, some said the man was a lonely romantic who lived only for his secret love. The police assumed he had no family because no one had come forward to report any relatives missing who fit his description. Most assumed he was homeless since there were no reports by landlords of missing tenants and unpaid rent. They were entirely mistaken.

Chief Inspector Guillermo Sedeño logged the dead man's belongings in his report: a navy-blue suit jacket with matching pants and tie, a white dress shirt stained with blood where he had been stabbed, black leather shoes, socks, an expensive gold watch with matching cuff links, and the bloodstained letter; and placed them into an evidence locker. The quality of his clothing indicated he was a man of means, but Guillermo Sedeño knew better than to immediately draw that conclusion.

"Too often it is the people who wear the nicest clothes that squander their money on appearance rather than save it for an emergency." Guillermo's father used to say.

The Chief Inspector led the murder investigation; it bothered him that the homicide occurred on his watch. If the unidentified man had any wealth then it was safe to say he didn't have any family, for it is known that where a rich man dies even his distant relations will find him. After several weeks without any new leads, the investigation was classified as an unsolved murder and the case was closed. The man's secret would have been lost to the shadows of time had the love letter not been stolen from police evidence a few days later.

Chief Inspector Guillermo Sedeño stormed into the heart of police headquarters when he received the call about the missing letter. His deep-set brown eyes darted around at the array of desks. Plain clothed and uniformed officers cast each other furtive glances when the Chief Inspector demanded everyone's attention. His thunderous voice echoed off the high ceilings of the station, a cathedral of iron and stone built to withstand the wrath of an angry god.

Light filtered in through the windows near the domed ceiling, illuminating the crowded room. Chief Inspector Sedeño searched the eyes of his subordinates for the familiar glance of betrayal he recognized in the eyes of suspects during previous investigations.

He towered over most men. A long brown coat draped over his broad shoulders and wide chest, the same color as his wide brim fedora that cast a shadow over his thick brow and strong chin. He lit a cigarette and took his time to inhale deeply before he spoke. The smoke lingered momentarily and followed him as he walked between the desks.

Thunderous silence echoed, save for his heavy footsteps on the hardwood floor. The arrays of desks were filled with papers, files and jars brimming with pencils. Filing cabinets lined the dark walls and trash bins overflowed with crumpled paper, torn folders and yesterday's tabloids. Chief Inspector Sedeño often felt that the disorganized appearance deceived suspects—who had been brought in for questioning—into thinking the truth would never be found amid the chaos. But he knew it was an effective technique that inspired overconfidence in the guilty.

He took a drag from his cigarette before he informed them about the missing letter from the evidence locker for which the culprit had better have a good reason for stealing. Then he looked Inspector Javier Villalobos straight in the eye from across the room, scrutinizing the alcoholic who had no qualms about voicing his resentment over Guillermo's promotion and said, "I will bury the man who tries to sabotage this investigation."

Inspector Villalobos met Sedeño's glare. Tension filled the room; for it was common knowledge the two men despised each other. In the presence of their superiors, they greeted each other with a curt nod, but mostly they avoided one another to prevent stirring up old memories.

Javier's thin sharp eyes were as dark as his pupils, keen and perceptive when he was sober, but in recent years his sobriety had been rare. He survived on a steady diet of coffee and cigarettes, which explained why his clothes appeared to drape over his slim frame like a heavy suit on a wire hanger. His black hair was slicked to one side with streaks of grey above the ears. He was surprisingly clean-shaven, save for the thin mustache that accentuated the natural hue of his lips.

Inspector Villalobos smirked before he lifted his coat from the back of his chair when he stood. Chief Inspector Guillermo Sedeño studied him for a moment, rage swelled within him as it had years ago in his futile struggle against fate.

"Is it happy hour already?" Guillermo said.

A few of the men snickered.

"Perhaps you should consider a 'happy minute'," Javier said over his shoulder. "Rumor has it you couldn't provide one for the ladies."

He pushed through the black wooden doors as the room fell silent. Outside the sun sauntered toward the western horizon and cast its golden glow against thin wisps of clouds over Old Sienna. Javier took a taxi to la cantina, where he expected to meet someone in a place no one would expect.

When he entered la cantina and the doors closed behind him, his eyes took a moment to adjust to the low lighting. A fog of cigarette smoke hung in the air and obscured the few faces that turned toward him.

A large man in a dark suit sat in the corner and eyed Javier Villalobos with keen interest. He puffed on his cigarette as he waved the inspector over. Javier turned to the barkeep and signaled for a double of his usual order. The bartender nodded as he threw a white cloth onto his shoulder.

"Inspector Villalobos, I presume?" The stranger motioned for Javier to join him.

"And you are?" Javier tilted his head before he took a seat

across the table.

"My name is not as important as who I work for," the large man coughed. "I have been sent here to procure something you were charged with retrieving for Señor de la Vega."

"We agreed that he would meet me in person. Instead, he sends an errand boy?"

The stranger shifted in his seat. He raised his chin before he spoke. "Señor de la Vega is a busy man."

"As am I." Javier moved his arm off the table when the bartender sat the drink before him. "Gracias Umberto."

Umberto nodded with a tense smile beneath his thick grey mustache. His dark grey hair with streaks of black and white complemented his white dress shirt, black vest, and matching bow tie.

"Another rum for you, Señor?" Umberto turned to the stranger. His round droopy eyes beneath bushy eyebrows met the stranger's gaze.

"No thank you."

Umberto returned to his place behind the bar.

"In any case, I don't have it with me." Javier took a sip from his drink. "I wouldn't carry an item of such importance with me to a bar."

"Where is it?"

"In a place only I know."

After studying Inspector Villalobos for a while, he replied, "People only keep secrets when they have something to hide."

"A philosopher and an errand boy," Javier smirked. "De la Vega must have acquired you at a bargain."

"We will be in touch, Inspector." The stranger downed the remainder of his rum and left.

After the stranger exited la cantina, Umberto returned to Javier's table with another drink. "A friend of yours, Inspector?"

Javier Villalobos scoffed. "You know the only company I keep resides on the shelves behind your bar, Umberto."

The barkeep glanced over his shoulder at the bottles of liquor lining the shelves. It was a sad truth, Javier Villalobos frequently joked that his best friends were Ron Bacardi, Jack Daniels, Jim Beam and Johnnie Walker. Too often the inspector wasted his nights drinking himself to the brink of consciousness. Then he'd miraculously stumble into a taxi and make his way home, but not before he'd spent hours rambling in drunken tirades about Chief Inspector Guillermo Sedeño and the politics behind his recent promotion.

The bad blood between the two inspectors ran like a river nearly twenty years in the making. Back to when they were cadets in the police academy and they pursued the heart of the same girl, Angelica Montana de las Fuentes.

They had seen her for the first time on the afternoon of April 16th, 1916 during the annual parade celebrating the birthday of Jose de Diego, the revered poet and political leader known as "The Father of the Puerto Rican Independence Movement."

Angelica sat beside her father on the float of the founding fathers of Old Sienna. Little was known about Don Enrique Montana de las Fuentes when he arrived in Patillas, also known as the emerald of the south because of its green mountains along the southeastern coast of the island, ten years earlier with a young daughter and an unmarried sister.

His wife had died during the sixth cholera pandemic in South America. He returned to his native Puerto Rico as an investor. With the small fortune he amassed on the mainland he became one of the founding fathers of the port city known as Old Sienna. Later he capitalized on the triple tax exemptions afforded to Puerto Rican bondholders under the Jones-Sharfroth Act of 1917 and helped expand the region's booming sugar cane industry.

Despite his commanding presence and distinguished features: clear blue eyes, white hair and thick mustache, all eyes focused on the beautiful young lady with almond shaped eyes. She wore a long red dress and sat like a queen on a moving throne. A single thick braid fell over her shoulder with a bow.

Javier and Guillermo were formally introduced to Angelica at her family's estate during the dinner Don Enrique hosted after the parade. The police commissioner's invitation had extended to his officers and cadets. Naturally he did this to win their favor and to obtain their services, off the books, for a later time.

Don Enrique had not anticipated how the events of that night would lead his legacy to be lost to the shadows of memory. For it was a defining moment in all their lives. The fates of Angelica, Guillermo, and Javier changed; if their destiny had been written in the stars before that night, it was a destiny erased by God and rewritten in the form of a love letter.

A cruel fate, which challenged their resolve, for it is said that obstacles define true love. In the years that followed, neither man allowed the memory of Angelica to fade from the world, and neither man forgave the other for her disappearance.

Umberto concluded that perhaps Javier Villalobos blamed himself for her untimely fate. The once promising career of the inspector whose family name had been among the most respected in Old Sienna faltered in the years after his wife had gone missing.

Whether he sought comfort at the bottom of a bottle or attempted to drown his guilt no one could say, for he seldom spoke of Angelica, or the circumstances surrounding her disappearance.

All that remained of the union was a daughter. Now a young lady, Olivia Esperanza Villalobos was the lovely heirloom of a loveless marriage. To help raise her, Javier invited his divorced sister, Katarina Villalobos, to live with them. After three stillborn births, the Church granted Katarina's husband his request for a divorce on the grounds that he was the last of his line and needed to preserve his family name. Unable to bear her own children Tia Katarina welcomed the opportunity to help raise her niece and she treated her as if she was her own. Even if her brother seldom expressed any form of love for his daughter.

Regardless of his emotional detachment, Olivia strived to please her father and win over his affections. Be it through academic accomplishment or the authority with which she ran the house and all its servants. She made every effort to live up to the nobility of the family name.

Even on nights like tonight when her father arrived too inebriated to stand on his own. The taxi driver pulled up to the front gates as he always had and summoned the male servants to help Javier into the home.

After climbing the flight of stairs to his bedroom and placing him on the bed, the servants left Tia Katarina and Olivia to remove his shoes, coat, shirt and tie. Tia Katarina instructed Olivia to leave the room when she prepared to remove his trousers, but not before she remarked that no daughter should see her father in this condition.

"He is my father regardless of his condition." Olivia emptied out his coat pockets. She placed the loose change on the dresser along with a watch chain, wallet, tiepin, cuff links, collar button and a handgun.

She was about to hang the jacket in the Italian Venetian Bombe Armoire when she felt a piece of paper through the folds. Perplexed, she searched the coat for a hidden compartment.

"Psst!" Tia Katarina waved Olivia out of the room.

Olivia nodded and closed the door behind her as she stepped into the hallway. She unfolded the paper carefully and felt the unfamiliar material between her fingers.

Is this blood? She studied the dry, dark red smudges on the edge of the page.

The cursive script was short and tight and slanted to the right. It was a man's handwriting, to be sure, but she did not recognize the penmanship. She concluded that the letter had not been penned by her father's hand. Not only because she knew his handwriting, but also because the words contained an elegance and romanticism her father did not possess.

"You know better than to pry into your father's private affairs." Tia Katarina said as she lifted Javier's jacket from Olivia's arm.

Startled, Olivia raised her eyes from the letter. "I don't believe this letter belongs to my father."

"How can you be sure?" Tia Katarina examined the letter when Olivia handed it to her. "Is this blood?"

"I believe so, but it isn't father's blood. You see, he doesn't have a scratch on his body."

Tia Katarina glanced over her shoulder at her sleeping brother as he laid on his back snoring. She pulled the door closed and ushered her niece into another room. Tia Katarina recognized the texture and the watermark embedded into the paper. She had first seen it years ago when her dearest friend, Veronica Castro de Garcia, had fallen into an impossible love with a married man.

They fell in love before he married, in a time when the hope that tomorrow belonged to them lived strongly within them. It was a love that would not be, for he had been betrothed to another in a period when marriage among the aristocrats was a social contract between families and not a matter of the heart. The circumstances, however, did not sway their desire to be together.

He promised to convince his father to break off the engagement, and she promised to wait until that day came. Over the following months they exchanged clandestine smiles and knowing glances. But that only intensified their longing and led them to search for ways to express their love beyond the watchful eye of their parents and the gossips.

Then it happened. A shadow moved among the cobbled streets of Old Sienna. Some said it was the spirit of Saint Valentine, and others speculated it was the spirit of Lorenzo Valentino himself, the Last Valentine, as they would say. For it is said the shadow appears before those who have fallen ill to the madness of love.

"According to legend, the shadow reveals the location of the Labyrinth of Love Letters to give the victims of true love a place to express the secret in their hearts." Tia Katarina said.

"How?" Olivia lifted her eyes from the bloodstained letter.

"They write each other love letters and hide them in the labyrinth for the other to find. By alternating their trips to the labyrinth, lovers avoid being seen together."

"Don't they ever see each other?" Olivia's brow furrowed. "When do they kiss and embrace each other?"

"Oh mija, you have plenty to learn about true love." Tia Katarina smiled ruefully. "Physical love requires the feeling of a caress, but true love is felt in the heart from a distance. That is when it remains pure."

Olivia glanced at the letter once more.

"Do you think your friend went to the labyrinth?"

"It's difficult to say." Tia Katarina held the letter up against the light. It was the same paper with the same watermark Veronica had used all those years ago. Tia Katarina shrugged as she stood. "Who knows? I think it's merely a local legend of a place that doesn't exist."

"What if it does exist? What if this letter belongs in the labyrinth?"

"That doesn't explain how it came into your father's possession. What is even more disturbing is that it doesn't explain the bloodstains. You had best return that letter to where you found it. Nothing good ever comes from discovering a secret that is not yours to keep."

"Didn't Veronica take you with her to see the labyrinth?"

"Heavens no!" Tia Katarina pulled her house robe closed at the collar. She declared herself a good Christian woman who didn't meddle in such scandalous affairs.

Olivia suppressed a smile. Her aunt walked over to the bedroom door. Before she pulled it open she instructed her niece to return the letter immediately. Olivia nodded as she stood and stepped out of the room.

It was there, in the lingering echo of silence between two women who shared the bond of mother and daughter—in a home where neither felt she belonged—that destiny and love conspired to lead them down a path that revealed the dangers of passion and a secret love.

That night, Olivia laid on her bed and read the letter repeatedly. Captivated as much by the contents of the letter as by the mystery behind the writer and the intended recipient. She wondered where they met and the circumstances surrounding their forbidden affair.

The words dripped with the desire and longing inherent in unrequited love, an unparalleled devotion. It was as if the pen had punctured a passionate heart and the ink bled into the fibers of the page. Etched into eternity where the gift and the curse of love became a narrative of secrets whispered among the shadows and only God was a witness. Word by word, carefully selected to convey a confession intended to be a reflection between hearts reminded Olivia of poetry that echoed through time.

In the darkest hour, just before dawn peered in through the window, she felt her eyes begin to close. As she tried to resist the sleepiness that beckoned her to fall into the sleeping city of dreams she thought about her best friend, Isaac Quintero.

She wondered what he would make of the letter. The echo of words left behind in the valleys of a broken heart reminded her of when he said, "The key to sharing a heart worth loving, is to share a love worth remembering." He fancied himself a writer despite never having published anything beyond a few poems in the local paper. But Isaac was a hopeless romantic with avid notions of love.

He believed the image of love at first sight lingered in the palace of our memories. And regardless of how many smiles captivate our eyes, how many kisses steal our breath, or how many times our hearts break, we will never forget our love at first sight. For a romantic, the enchantment of that moment will always emerge from the shadows of memory the way light breaks through a heavy fog to guide us safely to the shores of our hearts. Perhaps Isaac would be inclined to help her find the labyrinth and ensure the love professed in the letter would always be remembered.

2

The only thing worth dying for is love. When Olivia woke, her first thought was of the bloodstained letter. It dawned on her that perhaps it was a piece of evidence from one of her father's investigations.

That doesn't explain why he had it hidden in his coat.

Despite his reputation for being a drunk, Inspector Javier Villalobos had a reputation for being a skilled investigator. He knew better than to keep a valuable piece of evidence on his person. Olivia's mind raced with wild ideas and questions. Did he forget he had it? Was he somehow involved in a crime and hiding evidence from his superiors? Was he being framed, and the letter was the only piece of evidence to prove his innocence? Or did he plan on finding the labyrinth to deliver the letter for its intended purpose?

A knock on her bedroom door interrupted her train of thought. She threw her house robe over her shoulders and answered the door. The servant, Clara Ruiz, a Dominican immigrant around Olivia's age, informed her that Chief Inspector Guillermo Sedeño waited in the greeting room.

"Where's my father?"

"He left shortly after dawn."

"What about Tia Katarina?"

"She is at the market."

Olivia's blank stare fell to the floor. *Could the Chief Inspector be here about the letter?* She met Clara's expectant gaze. "Tell him I am not prepared to entertain company."

"I did, but he said this is an urgent matter and he will wait until either you come down, or your aunt or father return."

"Coño!" Olivia cursed under her breath and rolled her eyes. "Fine. Inform him that I will be down momentarily."

Clara nodded, turned and raced down the wide staircase. She froze at the foot of the stairs when she found the Chief Inspector pacing in the greeting room. He held his wide brim fedora with his hands behind his back. When she saw him still wearing his long trench coat, she surmised that he declined the other servant's offer to take it.

He studied the oil paintings hanging on the walls. Each portrait was of the husbands and wives of the Villalobos family going back several generations. Guillermo stopped before the painting of Javier and Angelica. It was a replica of the photo taken on their wedding day, which he had seen in the local paper announcing their marriage eighteen years ago.

Javier stood proud and triumphant like his Conquistador ancestors, laying claim to that which did not belong to them. In his youth, he possessed an air of nobility that had been lost in the years following Angelica's disappearance. His good posture in the photo reminded Guillermo of their time together at the Policeman's Academy. Javier excelled, both physically and academically, without much effort in contrast to his fellow cadets. Envious of his high marks, they believed that having been born with a silver spoon in his mouth made everything in life easier for Javier.

Guillermo never bought into that philosophy. He acknowledged Javier's performance as a result of his natural talents and intellect. An advantage he inherited through his genetic pedigree and competitive nature, which motivated Guillermo's assiduity to eclipse Javier's accomplishments.

Though their rivalry extended beyond the academy and later their vocation as officers of the law, it was in their attempt to win Angelica's heart that their disdain for each other grew fiercest. Despite Guillermo's ascension through the ranks, he never recovered from the heartbreak he endured when Angelica married the son of an aristocrat. She had been his only need, his only love, but seeing the sadness in her eyes as depicted in the painting made him wonder if she regretted her decision.

He remembered their last conversation as if it was only yesterday. In the atrium of the cathedral of Santa Maria, where she asked him to meet her just before sunset, they held each other's gaze without touching for what felt like an eternity. A thunderous silence hung in the space between them. It wasn't until the sun kissed the horizon—a long beautiful kiss that illuminated the sky for a brief instant—that she finally said, "I have always loved you, and I always will." Then she fled into the night. She did not wait for his reaction. She did not let him fight for her love one last time. The sadness in her eyes remained from that night, captured forever in a photo and a painting, a truth hidden in the darkest corner of his heart.

Clara Ruiz cleared her throat and interrupted the Chief Inspector's train of thought. She felt his intense gaze scrutinize her when she informed him that la Señorita Olivia would be down momentarily. Guillermo eyed her briefly before he nodded. She spoke Spanish with a slight variation in the syntax, which he identified as Dominican Spanish. He heard it spoken in the Dominican quarter where the influx of immigrants resided when they arrived from the neighboring island.

The young woman wore a long white nagua style dress

common among the Taínos, which explained her African features and humble status. She offered the Chief Inspector refreshments, but he politely declined. Clara Ruiz bowed and took her leave.

When Olivia finally appeared on the staircase she descended with an air of elegance that reminded Guillermo of her mother. "Good morning Chief Inspector Sedeño. To what does our home owe the pleasure of your company?"

"Señorita Olivia," the Chief Inspector bowed his head. "Please accept my apologies for the intrusion. As I'm afraid the purpose of my visit is for business and not pleasure."

Olivia motioned for him to have a seat. The Chief Inspector politely declined and said he only needed a moment of her time. At this, Olivia did not know whether to sit or remain standing. She wondered what could be so urgent that required her immediate presence, yet so short that he didn't need to sit even though he had been willing to wait several hours for her father to return.

Guillermo observed her uneasiness. He smiled inwardly, for he knew she had to be hiding something if she suddenly felt uncomfortable in her own home. *Does she know Javier took the letter?* He studied her in silence. He couldn't believe the striking resemblance to her mother. It was as if Angelica Montana de las Fuentes had been reborn. Her hair fell in the same gentle waves to the small of her back with the same features of her mother's smile. Although her eyes were the same shade as her mother's, she did not inherit the shape of her eyes and her brow from Angelica, or Javier.

Olivia cleared her throat. She avoided his eyes as she walked around him. She looked at the oil paintings, which she had seen her entire life as she circled the room with her hands behind her back. "How may I be of service, Chief Inspector?"

"A man was murdered recently." Guillermo's gaze followed the young woman.

"Yes, I've heard. The latest in a string of many recently, such a shame, really." She did not turn to face him. "And his identity remains a mystery, correct?"

"Indeed it is." Guillermo turned as his eyes followed her movements. "Though he did leave a clue, which may reveal his identity."

"Is that so?" Olivia feigned indifference. She continued to circle the welcoming room. Her heart pounded against her chest and her mind raced with ideas about the man's identity, and if the Chief Inspector knew she had the letter.

"My quandary, however, is that someone stole that valuable piece of evidence." Guillermo paused and watched, as Olivia grew stiff. "Without it, I cannot identify the man whose life was taken in such a violent manner, and unless I can do that I will be unable to bring his killer to justice."

"What does any of this have to do with your visit to our home?" Olivia said over her shoulder without meeting the Chief Inspector's gaze.

"Nothing, if you don't have that piece of evidence in your possession."

"How could I possibly come to possess such a valuable piece of evidence, Chief Inspector?"

"How, indeed, Señorita?"

She turned and met his intense gaze. His eyes and brow looked familiar just then, as if she had recognized their shape her entire life. Before she could say anything to him, or he could say anything to her, Tia Katarina returned home from the market with two servants at her side. She froze when she saw the Chief Inspector upon passing through the door. She wore a blue dress that fell just below her knees and accentuated her blue eyes. Her light brown hair fell past her shoulders with a yellow flower tucked within the gentle waves. Chief Inspector Guillermo Sedeño greeted her kindly before he thanked Olivia for her time and excused himself.

After the door closed behind him, Tia Katarina instructed the servants to take the groceries into the kitchen. She rushed to her niece's side and demanded to know what he wanted as they sat together on one of the couches.

"He's investigating the murder of an unidentified man, but someone stole a piece of evidence that could help him find the killer."

"Why would he come here?" Tia Katarina wondered. "God knows Guillermo would never seek your father's help."

"Do you think he suspects father of stealing the piece of evidence in question?"

"Your father would never do such a thing." Tia Katarina reproached her.

"What about the bloodstained letter?"

Tia Katarina's blank stare fell to the cyan tiled floor. "Aye, Dios mio." Her head fell into her hands. "If your father—"

"I know." Olivia stood.

"Where are you going?" Tia Katarina watched her niece approach the front door.

"Wherever the wind takes me," Olivia said over her shoulder.

3

Isaac Quintero was at his uncle's house for his daily lessons when Olivia arrived. His eccentric uncle, Gabriel Aquino, lived alone in a small boathouse near the beach. He purchased it with his earnings from his time as a schoolteacher in America. When he returned to Puerto Rico, he preferred to live as far away from Old Sienna as his feet could take him; he loved his privacy and distance from the town gossips.

"Old Sienna didn't exist when I left for America. Why should I want to live there in my old age with a bunch of people whom I don't know?" Gabriel had said to his nephew when Isaac complained about the long walk.

Olivia sympathized with Señor Gabriel Aquino. He resented the fact that the small town he called home had been stomped out of existence when Old Sienna was founded.

"Why do they call it 'Old Sienna,' when it's a new city?" He'd gripe when his bottle of rum ran empty.

Aside from his rantings about the city, he was a cheerful man who loved to talk about literature and history. His unruly grey hair framed his oval face with beady brown eyes, and a long broad nose. His friends called him "El Prieto," a nickname his late wife—Ariana Aquino—gave him because of his dark skin, which accentuated the perpetual stubble of silver hair that grew around his full lips.

He stood knee-deep in the water with his white pants rolled

up. The sea sprayed its mist of salt water as he stared at the horizon where the blue-green water met the clear blue sky. His white button down shirt billowed in the breeze. He was a slim man, nearly two meters tall with a body as sharp as his mind despite his grey hair.

Three times a day he stood in the water with a pensive look in his eye. At dawn, at noon, and at sunset he stepped into the cool refreshing sea.

"You are always out here, without fail, Señor Gabriel Aquino," Olivia said as she approached the shore.

"God's gift is the world, and life is merely a consequence of that gift. To show appreciation for what God has given us, we should endeavor to admire the beauty of His creation." Gabriel turned to face her.

Truth be told he always claimed God's favorite creation was rum. He once told Isaac, "When it comes to the ladies, always have a glass of rum at the ready. Aside from being liquid candy, it will provide you with the courage God didn't give you when he made you."

"Is Isaac still completing his studies?" Olivia asked. She knew that his uncle gave him a quiz at the end of each session to ensure he retained the information.

"The boy moves at a snail's pace. Whether it's with his schoolwork, or with the ladies. I keep telling him if he waits any longer he's going to lose any chance he has of winning your heart."

Olivia laughed. She appreciated Señor Gabriel Aquino's jovial nature. She found it a refreshing display of kindness and acceptance in contrast to the judgmental and watchful eyes of the aristocrats of Old Sienna.

"We are just friends, Señor Gabriel." She smiled as she

moved a strand of hair away from her face.

"Is that what they call it these days?" Gabriel winked. "He's inside. Go on in and make yourself at home."

She stepped inside the boathouse. It was made entirely of wood, with windows on all four sides and two chairs on the patio facing the water. The interior was sparsely furnished with a small couch and rug in the main room. A bookshelf against the far wall was lined with books written by the Romantics of the previous two centuries. From English brothers Joseph and Thomas Warton, Lord Byron and John Keats to the American greats Hawthorn, Emerson, Thoreau, and Edgar Allan Poe. Countless other names Olivia did not recognize from Russia, France, and Spain were etched onto the spines.

In the kitchen, there was a small stove and an icebox, along with a table accompanied by a single chair. Of the two rooms to the rear of the home, one was Señor Gabriel's sleeping room, which had the door closed, and the other was a classroom for Gabriel Aquino's lone student, his nephew, Isaac Quintero.

Gabriel returned from America when his sister, Maricela, had succumbed to smallpox. That left his brother-in-law, Rolando the hat-maker, to raise their only son alone. In the wake of her absence, the three felt her warmth and radiance like a spirit that watched over them with permission from God.

Señor Gabriel Aquino remained in Puerto Rico; for a while, he taught literature in the secondary school. Now he only provided lessons to his nephew, whom he wanted to succeed in academia in lieu of slaving away in the fields beneath the unrelenting sun.

She found Isaac sitting at his desk writing in his journal. It was a letter to his mother. Despite having no memory of her, he wrote her every day. His uncle had encouraged him to keep a daily journal for self-reflection and to help him develop his writing. Isaac used it to remain connected to his mother, for even in her absence she would know the secrets of his soul.

Olivia stood silently with arms crossed as she leaned against the doorframe and watched him in silence. His short brown hair, the same color as his eyes, lay combed to the side. He was tall and slender like his uncle, but he had his father's smile and indentation on the chin. Everyone said he had his mother's eyes; only it wasn't just their shape and color that people referred to, but also the deep, pensive gaze that were like windows into an old soul.

He laid the pencil down when he finished writing the last sentence and smiled at Olivia. The prominent dimple on his right cheek had always been her favorite feature. She always teased that it gave him a "good side," and he always replied that she used it as an excuse to compliment him without revealing her undeniable attraction.

"Are you ready to leave? I have something to show you." Olivia turned and walked away.

Isaac gathered his journal and his books into his carriel, a small leather satchel his uncle brought from a recent visit to Colombia as a gift. He followed her outside where Uncle Gabriel had returned from the water.

"Where are you off to in such a hurry?" Uncle Gabriel asked as he sat on one of his patio chairs.

"We're off to find the secrets of the Romantics," Olivia said over her shoulder.

"Be careful nena, for the Romantics are a dark breed and their secrets are even darker than the valleys of their souls."

Isaac and Olivia shielded their eyes from the afternoon sunlight as they looked at each other and searched for a suitable reply. It dawned on them; Gabriel Aquino was growing old. He sat in his chair and turned toward the ocean. His somber gaze revealed a longing to be reunited with the love of his life.

They had been children together. They were friends first. Attended the same schools, wandered the same dirt roads, and lingered along the same shores. Then he left. In 1897, he pursued his ambitions in America. Like so many others who left Puerto Rico and migrated to New York in search of a better life, he claimed he would see the world.

Years passed as Puerto Rico endured political unrest amid the cries for independence from the Crown of Spain. He wrote to Ariana on occasion, but he seldom spoke of love; instead, he would remind her that life should be lived, because time waits for no one, and love has no regard for time. She dismissed his rantings and continued to write him back. As far as she was concerned, if love had no regard for time, then neither would she.

When he completed his studies, he traveled abroad to Europe. He continued to send letters home, but he rarely remained in any one place long enough to receive a letter at a return address. He ventured to Arabia on a pilgrimage to Medina, "the radiant city," with hopes of visiting Mecca, but his plans were short-lived when Abd-al'-Aziz began his conquest of the Arabian Peninsula to establish the Kingdom of Saudi Arabia.

Shortly thereafter, he received a letter from home that the Spanish-American War had claimed the lives of most of his immediate family. Left only with a three-year-old sister and an aunt and uncle, he returned to Puerto Rico in 1903.

He arranged for his aunt and uncle to raise Maricela since they had no children of their own. After that, he prepared to leave Puerto Rico again. It was then that he sat down to read the letters from Ariana Jimenez; they finally caught up with him after chasing him around the world. She had written him a letter every day and every night. She described the sunrise and the sunset, the market and the shore. She told him that none of it was the same in his absence. She confessed that she was not the same without him either.

She said her letters to him were her secret diary entries and only he possessed the key to her soul. Her final letter ended with the words: "The day waits for the sunrise and the night waits for sunset. This is how I wait for you, without regard for time, because I know you will return to me when you are ready."

The day before his departure he went to the market. He saw Ariana at her father's stall haggling with customers. She possessed a natural haughtiness, which she used to negotiate prices to her father's advantage.

Her long brown hair and caramel complexion complemented her hazel eyes. She had a smile that stole men's hearts and a gaze that broke them a second later. Despite the afternoon heat, she dressed modestly, which Gabriel had always admired. They shared a conservative disposition and a love of literature. When they sat, and talked, their conversations were about ideas and themes in lieu of people and rumors.

He approached the stall and insisted on speaking with Ariana's father in private.

"Good God, can't you see I'm busy?" Miguel Jimenez reproached him.

"It is a matter of great importance, Señor. It will only take a moment," Gabriel pleaded.

"Not now. I'm busy." Miguel waved him off.

Ariana watched the exchange with keen interest. She tried to suppress a smile despite her shock at Gabriel's boldness. No one ever dared to interrupt Miguel Jimenez while he was conducting business. Not even God.

It is said that Miguel once told his wife, "If the good Lord—Jesu Christo—ever attempts to strike me down with a heart attack, he too shall wait until the end of the business day."

Gabriel Aquino did not relent. He held out his arms to usher the patrons back and declared his love for Ariana Jimenez. The market fell silent. Everyone watched with a wide-eyed expression as Miguel shot Gabriel a cold stare. He warned the young man to leave or suffer the consequences.

"You will either kill me or give me your blessing for your daughter's hand. Either way, I'll be in heaven." Gabriel proclaimed.

Thirty-two years had passed since that day. Twenty-three of those years he had shared with Ariana. They remained in Providencia for a decade until Miguel Jimenez passed, which allowed them to watch Maricela grow. Ariana then traveled with Gabriel to New York; he found work as a teacher, and she tutored the children of underprivileged families in their East Harlem neighborhood. Despite not being blessed with children of their own, they were happy and in love.

Tension between the Jewish and Puerto Rican communities came to a head during an economic downturn in a prelude to the Great Depression. In the middle of summer, Gabriel Aquino had been out searching for work when the Harlem Riots of 1926 ignited a fire that claimed hundreds of lives. The one that mattered most to Gabriel had been the love of his life. He sat in his chair on his patio looking out at the ocean thinking of her.

After a long moment, Olivia motioned for Isaac to follow her.

"Come, I have something to show you."

They followed the road, Carretera Central, leading them back to Old Sienna. This historic road was the first highway to cross the mountains and had been in use since 1886. Remnants of the Spanish-American War remained scattered near the roadside from when the American land forces moved north against the Spanish Army. The road winded along the uneven terrain, flanked by forestry on both sides. Occasionally they would pass mule-drawn wagons headed in the opposite direction towards the docks, loaded with guayaba, anon, jobo and piña, for exportation to the Americas and Europe.

"I assume you heard about the man found dead in an alley recently," Olivia said as she peered over her shoulder.

"Who hasn't?" Isaac shrugged. "It's all anyone wants to talk about."

"What have you heard?"

"Not much. Only that his identity remains a mystery and the investigation is closed."

Olivia led him down a dirt road that branched off from Carretera Central, leading them west to the Cemetery of the Nobles. The cemetery was first established in the wake of the Spanish-American War, to honor the men who fought bravely for Puerto Rico's independence from Spain. However, after the founding of Old Sienna, the aristocrats now use it to bury their dead, away from the lower and middle classes. Some claim the cemetery is haunted and that it wasn't the living that established the graveyard, but rather the souls of the dead who buried their own bodies in the hallowed ground.

"What are we doing in a cemetery?" Isaac asked as he and Olivia walked under an archway lined with black roses and dark green vines. The brightness of the day faded within the boundaries of the black iron fence that circled the graveyard. A light fog lingered over the statues and headstones of the necropolis, through which the gleam of sunlight filtered down in slanting streaks.

"Some secrets should only be revealed in the presence of the dead."

"As if I don't already hear enough of the macabre from my uncle." Isaac shook his head.

"You mustn't tell anyone what I am about to show you," Olivia said as she took his hand and led him to a stone bench.

A statue of an angel loomed over them like a sentinel with outstretched wings. The stare made Isaac feel uneasy.

"Promise me." Olivia insisted.

"Okay, I promise." Isaac nodded.

"Not your friend Memito, or even your Uncle Gabriel."

Isaac looked at her perplexed. Memito Linarez had been his best friend since the age of five. His father was a baker, and they had lived a few doors down before his parent's untimely deaths. Isaac and Memito remained close despite the tragedy and told each other everything. It was the same with his uncle. Isaac trusted Uncle Gabriel as much as he trusted his father.

"It's not that I don't trust them. I just don't want to get them in any trouble."

"Oh, but you're willing to expose me to such problems," Isaac said playfully.

"It's not that, silly. I'm just saying, the fewer people that know, the better."

"Okay, fine. The suspense is killing me already. What is it?"

She glanced over her shoulder once again. She felt an unseen presence nearby, a lost soul searching for peace and company, in a world where the echo of true love faded into eternity. Olivia revealed the letter from within the folds of her dress.

"I believe this belonged to the man who was found dead in the alley a few days ago." She held the bloodstained letter between her fingers.

"How do you know?" Isaac eyed the folded paper suspiciously.

"I found it in my father's coat last night. Then, this morning, Chief Inspector Sedeño arrived at my house and alluded to a missing piece of evidence that would help identify the man."

"Why would your father steal evidence?"

"That's what I've been trying to figure out. As far as I know, my father had no association with the man." She looked at the folded letter in her hands. "I wanted to show you this because it's a love letter. A love letter the man wrote for a woman as if he knew it would be the last correspondence he would ever share."

"A love letter?"

Olivia nodded. "What I can't understand is what would my father want with a love letter written by another man for a woman he probably didn't even know?"

"Unless he *did* know her," Isaac said.

Olivia had wondered about that too, but she concluded that her father was incapable of committing a crime of passion. Not only because he lived in a perpetual state of intoxication, but also because the only woman he had ever loved was gone.

When Olivia handed him the letter, Isaac eyed the peculiar paper with what appeared to be bloodstains along the edges. He turned to her perplexed. "Is this blood?"

"Go ahead, open it."

Isaac unfolded the letter. He was careful not to disturb the emotions trapped on the page by tearing the paper. As he read the letter in silence, the shadow of secret love reminded him of his private affair. The longing in a stolen glance, the confession lingering on his lips, and the agony of unfulfilled desire swirling in his heart, like a breeze on a deserted mountainside. At that moment, he realized another shared his pain.

Isaac sat motionless for several minutes. As he stared at the letter in silence, he remembered what his uncle had once said, "According to the Mahabharata, 'Desire is poison.'"

When Isaac shook his head and told his uncle he did not understand, Señor Gabriel Aquino was only too willing to clarify.

"Love is a potion, and many ingredients are used to enhance its potency, or alter the flavor. Infatuation makes it sweet, longing makes it strong, and agony makes it bitter. But desire is poisonous because it leads one to confuse lust for love, which always leads to heartbreak."

When he finally met Olivia's gaze she appeared to be lost in thought. He felt as if she was looking into his soul and caught a glimpse of his secret. He remained silent, for he did not dare interrupt her journey into his heart. He wondered if perhaps she might find the flowers he saved for her in the corridor where the whisper of her name lingered like the ghost that haunted his dreams.

"Well, what do you think?" She finally spoke.

"I think you should return this to the police."

"Are you crazy?" Olivia looked at him incredulously.

"No, but *you* must be crazy to risk being caught in possession of stolen property." Isaac folded the letter and handed it back. "Especially when the item in question is evidence in a murder investigation."

Olivia shook her head and hid the letter within the folds of her alpaca dress. "I can't believe you, of all people, are not willing to help me."

"Help you with what?"

"Help me find the Labyrinth of Love Letters to ensure this letter is received by the intended recipient."

"The Labyrinth—" Isaac whispered. "Wait a minute. You do realize that place is just a myth, don't you?"

"No, it is not. It is an actual place. I feel it in my heart." Olivia insisted.

She stood and stormed away.

Isaac hurried after her along the winding, cobbled path.

"Olivia, wait." He followed her without hesitation.

She marched on and ignored his pleads. Regardless of where the letter belonged and despite its classification as a stolen piece of evidence in a murder investigation Olivia Villalobos would not be dissuaded. She believed the Labyrinth of Love Letters existed and she fully intended to discover its location.

Isaac pursued her through the necropolis. A church loomed in the east like a sentinel watching over the city of the dead. He caught up with her and took hold of her hand. She stopped. He turned her toward him, but she lowered her gaze. She felt embarrassed, silly for believing in a myth like the last in a group of friends to discover Santa does not exist.

"Okay, look, if it means that much to you—"

"I don't need your pity." She snapped.

"I'm not doing this out of pity. It's just—" Isaac sighed. His eyes scanned their surroundings before turning to her again. "You're talking about finding a place no one we know has ever seen. Finding the labyrinth is not going to be easy."

"I never said it was going to be easy."

"Where do we begin?" He looked again at the myriad of headstones and statues.

She bit her lower lip and contemplated his query for a moment. "We begin at the scene of the crime," she said remembering a quote from the detective novels her father collected but never read.

Javier Villalobos had been an avid reader in his youth. Fond of detective novels since first reading a Sherlock Holmes short story titled: The Adventure of the Devil's Foot, at the age of ten. He amassed an extensive library of detective novels over the course of a decade. For close to twenty years, however, Javier had not read a single story. The books sat on the shelves and collected dust until one humid afternoon when the air was filled with mist and incessant rain.

Olivia lifted a book off the shelf. The texture of its hardcover felt rough against her fingers, as she leafed through the yellowing pages the faint odor of mold filled her nostrils. By sunset she had read two dozen short stories and fell asleep while reading a third novel sometime after midnight. She had read them all in the years that followed and believed she possessed all the know-how to conduct a proper investigation. With the conviction of the Holy Spirit, she set out to identify the man who died for love and discover the location of the Labyrinth where he intended to hide his heart's confession.

4

In the haunted mist of the graveyard, Olivia and Isaac plotted to uncover a secret that belonged to the torments of love. While he gazed into her brown eyes, enchanted, she explained how Sherlock Holmes used astute logical reasoning to solve different cases.

"Sherlock Holmes?" Isaac cast her an incredulous glance. He too was familiar with the popular detective created less than fifty years ago by Scottish author, Sir Arthur Conan Doyle. "That's a bit ambitious don't you think?"

"I suppose, but then again, Sherlock's career began as an amateur investigator when he was an undergraduate."

They continued talking about a fictional character while standing in the middle of the graveyard. Plotting their investigation as the day wore on, away from the watchful eyes of local authorities and town gossips. Given Chief Inspector Sedeño's suspicions that Javier Villalobos had the letter in his possession, extra precautions were necessary. They agreed to avoid falling into a routine and needed to take different routes each day to avoid being followed.

Her father, a skilled detective in his own right, had a reputation for keen powers of observation, despite being in a perpetual state of intoxication. In Old Sienna, no detective possessed a better record for solved cases—save for Guillermo Sedeño—than Inspector Villalobos. Some speculated his disposition as a drunk, was merely an act to remain innocuous and mislead criminals into underestimating him. Others considered his proficiency a gift from the devil, for no good Christian would poison his body and maintain his dexterity without consequences. Javier had a good understanding of human nature and knew that the best way to catch a thief was to give him the impression he wasn't being watched. It was for that reason Olivia devised her plan with a German's precision, and without underestimating her father.

She decided to proceed in secret and leave Tia Katarina in the dark, hoping to provide her aunt with plausible deniability. As the afternoon light faded, the haze that lingered over the graveyard morphed into thick fog and fell like a thick blanket.

When Isaac and Olivia had finally worked out the details of their plan, it became apparent to them that neither had ever truly been in love. Though each had felt the trickle of young love during their early adolescent years, neither had danced in the rain during a torrential downpour of emotions. The agony of desire, the longing to be together, the need to find a way to make it last, all the aspects of *amour* that remain after the initial excitement of falling in love has faded, was foreign to them. The madness of love had never consumed and driven them to risk everything for the sake of it.

At least not yet.

The clattering of hooves on the cobblestones pierced the silence. A horse drawn carriage came to a halt beneath a white willow near a church. It stood beside the path that ran parallel to the one they had walked. The two brown steeds snorted as the carriage door opened. The chauffeur, a middle-aged man with a thick mustache, wearing a dark suit, helped a woman climb out of the carriage. She donned a long black dress with a black veil that concealed her face.

She proceeded along the cobbled path, with the wave of her arm she motioned for the chauffeur to remain with the carriage.

Olivia and Isaac watched as she followed the winding path. They turned to each other and with a knowing glance they stood and trailed the woman without alerting her escort. It was not their intention to spy on the woman for the purpose of invading her privacy. However, there had been no recent deaths among the aristocrats of Old Sienna, and they wondered if she had come for the unidentified man found dead in the alley. That would be of no consequence if people frequently visited their loved ones who had passed away. Sadly, the dead know they have forever to wait for the living that are too busy to remember them and where they rest.

Darting behind statues and tall headstones, Olivia and Isaac followed the mysterious woman stealthily. The fog provided additional cover, along with the darkening sky. The trees surrounding the cemetery remained motionless. Overhanging branches rested on the black iron fence. Only the snorting of the horses broke the silence.

The woman turned off the path and approached a lone grave beneath another white willow. She knelt before the standing gravestone; unlike any they had ever seen. The black granite headstone was shaped like a broken heart. Cracked down the middle, as if a lightning bolt had struck it in the night, and two dolphins had been carved out of the slab along opposite edges of the heart.

Isaac and Olivia maintained their distance. They huddled behind adjacent tombstones far enough to remain hidden, but close enough to hear her offer a prayer. Though they could not make out her words, they assumed she had been praying when she crossed herself before touching the stone. Her body shook as she wept. Her tears hidden from the world and her heart tortured with inconsolable grief.

She cursed under her breath. She cursed death for taking her love. She cursed life for keeping her. And she cursed her lover for leaving her alone to swim in the sea of his memory, without the moon of his smile to comfort her, without the stars of his eyes to guide her, and without the shore of his embrace to hold her when she grew weary.

She offered the secrets of her heart, which he had promised to take to the grave, but she had no assurances he could hear her. Even if he was listening, no one knew for certain if the dead could hear the voices of the living from the other side of the veil. She hadn't heard his voice in months, or he hers, for they had agreed to communicate only through letters after they were nearly caught whispering to each other at a dinner party. It was during the celebration of el Día del Descubrimiento de Puerto Rico, the national holiday that celebrated the Discovery of Puerto Rico by Don Cristóbal Colón. Their secret love had been relegated to voiceless confessions trapped on a page and hidden with invisible ink.

Their affair was doomed from the moment Cupid's arrow was dipped in the poison of passion and pierced both their hearts. She, Carmen Alicia de la Vega, a woman of status who was married to Fernando Gonzalo de la Vega, a deeply religious man and politician whose surname launched his career and whose dealings cemented his reputation as a powerful man. Nothing happened in Old Sienna without his knowledge nor his permission. If any man had an agreement with the angel of death, it was Fernando Gonzalo de la Vega; it is believed he kept a list of names given to him by Saint Peter with the authority to cross a name off the list at his own discretion.

There he laid, the man with no name, in an unmarked grave,

his secret revealed. His life destined to become a memory that belonged to no one. His love letter lost in the wind carrying the last words he would ever say to the woman he loved. She secretly arranged his burial to secure his safe passage into heaven.

Luis Alfredo, the mortician, agreed to inter the body under the cover of night. He was Carmen's older cousin on her mother's side and—despite his vocation—was a hopeless romantic. By day, he prepared the dead for the ferryman with such care and precision that his reputation as an agent of God sometimes eclipsed the rumors of his private endeavors. Unmarried, in his early-60's, had never been seen in the company of a woman, and whose flamboyant nature raised the occasional eyebrow. No one else knew he had already known, and lost, his one true love many years ago.

He revealed to Carmen Alicia de la Vega, his favorite cousin, the location of her lover's resting place. He did this for two main reasons, to ease her suffering and out of spite for her husband who made it a point to ridicule Luis Alfredo for his effeminate disposition at any given opportunity.

He prepared the body according to standard procedure and took extra care with the heart. Since there would not be a funeral service, Luis Alfredo placed two coins on the hallowed eye sockets before he offered a prayer and sealed the casket. After Carmen had selected the headstone, her cousin had an inscription engraved on it that read: *The only thing worth living for, and dying for, is love.*

5

Carmen knelt beside the unmarked grave barely able to hold back her tears while she read the letter aloud that she had written for her love before his untimely death. She began to write it—like she had written all the others—while her husband slept in the dark hours before dawn. And she continued to write it during the day when Gonzalo left her in the morning without a kiss. She completed it in the evening when Gonzalo failed to return home at a decent hour.

He attended private meetings with members of his inner circle. Though he claimed they deliberated over civic matters on their personal time—as a show of commitment to Old Sienna—Carmen knew the truth of it. In part because the other wives had grown suspicious of their husbands who arrived home smelling of rum and perfume, which led to allocating funds for a new bath house in the basement of the civic center where the private meetings were held, and in part because Gonzalo had a penchant for talking in his sleep when he consumed too much rum.

Gonzalo muttered their names in a haze of dreams and shadows. Lorena, Claudia, Cecilia, Fermina, Gabriela, Magdalena, Patricia, Teresa and Beatriz. His whispers—a litany of empty promises and flattery to persuade the women to fulfill his desires—broke Carmen's heart, killing her softly in the bed where he laid beside her, but refused to touch her.

She fell asleep shedding silent tears wondering why her

husband did not want her and what she had done to lead him astray. It wasn't until after she met El Prieto, Señor Gabriel Aquino, one morning when her carriage took her to the sea that her life had changed. She had never seen the man before that day, for he had just returned from America to bury his wife. He was standing in the water watching the sunrise when her carriage approached. He introduced himself when he returned to the shore and noted the redness in her eyes.

Carmen wiped away her tears but she could not hide the weariness in her gaze. She hadn't slept in days. For several nights, she lay in bed waiting for her husband to return and she laid awake—pretending to be asleep—waiting for his caress. His snoring broke the silence and his whispers broke her heart.

She'd watch Gonzalo sleep. He always slept on his back. His round lips partially open beneath his thin black mustache with streaks of grey despite his youth. His short coarse hair also peppered with streaks of grey around his forehead complimented his caramel complexion. Gonzalo was a tall man with a robust frame who went to bed late and rose before the dawn.

Carmen laid in bed silent. She wanted to question him about his late nights and early mornings, but she feared his temper. Instead she waited until after he left before she climbed out of bed and had her carriage take her to the sea. She contemplated suicide by drowning, similar to the legend of La Llorona—the Nahua woman who served as Hernán Cortés's mistress, only to be abandoned by her lover so that he could marry someone else—which spread throughout the region after the Spanish colonization of the Americas.

It was there in the early morning light when Gabriel Aquino ambled up to her on the sandy shore. He inquired about the sadness in her eyes. She averted her gaze and avoided his questions, but the man persisted with a gentle voice as calm as the ocean breeze. "No one comes to the water without questions in their heart." Gabriel prepared to offer the compassion she needed. It would not be the first time he offered advice on matters of love, nor would it be the last.

Her tragic beauty surprised him. Lovely in her natural splendor like a flower left to grow in the wild and to be loved by no one.

"It is not appropriate for a woman to discuss her marital troubles with another man." Carmen said without meeting his gaze.

"Indeed you are correct." Gabriel Aquino turned toward the horizon. "Though I can assure you I have no intention of dishonoring your name."

Carmen cast him a sidelong glance. In the four years of their marriage, Gonzalo had never said a kind thing to her. Here a stranger treated her like a woman, and she wondered about his motives.

"Only a man who does not understand the true nature of love will attempt to seduce another man's woman under the guise of friendship."

"What makes you an expert on such matters?" Carmen eyed him suspiciously.

"I would hardly consider myself an expert, but I daresay heartbreak is a great teacher."

"What do you know of heartbreak?"

"It is the purest form of pain. It will shatter your soul and leave a scar on your heart that never heals."

They sat on the patio of his boathouse facing the open sea. They conversed like old friends aware of each other's lot in life. Gabriel Aquino met her at a time when she wanted to love her husband, even though Gonzalo had no intention of reciprocating her affections. And Carmen met Gabriel in a time when he was no longer open to falling in love, for he had already experienced that perfection and did not wish to taint the memory of his late wife by searching for love with another woman.

In that moment Gabriel became the brother she never had and they spoke without concern for the time that passed. She asked about the motives of men to better understand her husband's behavior and he clarified the fragility of the male ego, which did not excuse immoral behavior, but provided the insight she sought. Insight he did not possess in his youth, for it is the wisdom that only comes with age and experience. He put on a pot of coffee with beans he brought back from his time in Colombia. The morning sun sauntered across the heavens as Carmen revealed her dilemma.

She was married to a man chosen by her father to secure her future without considering her need for love.

"Love is a fickle notion at your age and marriage under such circumstances never lasts." Her father, a Colonel in the Army, had said. "You will marry for the future. It is there that love will greet you after your husband has exhausted his body's desires and all that remains is his need for your company in the winter of his life."

"What about my needs?" Carmen had protested.

"Your priority will be your family. Your needs will be theirs."

Gabriel Aquino listened without interrupting, like a preacher in a confessional, as Carmen revealed her pain to a man she did not know. For it was as it has always been that we reveal more to strangers than we reveal to those we know. What she did know was that despite the dichotomy of their personal circumstances they shared a longing for love inherent in the heart of every romantic.

She understood this by the way he remembered his late wife. Her memory lingered like a ghost. He saw her often and felt her presence, but when he whispered his affections she did not reply. When he apologized for not being a better husband she would not forgive him. He never felt lonelier than when he woke in the morning and fell asleep at night.

They spoke about everything; in accordance with the method strangers use to become friends. What impressed him most about the well-educated Colonel's daughter who possessed a natural instinct for love was her ability to articulate her thoughts and feelings as only someone who said intelligent things knew how to do.

She gained a profound understanding in that moment that it was possible to speak with a man about love and not have him misconstrue the conversation as an invitation to betray her vows.

Over time they came to enjoy each other's company. Meeting on Saturday mornings at his boathouse to drink coffee and discuss literature. They conversed about the Romantic Period, the literary and intellectual movement of the second half of the 18th century and the implications the movement had across Europe. They debated whether Puerto Rico would have had greater success in achieving independence from Spain, and later the United States, through intellectually-inspired means, in lieu of the series of unsuccessful revolts and attacks that began with the Taíno rebellion of 1511 and continued protests during the American acquisition of Puerto Rico, which had been justified by American politicians as part of American Manifest Destiny.

It was difficult to imagine that a woman of noble standing would risk a scandal with her friendship to a widower who lived beyond the city limits and visited him on a weekly basis. Nevertheless, their friendship blossomed and when her chauffeur suggested if perhaps it would have been more prudent to cease her weekly visits before her husband learned about them and assumed the worst, she thanked him for his concern and carried on for several years with her innocent interactions. She did so with the same confidence she possessed when she engaged in intellectual discourse, certain of her position and certain about the outcome.

That certainty, however, was lost to her the day she met the love of her life. She was at the market in the Plaza of Los Rios. She navigated through the crowds with the grace of a swan dismissing the urgings of the merchants, the snake charmers and the charlatans. She negotiated prices in her favor for the items she needed, and paid with pieces of gold to remind the shopkeepers they needed her more than she needed them.

It was in that moment—with permission from God—when destiny and love conspired to answer her prayers.

He first caught her eye when he stood beneath the archway leading into the Alley of the Angels. The alley ran from the marketplace in the church square at the center of Old Sienna to the eastern entrance of the Cathedral of Santa Maria. The white and brown cobblestone path complimented the stonework of the buildings linked by the archway. Statues of angels stood in the crevices carved out of the alley walls as the midday sun cast angular shadows against the stones.

She froze at the sight of him. To her he seemed so handsome, so seductive, so different from any other man she had ever seen, that she could not understand how he stood there virtually unnoticed by every other woman in the crowd. His dark brown eyes locked with hers. He resembled a bronze statue with his caramel complexion and stoic expression as he studied her from a distance. The man remained motionless in his vest and dustcoat, with a thin beard and his hair parted neatly down the center.

She lowered her eyes when she met his intense gaze. That brief glance was the beginning of a tragic love that altered the fate of Old Sienna.

After she recovered from the seismic tremor of love at first sight Carmen Alicia de la Vega made to return to her carriage. She navigated through the bustling crowd forgetting to breathe. Absent was the doe's gait she possessed moments ago. She bumped into people and they collided into her. Shoving her this way and that in the clamor of the market.

She glanced over her shoulder, but the stranger no longer stood beneath the arch. He hurried after her without letting himself be seen. Keeping her in his line of sight as he maneuvered through the crowd hoping to catch her before she escaped.

Amid the haggling between merchants and shoppers a thief was spotted and the crowd bottlenecked as an argument ensued. Carmen arrived at her carriage. Her chauffer held the door open. She stood in the carriage entrance with one foot on the ground and the other on the footboard. She turned back to face the crowded market and scanned the sea of unfamiliar faces. She hoped to catch another glimpse of the stranger, to gaze into his eyes and feel the intensity of his stare as he looked into her soul.

She spotted him, cornered and trying to push through the crowd. Their eyes met. He froze. A hint of a smile played on his lips. He shrugged. He surrendered the authority of his presence to the chaos and allowed himself to be carried away with the momentum of the mob. He lifted his satin top hat to bid her farewell.

Carmen struggled to suppress a smile as she climbed into the carriage. She stared, lost in thought, through the window on the opposite side of the carriage. It rocked as it traveled over the cobblestone streets. The moment was as Hesiod wrote in the Theogony, "From their eyelids as they glanced dripped love."

6

The carriage made its way to the shore through a floating blanket of fog. The sun had barely peered over the horizon when Carmen saw her friend, Gabriel Aquino, standing knee-deep in the water. He stood with his hands on his hips and his white pants rolled up to his knees as he watched the sunrise.

"Men and their routines." She muttered to herself.

Despite being a Colonel's daughter, she never understood the nature of men as creatures of habit. Her father followed the same daily routine until the day he died. A daily ritual of exercise before breakfast—in the predawn darkness—followed by one cigarette before his shower. He shaved every morning and pressed his uniform every night. The soldiers respected him because he led by example and held himself to the same standard of expectation he set for them.

The only day he broke from his routine was when he died in his sleep. Carmen liked to think her father died because he missed his wife, who had passed three years ago. Others believed his long life was attributed to his heroic service during the Spanish-American War. As a local hero, he led a quiet life in Old Sienna. Even during retirement, he maintained his military inspired demeanor. Despite the pleas of town officials, he refused to enter the political arena. He believed politics was for ambitious men who cared more about their legacy than for the people they claimed to serve. So, it came to pass that when the vapors of death filled his lungs he was remembered by the public for his service, and by his daughter for his personal proclivities.

When the carriage arrived at the boathouse Carmen waited until Gabriel returned from the water before she emerged. After he set their cups of coffee on the table and they took their seats on the patio he looked at his guest and recognized that something had changed.

She stared ahead with a pensive look in her eye. The ocean resembled a grey mirror reflecting the golden glow of dawn that spilled across the heavens through a cloudy sky like molten lava.

Everything seemed different from when she last visited Gabriel. The world was now filled with endless possibilities. Hope filled her heart and in the wake of feeling something indefinable she knew—without knowing—that unfulfilled dreams and regrets would no longer haunt her life.

She confided in Gabriel what had occurred in the market. She described the unnerving gaze of the handsome stranger who looked at her as if he peered into her soul and recognized her from a lifetime before.

"It was utterly different from the way Fernando looked at me when we first met," she paused.

Gabriel listened without interrupting.

"Fernando seldom looks at me now. He doesn't even attempt to make eye contact when we're in the same room. It's like he doesn't even see me, or if he does he has grown tired of the view."

After she returned home from the market she fell asleep that night replaying the moment in her mind. She manipulated the memory with various outcomes. She dreamt the stranger stood beneath her balcony and serenaded her in the moonlight. She woke before dawn and raced to her balcony, but instead of the handsome suitor she only saw her husband climb into his carriage and leave without giving her a second glance.

She returned to the market each day, but to no avail. The mysterious stranger had not been seen. Who was he? Where did he come from? Where did he go?

"How is it that this man consumes my thoughts?" Carmen turned to Gabriel. "This is madness!"

"There is always some madness in love."

"Are you mocking me with a Nietzsche quote?"

"My dear Carmen, I am a romantic. I would never dare make a mockery of love."

Carmen sighed. She could not believe she permitted herself to be unhinged by the sight of a man she had never formally met. Her memory of him persisted in the mornings and in the evenings. When she woke thinking about him she realized that her desire to know him was more than a simple curiosity, or the infatuations of a schoolgirl experiencing her first crush. She could not avoid a profound feeling of longing that caused her to stop in the middle of whatever she was doing and surrender herself to the silent fantasies of her day dreams.

She did not endure the silent torture alone.

Days turned to weeks and the time had been agonizing for him as well. The stranger had wandered aimlessly through the cobbled streets of Old Sienna searching for another glimpse of the enchanting beauty he saw in the market. He was a foreigner in the city to where destiny had brought him. His business was his own, but it required him to travel throughout the Caribbean. In the sudden silence of other voices, he became familiar with the growing port city on the southeastern coast of Puerto Rico.

At night when the wind was calm and the stars emerged in

their places beyond the clouds he heard singing around every corner. He needed to see her again. He needed to soothe his soul with another glimpse of her exquisiteness. He needed to look into her eyes and lose himself to the hopelessness of love lest he find himself trapped in the catastrophe of what could have been.

At the end of another week he wandered through the Park of the Saints. Night had fallen and the moon emerged to guide him. He found a seat beneath a tree and there he remained until he woke the following morning on a bench to the sound of church bells. It was then that he saw her emerge from the carriage behind a man whom he could only assume was her husband. He recognized the man from his business dealings in the Capitol Building. Fernando Gonzalo de la Vega dressed in a dark suit with a matching vest and tie appeared more concerned with the adoring crowd than with his wife.

The mob swallowed him as Carmen Alicia de la Vega stood in the carriage entrance and scanned her surroundings. The sadness in her eyes searched for hope and for the stranger who studied her from a distance. She dismounted from the carriage with the help from her chauffer.

"Gracias Miguel." She thanked him with a smile.

Miguel nodded and returned to his place at the front of the carriage. The horses trotted off through the gathering congregation. The people parted to let him pass. After the carriage disappeared around the corner, the stranger in the park raced to the fountain in the center of the plaza. He splashed water on his face and looked at his reflection in the water to straighten his tie and wet his hair.

After squeezing his way into the cathedral, he maneuvered among the standing attendees along the rear and sidewalls. The pews were reserved for the aristocrats who made generous donations to the church over the years. It was near the front of the church where the stranger spotted Carmen seated beside her husband. He watched her amid the intermittent silence and echo of the priest's voice off the high ceiling. Her breathtaking beauty captivated him and it wasn't until halfway through the mass that she noticed him leaning against a pillar. For the remainder of the service they exchanged stolen glances. It was there in the breaths between heartbeats and in the presence of God when their love affair began.

7

Carmen pulled her hand away from the gravestone and wiped away her tears. "You swore to love me forever. Now you are gone, and I'll never know if you kept your promise." She stood and returned to her carriage.

Miguel, her chauffer, opened the carriage door and assisted her with climbing inside. They disappeared into the fog and left the cemetery. Isaac and Olivia emerged from behind the headstones and approached the unmarked grave. When they stood where Carmen had knelt Olivia brandished the bloodstained letter. She looked at it in silence as a soft breeze blew past.

"Do you think he is the man they found dead in the alley?" Isaac finally said.

"I don't know." Olivia said pensively. She glanced over her shoulder. "It seems strange that a woman would visit an unmarked grave wearing a black veil."

"Unless she wanted to conceal her identity," Isaac said.

"To what end?"

"Perhaps she is married to someone else."

"Don't say that!" She reproached him.

"Let us return tomorrow and see if she comes back."

After a moment of deliberation Olivia agreed. They left the cemetery amid the setting sun and deepening shadows. When they returned to Old Sienna nightfall had cast a dark blue blanket across the sky with the sparkle of Caribbean stars scattered about.

"Meet me in the atrium of the cathedral after your lessons."

Isaac nodded and waited for her to enter her home before he disappeared into the night. He wandered through the deserted streets of Old Sienna with an innocent heart that had not yet been broken by love.

He thought about the woman in the cemetery and he thought about the person buried in the unmarked grave. The way she mourned him, shedding tears and sitting alone without concern for the time that passed, as if she did not want to be anywhere else in the world than by his side. It reminded Isaac of how his father, Señor Rolando Quintero, whispered to his late wife in the darkness after he thought Isaac had fallen asleep. He'd tell her about their day and about Isaac's academic progress before he cried himself to sleep in silence confessing he still loved her as fiercely as he did on their wedding day.

"Love is the only memory one never loses, Isaac." His father had said. "Because even if one loses his mind the memory always remains in the heart."

Even though Señor Rolando Quintero made a decent living as a hatter and had quite the reputation for the quality of his work, Isaac recognized the loneliness in his father's eyes. Known as the Mad Hatter of Old Sienna, he occupied his time making Ascot caps, Bowlers, Panamas, Top Hats, sombreros, and his most popular item the fedora. His heart and thoughts, however, remained occupied by the memory of his late wife Maricela Aquino.

They had grown up together in the small town then known as Providencia before it was stomped out of existence by the emergence of Old Sienna. Despite the change they stayed, they fell in love, and they married. When his father passed, Rolando sold his father's lot of land and used the proceeds to establish his hat shop. Three years later, they were blessed with a son, and all felt right with the world until a bout of small pox struck the budding city.

Some claimed it was punishment from God for erasing the memory of Providencia, but others believed the sickness arrived at their port city with cargo from infected parts of the world. For a brief time after Maricela's passing the hat shop remained closed. No one had seen Rolando for several weeks while he mourned the loss of the love of his life.

It wasn't until his brother-in-law, Gabriel Aquino, intervened that everything had changed. He arrived at the back door of the shop where their living quarters had been, and invited himself inside carrying a bottle of rum and two glasses.

"Let's put my nephew to bed. Men must talk."

Rolando looked at his brother-in-law perplexed. He always found him to be a peculiar man, but if he had to be honest he found Gabriel to be good company. And so, it was that after they laid Isaac in his crib, Rolando and Gabriel polished off a bottle of rum while reminiscing about Maricela. They mourned her death, but more than that they celebrated her life, which based on the way she lived is what she would have wanted.

Despite the hangover Rolando reopened his shop the following day. His first customer was his brother-in-law who arrived with a special request, and coconut water.

"Drink up!" Gabriel had said. "Coconut water is the best remedy for a hangover short of death."

"What is it with your fascination with death?" Rolando said remembering Gabriel's area of study.

"It is the only guarantee in the world aside from taxes, but beyond that it is as Edgar Allan Poe once said: 'Love acknowledges no limits—not even the grave.'"

The quote had always been Gabriel's favorite. Isaac heard him repeat it every day and twice on Sunday. It dawned on him that perhaps his uncle, or rather Edgar Allan Poe, had been correct in his assessment. Isaac reflected on his lessons. *How is it that death and love are so deeply intertwined?* Miguel de Cervantes compared love and war in 1604 when he wrote in Don Quixote, "Love and war are all one." Two hundred and fifty years later Frank Smedley wrote, "All's fair in love and war." Isaac contemplated the analogous nature of love and war and wondered if it is true that nothing is the same after war and nothing is the same after love.

Seeing the woman in the cemetery reminded him of his father and his uncle. Death claimed the people they loved the way war claims lives, yet love remained suspended at the edge of space and time. He wondered about his own destiny. Would he suffer a similar fate in love?

A figure emerged from the darkness and the streetlight cast his shadow across the cobbled street. His silhouette consisted of a long coat and wide brim hat. The man was tall with broad shoulders and appeared to have a hand in his coat pocket. The glow of a cigarette reflected in his eyes, but the street lamp behind him obscured his features. A breeze made his long coat flutter. He studied Isaac silently.

Lightning flickered in the distance. Storm clouds gathered over the open sea. The scent of fresh air and sea salt carried by a cool breeze filled the air. The mysterious figure turned down an alley and disappeared into the shadows. After a moment of hesitation Isaac sprinted after the man. He arrived at the alleyway where the stranger had been swallowed by the darkness.

Isaac briefly contemplated chasing after him, but he decided to return home. The hour was late and his father would be worried. When he entered the home to the rear of the hat shop there was only darkness save for one candle next to a plate of food. There was a note from his father reminding him to eat and wash his plate before bed.

After his meal Isaac sat in his father's armchair. It was identical to the one his uncle had in the boathouse. The upholstery was short pile velvet with a rusty peach accent on the cushion. Isaac leaned against the comfortable vintage wing back of the chair. He gazed through the window and watched the storm clouds approach like a floating city of flickering lights.

Curtains billowed when fresh air blew through the window. He dozed off in the chair and fell into a dream. It began as a dark and tenuous dream. Isaac found himself in an unfamiliar place. A train station built like a cathedral of iron with dim lighting and deep shadows. A series of cylindrical metal carriages waited like giant snakes made of steel. Crowds of soldiers bid their loved ones' farewell on the platforms amid clouds of mist and the hissing of steam.

Isaac recognized himself standing beside a woman. He appeared to be a few years older. Taller, stronger, more refined. He stood with an air of dignity and confidence he did not recognize in himself.

The woman was unfamiliar with her dark brown hair pulled back in a bun. Her hazel eyes accentuated her china doll's complexion as she gazed at the older Isaac adoringly. She stood in his embrace, perfect, elegant with soft features; it was as if Saint Catherine of Bologna—Patron Saint of the Arts—sketched her into existence with a gentle stroke guided by the hand of God.

He figured she must have been about twenty-three, yet there was something about her demeanor that reminded him of the ageless beauty of an angel. Her long red dress covered her shoulders and fell to just below her knees.

"Did you know that no one in the history of the world has ever seen the love of their life before meeting them?" Said an unfamiliar voice.

Isaac turned and saw the mysterious figure from the darkened street now standing beside him. His face remained hidden by a veil of darkness. A shadow fell over his face cast by his wide brim hat.

"Who is she?" Isaac turned back toward the woman.

"She will be the love of your life."

"Love of my life?" Isaac looked perplexed. "But I'm in love with—"

"I know." The stranger cut him off. He walked away and disappeared among the crowd.

Isaac glanced over his shoulder at his future self before he raced after the stranger. The man had walked through a set of double doors. Isaac pushed his way through the throng of people bottlenecked at the entry-exit doors. When he crossed the threshold, he found that he was no longer at the train station.

The crowds had vanished. When the doors slammed shut behind him, Isaac stood on the front steps of the Cathedral of Santa Maria. The empty plaza stretched before him beneath a clear blue sky. Stone benches were assembled in the shade of fruit trees surrounded by bushes. Patches of grass stretched across the plaza and surrounded the fountain. Passages of stone neatly carved among them lined with petunias and roses like a garden. A dove sat perched on the arm of the statue of an angel in the center of the fountain. The dove flapped its wings and shook its head when droplets of water from the steady stream splashed up at him.

"Why is he alone?" Isaac muttered to himself.

Why indeed? The voice of the stranger echoed in Isaac's mind.

Isaac scanned his surroundings. He saw the silhouette of the man before he disappeared behind a set of tall bushes. He pursued him through the plaza until he found him standing underneath a canopy of trees. The stranger stood with his back to Isaac and his hands clasped behind his back.

"Are you going to tell me about the woman at the train station?" Isaac asked.

"I would, but I cannot ruin the magic you will experience when you discover love as a man."

The stranger sensed Isaac's confusion.

Isaac hesitated before he said, "But I have already discovered love."

"You have only felt the feverish palpitations of young love. That is but a flame that flares when a match is struck."

"That doesn't make it any less real," Isaac said.

"I never said it wasn't real. I'm only saying it is different."

"Different how?"

"You must discover that in your own time, for it is the nature of love to be understood with age."

"Then why did you show me the woman in the train station?"

"I gave you a glimpse of your future to give you hope."

"Hope?" Isaac whispered.

"You are headed down a dark path. A path of love and ruin

that only the true Romantics have experienced. It is a journey that drives most men mad and leads others to an early grave."

"What does that mean?"

"You will know when your heart breaks."

Isaac lowered his eyes momentarily. "Who are you?" Isaac said, but when he looked up the stranger was gone. Isaac's eyes darted back and forth. He saw only the empty benches beneath the trees and the gazebo made of stone. He contemplated the stranger's cryptic message, but remained as confused as ever. He had no idea that the glimmer of hope the stranger revealed would someday bring him back from the deepest recesses of his soul.

8

Isaac woke to the sound of thunder rumbling in the distance. The worst of the storm had passed north and east of Old Sienna. The cobblestone streets still shone, and raindrops clung to the leaves beneath an overcast sky.

Isaac shifted in the armchair. A blanket covered him from his shoulders to his feet. His father must have placed it on him before he opened the hat shop. Isaac looked at the clock. He kicked off the blanket when he realized it was almost time for his Saturday morning lessons with his uncle.

Even after seven months Isaac was not accustomed to waking up early on Saturday mornings to walk the mile to his uncle's boathouse. After he washed his face and brushed his teeth he grabbed his satchel and bid his father a good day.

Isaac froze when he arrived at the turn in the road along the beach. He couldn't believe his eyes when he saw the same carriage from the cemetery parked behind the boathouse. His uncle walked the woman back to her carriage. She wore a long black dress and her face remained hidden by a matching veil. The horses pulled the carriage away as Isaac approached.

"Who was that?" Isaac asked.

"A friend."

"How come I've never seen her before?"

"She hasn't visited since before your Saturday morning

lessons began."

"What's her name?"

"That is not your concern," Uncle Gabriel winked. "Come, you're late."

Isaac followed his uncle into the boathouse. He told his uncle about his dream as they walked through the main room.

"Aristotle once said, 'Hope is a waking dream.'" Uncle Gabriel said over his shoulder.

"What does that mean?"

"It symbolizes that in your heart you believe anything is possible."

"Who do you think was the stranger in my dream?" Isaac asked. "What do you think he meant when he said I was heading down a dark path of love and ruin?"

When they entered the study room Uncle Gabriel turned to his nephew and studied him momentarily. "What do you remember about the Metamorphoses concerning love?"

Isaac looked at his uncle perplexed. He remembered the 2nd century Latin novel by Apuleius and the story about the love between Psyche, who represented the soul, and Cupid, who represented desire. "I believe the moral of the story is that without trust there can be no love."

Isaac remembered the story well. Cupid made only one request. He asked Psyche to trust him without question and not look upon his face, but at the behest of her sisters Psyche defied him. As a result of going against his wishes she lost him. She embarked on a series of tasks designed by Venus as punishment, but in the end, they are reunited and marry.

"Many Renaissance era paintings and sculptures were

inspired by centuries-old poetry and literature. Michelangelo, Caravaggio, Giovanni da San Giovanni and other artists had patrons like Lorenzo de Medici and the Mattei family commission them to create priceless works of art. Among them was the Sleeping Cupid by Michelangelo, but it was Donatello who infused the form with Christian meanings. Amid this artistic explosion Caravaggio gifted us with *Victorious Love*, which was directly inspired by the ancient Roman poet Virgil's most famous quote, 'Love conquers all, and so let us surrender ourselves to Love.'"

"What does any of this have to do with my dream?"

"Funny you should ask." Uncle Gabriel smiled. "In the ancient classical world of art, winged infants known as Putti were believed to influence human lives. Later, in the Renaissance era, the Putti were depicted in the form of Cupid. Cupid, as you know was also the Roman type of messenger being who traveled halfway between the realms of the human and the divine."

Uncle Gabriel grabbed a heavy book off the shelf and flipped through the pages as he continued to speak. "Given Cupid's marriage to Psyche it's quite plausible to interpret your dream as a moment when the messenger of love brings knowledge of the unknowable and presents it to you in your subconscious, your psyche."

He handed the book—the Encyclopedia of Angels—to his nephew.

"What is Cupid's true name?" Uncle Gabriel asked.

Isaac glanced at the page to which his uncle had opened the book. He looked up at his uncle's mischievous grin.

"Eros." Isaac whispered.

"And what are some of the synonyms associated with Eros?"

Isaac read the list of words from various languages: amor,

amar, love, Dio, Dios, Cupid.

"That's who came to visit you in your dream, my boy. It means you're in love!" Uncle Gabriel patted him on the shoulder.

Isaac lowered his eyes embarrassed.

"Don't fret. We all experience it. We must. For despite our humanity love is the only way we can be like gods. It is in love that we glimpse heaven during our lifetime and have proof that there's something worth looking forward to in the end."

Isaac nodded pensively.

When Isaac completed his assignment a few hours later he placed his notebooks in his satchel and prepared to leave. He glanced at the Encyclopedia of Angels on the desk and remembered his dream. *You are headed down a path of love and ruin*, the voice of Eros echoed in his mind. He replaced the book on the shelf and left the boathouse.

Uncle Gabriel Aquino stood knee-deep in the water beneath the midday sun. Gabriel stared off into the distance. His eyes pensive, his breathing steady, and his mind clear. The sea breeze felt soothing as the water lapped the shore.

Isaac looked around. The trees swayed beneath scattered clouds. The storm had retreated beyond the horizon. He considered telling his uncle he had completed his assignment and was leaving, but decided against it.

"Never interrupt a man's conversation with God," his uncle once said. "You'll piss them both off."

Isaac headed back to Old Sienna. The clamor on the docks to the north drew his attention. He caught a glimpse of the stranger with the long trench coat and wide brim hat amid the crowd of merchants and dockworkers. When Isaac blinked, the man had vanished. His eyes darted back and forth, but the man was nowhere to be found. A shiver ran up Isaac's spine before he turned and headed up the road. He looked over his shoulder then continued in silence.

When he arrived at the Cathedral of Santa Maria the plaza was filled with Believers and shopkeepers and prospective buyers. The steady stream of the fountain was nearly drowned out by the clamor of haggling over prices and various other conversations.

Isaac climbed the steps of the cathedral and pulled the heavy wooden door open before he slipped inside the church. The door slammed shut behind him with a thunderous boom that echoed off the high ceiling. The smooth whitewashed walls extended to the high-arched ceiling lined with a series of crisscrossing patterns carved out of the stone. Sunlight accentuated the colors of the stained-glass windows and filled the church with natural lighting.

A couple sat in a nearby pew. The man huddled over a woman as they spoke in hushed tones. An elderly woman lit a candle in the far corner and offered a prayer. A padre shuffled his feet as he made his way past the confessionals lost in thought.

Isaac walked briskly along the far wall behind a series of pillars. He reached a small door off to the left of the altar. It led to an open corridor and the atrium. He glanced over his shoulder as he crossed the threshold. He shielded his eyes from the sun and scanned the courtyard. Pillars lined all four sides, interconnected by arches with open corridors above them. It wasn't until he reached the far end of the passageway that he found Olivia sitting on a bench reading the letter.

"Do you think it's wise to be reading the letter in public?" Isaac approached.

"There's no one else here." Olivia looked around. She tucked the letter into her pocket and stood. "How was your lesson?"

"Interesting to say the least."

"How do you mean?" She asked as they proceeded to walk. They exited the atrium through the east doors that led to the Alley of the Angels.

Isaac stared ahead pensively before he spoke. He told her about his dream and his uncle's interpretation. The mysterious figure, the train station, the ominous message, and the conclusion in the plaza at the stone gazebo all left unanswered questions about its meaning.

"And your uncle is certain Eros was the messenger in your dream?" She glanced at the statues of angels along the wall.

Isaac nodded. They walked together in silence. When they arrived at the cemetery they sat on the same bench as the day before without saying a word. She rested her head on his shoulder and together they waited for the carriage to return. That was the nature of their friendship. They could sit together for hours and discuss many things, or they could sit for hours without saying a word.

The air in the cemetery was cooler, for it seemed to always be covered in perpetual mist. The day wore on and they dozed off sitting beside each other on the bench. The sound of horse hooves clattering on the cobblestone path roused them from their nap. They exchanged a curious glance before the carriage emerged from the fog and came to a stop before the church.

The chauffeur walked around to the side of the carriage and opened the door. The woman stepped down and motioned for him to stay with the carriage. She wore a long black dress and a veil concealed her face. She walked slowly toward the unmarked grave.

Isaac and Olivia stood and proceeded down the parallel path after her. When they saw her turn off from the cobblestone path they crossed the field of headstones and statues between the two paths. They ducked behind taller headstones when they drew near and listened to the woman cry.

After a few minutes, she began to speak. Though they could not discern what she said they heard her talk for a long while. Then she fell silent for a brief period before she continued crying.

Finally, she offered a prayer and made a sign of the cross on the headstone before she stood and left. They watched her disappear into the fog before they approached the black gravestone.

"This must be where they buried the unidentified man found dead in the alley and this letter *must* have been written by him." Olivia insisted.

"We don't know that," Isaac said.

"Did we just not witness the same thing?" Olivia cast him an incredulous glance.

"It's one thing to know what we see, but it is another thing to prove what we know."

"Great. You sound just like your uncle."

"Look, I'm just saying that we can't assume to know who is buried here without any proof. For all we know this could be a relative."

"Then why the unmarked grave?"

"I don't know, perhaps he committed a crime, and she is protecting his identity, or what if he was ex-communicated and isn't supposed to be buried here."

"Crimes against the Church? That's ridiculous," Olivia shook her head. "I swear Isaac you have the most active imagination I have ever seen. Where do you come up with these wild ideas? I suppose you truly are a writer."

Isaac gazed at her momentarily. Despite the years of their friendship her beauty enchanted him from the first. The workings of a poem stirred in his heart as he looked at her. He liked that Olivia knew him better than anyone else and that she accepted him for whom he was despite his eccentricities. Even at the tender age of seventeen he understood the rarity of that quality. Not necessarily because he possessed unique insight into the relationships between people. Rather it was because his uncle had once told him, "People capable of true friendship accept you not despite your proclivities, but *because* of your proclivities. This is the reason best friendships make a great foundation for marriage. Between best friends there's a trust that will never be broken, a respect that will always be shared, and an understanding that to hurt the other is to hurt oneself."

They had been friends for nearly ten years. A friendship that began with a chance encounter—when her father, Javier Villalobos, walked into the hat shop—to meet Rolando Quintero. He had originally planned to go alone to speak with the Mad Hatter, but Olivia insisted that he take her with him. When they arrived, the young girl browsed through the wide selection of hats. She was mildly impressed for it appeared to be a small shop from the outside with only a half dozen hats able to be displayed in the shop's sole window.

Inside, however, the shop stretched like a long corridor with hats lining both walls and others situated on long thin wooden tables. Isaac first saw her trying on a hat that fell over her eyes when she stood before a mirror. He approached her with a smile and introduced himself.

Javier Villalobos eyed the boy suspiciously from a few yards away.

"There's no cause for alarm." Rolando Quintero introduced himself when he approached the detective. "That is my son, Isaac. He helps after his studies. How may I be of service?"

Javier Villalobos avoided small talk. He inquired about Rolando's business with Guillermo Sedeño. Rolando had stated his business with Guillermo was the same as with everyone else, that of a shopkeeper and his customers. Unsatisfied with Rolando's reply, believing the shopkeeper-feigned ignorance, Javier instructed Rolando to refrain from continuing to do business with Guillermo in the future.

Not to be intimidated Rolando made it clear he ran his business on his own terms and would continue to do so for the rest of his days.

"You had just better hope they aren't numbered," Javier muttered.

Rolando ran the detective out of his shop. He stormed after him in a tirade of obscenities, which caused quite the scandal because Rolando was well known for his calm disposition.

In the presence of his daughter, Javier maintained his composure, but secretly he vowed to make Rolando pay for the embarrassment. His veiled threat, however, never came to fruition and not for lack of desire.

Once word had reached then-Junior Inspector Guillermo Sedeño of the incident he applauded Señor Quintero and assured him that Javier's words would remain an empty threat.

In the weeks that followed Isaac and Olivia ran into each other on several occasions. Despite attending different schools, their circle of friends overlapped, which led them to frequent the same places. When her father saw them together at the town malt shop, La

Fuente de Azucar, he forbade her from seeing him again. Naturally, this only led her to do the exact opposite. And so, it came to pass that in the excitement she found in the shadows of secrecy Olivia Villalobos grew fond of her new friend, Isaac Quintero. Their friendship blossomed over the years and eventually her father's watchful eye focused more on the bottles behind Roberto's bar than on his daughter's activities.

She would later say, "It's because of who he is that I enjoy his company, peculiarities and all."

There were times he felt she knew him better than he knew himself. Though he could never explain it he equated her with an angel sent just for him. He studied her in silence as she stood before him. *God, you're beautiful.* He loved the way her hair fell over her shoulders and billowed in the breeze.

She met his gaze and cast him a curious glance. "What?" She broke the silence.

"Huh?" Isaac flinched. "Oh nothing."

"Are you okay?" She tilted her head.

"Yes, I'm fine."

"Any ideas how we're going to figure this out?"

"I don't know, perhaps we should see if this woman returns tomorrow, and if she does we should follow her carriage when she leaves."

"Are you crazy?"

"What?" Isaac shrugged.

"Don't you know how difficult it is to keep up with a horse-drawn carriage on an uphill slope, even when the horses trot?"

Isaac had never put much thought into it. Few carriages had ever passed through his neighborhood in Old Sienna. The occasional automobile had been seen more frequently than carriages, and even then, they were mostly relegated to the wealthy quarter of town.

"What do you suggest?" Isaac said.

"I say we approach the woman and introduce ourselves. We could ask a few questions—"

"Oh, yes, *that* should go over well." Isaac cut her off. "Excuse me. What's your name? By the way, is it possible the man buried here wrote you this blood-stained love letter?"

"What if he did?"

"We don't know that," Isaac said. "And it wouldn't be a good idea to reveal the letter because we can't risk her telling someone about it."

"You're being paranoid." Olivia rolled her eyes.

"I'm being cautious. We're in possession of stolen evidence, remember?"

"You said, 'we,'" Olivia smiled.

"Well, yeah, we're in this together."

"All right," Olivia sighed. "We'll come back tomorrow and play it by ear."

"That's what scares me."

9

The following day as church bells tolled in the distance Chief Inspector Sedeño entered Rolando's hat shop. He removed his fedora and scanned the shop until he saw Isaac. He nodded and asked for Señor Quintero. Rolando emerged from the backroom and greeted the Chief Inspector with a smile and a firm handshake.

"Señor Quintero, the Mad Hatter. How are you, my friend?" The Chief Inspector smiled.

"I don't know why you insist on calling me that," Rolando shook his head. "That was years ago."

"I remember it like it was yesterday." Guillermo smiled.

"I have your order." Rolando changed the subject. He retrieved a box from behind the counter, opened it, and pulled out a white summer straw fedora with a gray hatband around the base.

Guillermo examined it with a keen eye as he ran his fingers along the one and three-fourth inch brim. "Exceptional work, as always, my friend."

"Well, I don't do it for free."

"After all the hats I have purchased from you throughout the years I *should* get this one for free."

"And risk being accused of attempting to bribe an officer of the law by your colleague, Javier Villalobos?" Rolando shook his head. "No thank you."

"Why would you ruin a good conversation by mentioning

that good-for-nothing drunkard?" Guillermo handed the fedora back to Rolando.

Isaac froze and cast the Chief Inspector a sidelong glance. His father placed the hat back inside the box as Guillermo continued.

"A man of his caliber would be more useful to the department if he would only put down the bottle."

"Every man has his vice," Rolando said. "That is a matter between him and God."

"True enough, but I need everyone focused right now and given the circumstances, I don't know who I can trust."

"That's not a good sign for a police department."

"No, it is not. Especially when a key piece of evidence in a murder investigation has gone missing."

Rolando arched an eyebrow without saying a word.

"A man with no identification has been murdered in my town and the only thing that could help me identify him has been stolen from the evidence locker."

He watched Rolando seal the box and write up a bill of sale. The Mad Hatter seemed more interested in packaging the box than in anything the inspector said.

"Señor Rolando," The Chief Inspector leaned over the counter. "Why don't you ever ask me for details about my cases. In all these years, you are the only person who does not question me about my work."

"I believe it is best I do not know."

"And it is *because* you are not nosey that I am comfortable discussing this with you," Guillermo said. "I know you won't babble to the rest of the world."

"You could be mistaken."

"If you weren't a recluse, I would be mistaken, but I'm not."

Rolando scoffed. "Very well, Guillermo have it your way. Reveal state secrets to me."

The Chief Inspector glanced over his shoulder at Isaac before he spoke. "I'm under extreme pressure to find a blood-stained letter before the end of the week."

"You only have five days, but why such a short time frame?"

"I'm expecting the renowned graphologist, Julian Aponte, to inspect the letter."

"Forgive my ignorance, Chief Inspector, but what exactly does a graphologist do?"

"He specializes in studying penmanship by comparing writing samples to determine the identity of the author."

"They can do that?" Rolando said with wide eyes.

"It's a new century, my friend. The advent of new skills grows with each day."

"I see," Rolando nodded.

"Once we identify the victim we will be able to identify his killer." Guillermo brandished his wallet and handed Rolando the money for his purchase. "There's even talk of implementing a new method of investigating by identifying criminals through fingerprinting."

"Fingerprinting?" Rolando looked at his hand.

"In the 1890's the French, British and Argentinians independently developed methods for investigating crimes and identifying the guilty through the series of arches and loops on our hands and fingers." Guillermo continued. "The death of a young boy in Buenos Aires is the first murder solved using fingerprint identification. The mother eventually confessed to the crime."

Rolando cast the Chief Inspector an incredulous glance.

"We may never understand the atrocities of man, Rolando, but no one deserves to get away with murder. Regardless if we know the identity of the victim, or not."

"Even forgotten souls deserve justice," Rolando nodded.

The Chief Inspector agreed as he gazed through the shop window at the passersby on the street. After having interviewed half the police force about who had access to the evidence locker on the day in question. He had a suspect in mind, but he needed more than mere speculation. To build a case he needed hard evidence. Especially when it concerned one of the most decorated officers on the force, even if he was a drunk.

10

Fernando Gonzalo de la Vega sat in a secluded corner of the near-empty café. His robust frame filled the bench on his side of the booth. He glanced over his shoulder at the barista who wiped the counter with a white cloth.

A waiter arrived at the booth. He recognized the governor and bowed before he took his order. Café con Leche with a dash of cinnamon. Fernando reached into the inner pocket of his jacket and retrieved a pack of cigarettes. He lit one after the waiter left.

A moment later, Javier Villalobos walked through the door. His eyes locked on the governor. They glared at each other momentarily. The inspector shrugged his shoulders and approached the booth.

"Do you have the letter?" Fernando studied Javier as he took his seat across the table.

"I did not come here to hand over the letter." Javier lit a cigarette of his own.

"Then why did you even bother to come?"

"I would like to renegotiate our terms."

"You have balls, Javier. I'll grant you that," Fernando nodded.

"After you decided to not show up for our previous meeting I decided that the price for this letter has gone up. Until we come to an agreement, I will hold on to the letter for protection."

The men stared at each other momentarily. The governor felt

the anger rise in his chest. He wanted to reach across the table and rip out the inspector's throat. Javier possessed the only thing keeping him alive and his unwillingness to surrender it hindered Fernando's plans.

"What do you intend to do with this extra money, Javier?"

"My business is my own." Javier said. He divulged nothing about his intention to flee Old Sienna with his sister and his daughter. Of all the wealthy families in Old Sienna that were affected by the Great Depression, his family had lost the most because of their investment in El Banco Español de Puerto Rico, which collapsed by the mid-1930's. The amount of money Javier demanded would provide them with an opportunity to start over in another place far from the reach of the corrupt politician. He slid a piece of paper across the table. "You just make sure you meet my demands."

Fernando lifted the paper off the table and unfolded it with his thumb and fingers in one hand. He scoffed and shook his head. "Do not press your luck, Javier. Your reputation as a mean drunk is already a strike against you in the court of public opinion. Think what the mob will do to a corrupt officer involved in a murder. Think of what will happen to that lovely daughter of yours?"

"I'm already near the bottom of the barrel, Fernando. Perhaps it is you who should be more concerned with the disgrace your family will endure over your wife's infidelity and your role in the death of her lover."

"Remember your place, Javier. I'm a man of status afforded the luxury and protection only my name, my position, and my money can buy."

"If you believe that then I will leave you with your delusions Fernando. You'll discover soon enough that you live in a house of cards."

11

After Guillermo left with his order Rolando closed the shop for lunch. He had prepared soup the night before—sopa de pollo con arroz—chicken soup with rice. This recipe called for large pieces of pumpkin and diced potatoes.

Father and son sat at the kitchen table. Sunlight filtered in through the open windows. The curtains billowed in the warm breeze. They ate in silence as Isaac contemplated telling his father about his dream.

"What's on your mind?" Rolando asked.

"Nothing," Isaac said without meeting his father's eyes.

"No one thinks of nothing," Rolando scoffed.

Isaac smiled. His father always seemed to know when something weighed on his son's mind. "Well, I had this dream."

Rolando listened as Isaac described the mysterious figure from the night before and recounted seeing him in his dream. The dream perplexed the father as much as it did the son.

"A path of love and ruin, huh? What do you suppose it means?" Rolando asked his son.

"I don't know," Isaac shrugged. "Uncle Gabriel says it's because I'm in love."

"He does, does he?" Rolando leaned back in his seat with a smile. "That uncle of yours is quite the character."

The two sat together and completed their meal. Isaac helped

his father with the dishes when Rolando finally asked, "Well, who is she?"

"Who?" Isaac turned to his father perplexed.

"The one with whom you are in love."

Isaac shook his head. "No one."

"Don't be coy with me, son." Rolando nudged Isaac. "By the age of seventeen every man has fallen in love once."

Isaac lowered his eyes and shook his head embarrassed. "Will you need my help in the hat shop this afternoon?" He changed the subject.

Rolando cast his son a curious glance. "Do you have plans?"

"Kinda," Isaac said without meeting his father's gaze. He continued to dry the dishes and place them on the counter.

"I suppose business will be slow enough today that you may have the rest of the day off. Who are you going to be with today?"

Isaac hesitated. Although he knew his father did not disapprove of his friendship with Olivia, in fact, he was quite fond of her; he simply did not want his son to have any run-ins with her father. "I'm meeting Olivia at the café."

Rolando pursed his lips and sighed. "Just be careful."

"Why, because her father carries a gun?" Isaac said. "Aren't you the one who always said guns don't shoot people?"

"No, it was you who said that." Rolando corrected his son. "I've said fathers with guns and beautiful daughters shoot people. Boys in particular."

"You worry too much, dad."

"One day, when you are a father, you will understand."

Isaac rolled his eyes as he walked into his room to change.

An hour later he met Olivia inside the café. They each

ordered Café con Leche and sat in a booth away from the window. The café was mostly empty save for the barista and the waiter who conversed quietly at the counter. Isaac and Olivia watched the passersby through the large window until they were certain no one had followed them.

When they arrived at the cemetery the carriage was already there. Miguel sat in his seat and appeared to be taking a nap. They hurried past the carriage after the woman. The horses snorted, but otherwise remained still. They could not see the woman through the perpetual mist, but they assumed she had returned to the unmarked grave.

They ducked behind large gravestones when she came into view. Olivia cast Isaac an anxious glance while they observed the woman's daily ritual. After a few minutes the woman called out to them.

"What are you doing spying on a woman in a cemetery? Shouldn't you be wasting away your days like normal teenagers getting into mischief?"

Isaac and Olivia stared at each other in disbelief. Olivia arched an eyebrow and Isaac responded with a shrug. The woman waited for their reply. They stood, walked around the gravestones and approached.

"Please accept our apology," Olivia said. "We did not mean to intrude on your privacy. It's just that we were looking for something when we first saw you and we grew curious about what brought you to an unmarked grave."

"What could you possibly hope to find in a cemetery?" The woman said. "The dead tell no secrets and the living seldom come to visit them."

Isaac and Olivia exchanged a furtive glance. He sensed that Olivia wanted to reveal the letter.

She saw his head shake almost imperceptibly before she turned to the woman and blurted out. "We're looking for the Labyrinth of Love Letters."

The woman stiffened. She studied them from beneath her veil.

"Olivia!" Isaac said. "Please excuse my friend. She has a penchant for speaking without thinking."

The woman laughed. "You are searching for the Labyrinth of Love Letters? You have a better chance of finding El Dorado, or the Fountain of Youth."

"You've heard of it then," Olivia said.

The woman hesitated. The memory of sitting in the Labyrinth and reading the letters her beloved had written for her remained fresh in her mind. She loved sitting on the benches of the dimly lit corridors reading his passionate professions of love in the candlelight. Occasionally a shadowed figure walked past, but aside from a polite nod, visitors to the Labyrinth seldom interacted. They understood the secret nature of its existence and respected the privacy of others.

"Of course I've heard of it. Who hasn't?" The woman said with a wave of her hand. "It's an urban legend."

Olivia turned to Isaac perplexed.

He shrugged.

"Why would you be inclined to search for such a place?" The woman asked.

"I have studied the Romantics under the tutelage of my uncle Gabriel Aquino, and I am curious about its existence."

Gabriel, Carmen thought to herself. *So, this is the nephew he spoke of during our Saturday morning conversations.*

"What do you hope to accomplish in this endeavor?" Carmen tilted her head.

Isaac and Olivia cast each other a curious glance. Olivia shrugged. Isaac turned to the woman who remained kneeling beside the unmarked grave.

"I want to better understand love. If it is true what they say about the Labyrinth and the hidden love letters, then I'd like to read them and learn about love."

"And you?" Carmen turned to Olivia.

Olivia bit her lower lip. "What he said."

"Well, I hate to break it to you, but that is not how you learn about love." She studied them momentarily. "You may read love letters and poems to gain insight into how someone else felt at the time they wrote those words, but to learn about love you must experience love. For you see, falling in love is a long and deep process where you surrender your soul and become completely vulnerable to another human being. You must keep no secrets in order to tell no lies. You must trust that they would never allow you to endure any pain and you must do the same for them. They become your strength and your weakness. You are exposed in such a way that when they go all-in to make you happy you believe you will conquer the world, but if they break your heart they can destroy you. When you have love, you are in heaven. When you lose it you are condemned to a lonely hell. Let it fill your heart and you will feel as though you possess the conviction of the Holy Spirit. Lose it and you succumb to the torture of your personal demons. You will never feel more alive than when you are in love and you will never feel more alone than when your love is gone."

"Is that why you're here," Olivia asked, "because your love is gone?"

"We are discussing your reasons for being here, not mine."

Isaac begged her pardon and apologized again for their intrusion. He motioned for Olivia to follow him as he walked away.

Olivia proceeded after him before she stopped and turned to face the woman. "Seriously." She cast the woman an incredulous glance. "Why do you visit an unmarked grave?"

"Olivia!" Isaac reproached his friend.

Carmen smiled beneath her veil. "Young lady, I don't know who you are that I would be inclined to share details about my private life with you."

"Well, my name is Olivia Villalobos. I am an only child. My father is Javier Villalobos, and my mother was Angelica de las Fuentes. This is my friend—"

"Wait." Carmen cut her off. "I'm sorry, but did you say Angelica de las Fuentes was your mother?"

Olivia hesitated, and then she nodded.

"I can't believe this." Carmen began to laugh, "Angelica de las Fuentes was *your* mother."

"I don't see what's so amusing about who my mother was." Olivia snapped.

"There's no amusement at all." Carmen stopped laughing. "It's just a happy coincidence, to say the least."

Olivia cast Carmen a suspicious glance. She turned to Isaac. Her brow furrowed. He shrugged. They turned their attention back to the woman whose face remained hidden behind a black veil.

"Your mother and I were schoolmates. Beyond that we were close friends. At least we were until your grandfather, Don Enrique, deemed me a bad influence and forbade your mother from being my friend."

"How come I never heard about you, or any of this?" Olivia approached.

"I suspect Javier has kept a close eye on you all these years," Carmen said.

Olivia turned to Isaac. Her father had indeed been watchful of her every move despite being drunk half the time. And like her grandfather, he had also prohibited her from carrying on a friendship with someone whom he did not approve of. "What do you know about my father?"

"I know many things," Carmen said. "More than you have been told, I'm sure."

Olivia asked the woman's name. The veiled woman stood and introduced herself as Carmen Alicia de la Vega, wife to Fernando Gonzalo de la Vega. After she shook both Olivia and Isaac's hands she walked past them to her carriage.

"Wait. Where are you going?" Olivia asked.

"It is getting late. I must return home."

"What about my mother? I want to know more about her."

"Another time, perhaps," Carmen said over her shoulder.

"Will you be here tomorrow?" Olivia called out.

Carmen said nothing more. She disappeared into the blanket of fog. Olivia made to chase after her, but Isaac took hold of her hand. Their eyes met. Olivia was at the brink of tears. Isaac embraced her. He assured her they would find the answers she sought. Unbeknownst to them both, he would be trusted with the secret of Old Sienna surrounding her mother's disappearance and forbidden from sharing it with his best friend.

12

Isaac walked Olivia to the front gates of her home. He told her he saw Carmen's carriage at his uncle's boathouse earlier that day. When she asked him why he failed to mention that earlier he explained that his uncle refused to reveal any details about the woman and the reasons for her visit. Olivia nodded with a pensive look in her eyes. She had been lost in thought momentarily, but a loud commotion coming from inside the house drew her attention.

"You better get home," she turned to Isaac.

"But, what about?"

"Don't worry about me. I'm sure my dad is just drunk again. I'll handle him."

He nodded as she pulled the gate open and ran to the front door. Tia Katarina's screams echoed in the night when the front door opened and closed again. Olivia froze at the sight of broken furniture, scattered papers, and tipped over bookshelves. The servants huddled in corners and hid behind curtains. Terror filled their eyes. When she asked about her aunt they told her she had fled into the courtyard.

Olivia navigated through the mess. Her father's shouts and grunts could be heard from upstairs. He shouted obscenities as he emptied out drawers and tossed over mattresses. She raced upstairs to confront him. When she arrived at the top of the staircase he stood at her bedroom door.

His eyes were bloodshot and his breathing heavy. He was

drenched with sweat and reeked of alcohol as he glared at his daughter. His slim shoulders hunched beneath a large suit jacket with his hand on the doorknob. Olivia shook her head in disbelief. Tears welled in her eyes.

Javier Villalobos released the doorknob and stormed past her without saying a word. A moment later the front door slammed shut. She ran back down the steps and raced to the courtyard. She found Tia Katarina sobbing on the bench with her head in her hands. Olivia embraced her and assured her that everything would be okay.

"I've never seen him like this." Tia Katarina shook her head without meeting her niece's gaze. "Not even when—"

Tia Katarina caught herself. There were things about Javier that Olivia did not know. Though Olivia had heard stories about Javier's involvement in drunken brawls she had never witnessed the full extent of his anger, for he had a fierce temper. The kind that turned him into someone unrecognizable, like a man possessed and incapable of love. Yet it was love, and the betrayal that comes with it that changed Javier Villalobos forever.

In his youth, he had been the most eligible of bachelors. A handsome young man with a noble pedigree, a fine education, and a list of accomplishments that set him apart from other men his age. The only exception had been Guillermo Sedeño the son of a field worker named Mauricio.

Aside from their ambitious nature they had nothing in common except for their pursuit of Angelica's heart. For Angelica, the choice was simple, until it wasn't. Though her heart had chosen the one she loved, her fate rested in someone else's hands and was already decided for her.

Javier Villalobos had never been happier than the moment

when his father announced the arrangement of marriage with Angelica de las Fuentes. He had sought to seduce her from the first, but neither his charms, nor his status, or his accolades impressed her. He overwhelmed her with gifts and flowers and flattery. And with every attempt he made to sway her heart he merely pushed her away. He knew not how to win her love, for it was a futile endeavor to be sure; and when he learned the truth of it he was never the same again.

He had gone from being blissfully married to the woman he loved to a man haunted by suspicion and jealousy. By the time she realized she was with child he had been so convinced by his premonitions that he did not feel the happiness a man feels when he discovers he is going to be a father.

When Olivia was born eight months later he made the customary appearance at the hospital, but one look at the child and he knew without knowing she was not his daughter. In the months that followed everyone had said she resembled her mother except for her eyes and brow. Some thought she inherited the features from a relative who had long since passed, and few suspected adultery, but never said it aloud.

Javier, on the other hand, recognized the eyes and brow, but he was too proud to admit it even to himself. When he questioned Angelica about her fidelity she swore on her mother's grave that she had never betrayed him. It was true. And he believed her for a time. Without proof and without question he accepted her declaration, yet deep down in the pit of his stomach he knew Olivia was not his daughter.

It became the source of discord in their marriage. As Olivia grew, Angelica and Javier became distant. With each day that passed they spoke less, and with each night that fell their touch became less frequent, until they became strangers in a house that was no longer a home.

They communicated with each other through the servants, and even then, they did not relay a direct message to one another. In the space between them a thunderous silence echoed. The void filled them with a fear not unlike the darkness one finds when time and memory is lost to the mind. The fear that gripped them distracted their thoughts, robbed them of their appetite, and made it impossible to sleep.

For her part, Angelica feared her husband would find the proof he needed to confirm his suspicions. Would he divorce her? If so, where would she go in light of the disgrace? Would he kill her in a crime of passion?

The truth was she did not know, because despite living together as man and wife she never truly had the chance to get to know Javier Villalobos. In the year and a half since they first met, he never spoke of his childhood, his dreams, or his fears. He only spoke of his cases, his ambitions, and his colleagues.

For his part, Javier also feared he would find the proof he needed to confirm his suspicions. Would Angelica ask him for a divorce? If so, how would he endure the disgrace of being left for another man? Would she go to Guillermo and surrender her body to uninhibited passion?

The mere thought of it tortured his soul. But the pain he felt in those moments paled in comparison to the heartache he endured when she left. At first he was appalled at her audacity to leave without warning and without her daughter in the middle of the night.

His suspicions bubbled to the surface. The following day, after he left Olivia in the care of the servants he reported to the police station for duty. When he realized that Guillermo Sedeño had taken a personal day he made a beeline for Sedeño's residence.

He switched beats with a fellow officer and waited, even past his shift, until someone left the house. Much to his surprise, when a woman emerged from the home it was not Angelica. Rather it was an attractive young lady Javier had seen before, but whose name he did not know.

He returned home and stayed up half the night. The following morning Olivia's cries roused him from his sleep. He instructed the servants to look after her and among them they arranged a system that allowed them to take turns carrying for the child while attending their duties.

As for Javier Villalobos, he slowly fell into a deep depression. Each day without Angelica was more difficult than the last. He laid awake at night tossing and turning, hoping she would emerge from the shadowed corners of their bedroom. In the mornings, he struggled to climb out of bed, lying with his head on her pillow in search of the slightest scent of her perfume. For a man who had never been in love prior to meeting Angelica de las Fuentes, heartbreak proved to be his undoing.

And it wasn't just his heart that ached. The heartache was merely the tip of the iceberg. He felt his chest tighten and his stomach twist in knots. He couldn't eat and he couldn't breathe. When he tried to speak to God his throat tensed, and his jaws clenched. He drew sharp breaths to fight back the tears, but his eyes burned when the shattered pieces of his soul fell from his eyes.

Eventually he turned to the bottles behind Roberto's bar. He sought to drown his sorrow and find comfort at the bottom of a bottle. A steady diet of alcohol and cigarillos replaced his meals. He poured

Brandy into his Café and grew well acquainted with the Whiskey from America and the Scotch imported from Europe.

After several weeks, he finally reported her missing. His superiors asked him why he waited so long, but he would not say. He would not reveal his pain. He was too proud—as Latin men tend to be—to allow anyone to see his broken heart. He would only say that he had expected her to return eventually, but when she didn't he knew he had to file a police report.

With the assistance of the entire police force of Old Sienna, including Guillermo Sedeño, the search for Angelica blanketed every quadrant of the city, but to no avail. After several weeks of long days and late nights she was never found. Although Javier had been cleared of any wrongdoing, rumors persisted that he was somehow involved with her disappearance. This led to the drunken brawls in La Cantina when others made offhand remarks that sparked Javier's temper. It was the flash of anger Olivia had never seen. Even Tia Katarina had never seen him so enraged. Not even when Guillermo Sedeño had come to the house on Olivia's first birthday and declared that she was his daughter.

He had no proof to substantiate his claim save for the memory of when he and Angelica had made love before her marriage to Javier. Guillermo knew Javier did not care for the girl. Word had reached him through the network of servants in Old Sienna that Javier spent very little time with Olivia. Javier dedicated himself to his work and spent his free time at La Cantina drinking himself unconscious.

Javier denied Guillermo his request, and instead invited his sister to come live with them to look after the girl. After the guests had left Katarina asked her brother why he turned Guillermo away if, in fact, he was telling the truth.

"I will not give him the satisfaction of knowing he had the best of Angelica, and the product of that moment. I will punish him as she has punished me."

"But what about the girl? Olivia deserves to be with her father."

"*I* am her father!" Javier shouted. "For all intents and purposes the girl will remain in this house and raised as a daughter of the Villalobos name. As my sister, you are obligated to honor my request and you will take this secret with you to the grave."

Tia Katarina nodded solemnly and kept her brother's secret. She raised Olivia as if she was her own. She grew quite fond of the jovial child as they formed a bond not unlike that of a mother and daughter. And like all mothers who know the secrets of a girl's father, she dared not divulge the truth that would break a daughter's heart.

13

A man arrived the following morning with a hand-embroidered envelope. It had an elaborate floral design and it contained a letter addressed to Olivia Villalobos. She opened it carefully as one of the servants approached.

"What is it, Señorita?" Clara asked.

"It's an invitation to the estate of Fernando Gonzalo and Carmen Alicia de la Vega." Olivia turned to her in disbelief.

"An invitation to the governor's mansion?" Clara said with wide eyes.

Olivia nodded pensively. "Yes. She humbly requests that I come to the mansion for a dinner party."

"That is quite an honor." Clara peered at the invitation. She cleared her throat when she noticed Olivia watching her. "We have nearly finished clearing all the debris from last night. What would you have us do with the furniture that is damaged beyond repair?"

"Send for the garbage collector and make arrangements for him to remove all of it from the property as quickly as possible."

"Si, Señorita." Clara nodded and left.

Olivia returned to her room. She sat on the edge of her bed and examined both the bloodstained letter and the invitation from Carmen Alicia de la Vega. She searched for a link between the two authors. In her heart Olivia felt that somehow the two were connected, but she had no proof.

She wanted to bring Isaac with her to the governor's mansion, but she didn't want to presume she had that right. *Should I tell Isaac about the invitation? What if he is offended over not having been invited?*

Her concern turned out to be inconsequential when she met with Isaac in the plaza an hour later. They sat together on a bench beneath a fruit tree. The bustling activity in the market drowned out the innumerable conversations throughout the plaza.

"What was your impression of la Señora de la Vega?" Olivia asked when they sat down.

"She seemed to be a kind enough woman." Isaac shrugged. "By the way this was delivered to my father's shop today."

He handed Olivia an envelope. It had the same embroidered design as the one delivered to her door earlier that day. When she opened it she saw the same invitation to the governor's mansion for dinner that evening.

"I received one just like this," she confessed.

"It says here they are sending a carriage for us after sunset." Isaac pointed at a special instruction near the bottom of the letter.

"Do you know what you're going to wear?" Olivia asked.

"I have one suit and I only wear it for important holidays and events," Isaac said proudly. "Father says he will gift me a hat for the occasion."

"A hat?" Olivia's brow furrowed.

"Yeah, he told me that an invitation to the home of an aristocrat is not to be taken lightly." Isaac smiled inwardly when he recalled the conversation he had had with his father earlier that day.

"No mijo, a Quintero does not dishonor his family, or disrespect anyone who extends such a polite invitation. Just because we are hung like horses that doesn't mean we piss where we please."

"What's so funny?" Olivia cast him a curious glance.

"Nothing," Isaac shook his head.

"What are we going to do about finding the Labyrinth?" Olivia wondered. "Do you think we should ask La Señora Carmen again?"

"She already said she doesn't know anything about it"

"No she didn't." Olivia corrected him. "She merely asked us why we were interested in such a place, and then she avoided any inquiries we made about her reasons for visiting an unmarked grave."

"Wouldn't you take umbrage with someone asking you about your personal business?"

"Only if I was hiding something," Olivia said.

"Either way, I think it would be rude to ask her about it in her own home."

"How else are we going to find out who wrote the letter?" Olivia glanced over her shoulder and lowered her voice. "How else are we going to find the Labyrinth?"

"That reminds me," Isaac smiled. "Memito came by the hat shop this morning."

"Your friend, Memito Linarez, the self-proclaimed procurer of information?" Olivia asked.

"Yep." Isaac nodded. "I asked him what he knew about the Labyrinth."

"Isaac, I asked you not to say anything about the letter."

"And I didn't," he assured her.

Memito entered the shop immediately after the mail carrier had delivered the invitation. He walked through the shop imitating a soldier's strut wearing a mischievous grin. He was a very thin boy, with short coarse hair and keen brown eyes. He wore an over-sized wool coat he acquired from a trade with a homeless man. He wasn't simply going to give the man money without getting something in return. As far as Memito was concerned the man only claimed to be hungry, but in truth was panhandling for money to buy rum.

Though he intended to provide the man with a few dollars regardless of the reason, Memito figured he'd get something out of the deal.

"You paid the man to give you that dirty old coat?" Isaac had asked.

"Let's just say I bought it off him." Memito shrugged. "I like the look of the coat."

"But it's filthy and worn."

"I like to think it has character. Besides it spared the man's dignity to make a deal." Memito said.

"As often as you rationalize your foolishness Memito, you should consider a career as a lawyer." Señor Rolando approached.

"These are tough times, Señor Rolando." Memito countered. "The Great Depression has affected many people all over the world. One mustn't be too picky about where he finds clothes to put on his back."

Memito had once lived on the streets after his father was accused of rape, and murdered by the girl's father. His mother committed suicide in the aftermath of the disgrace. It wasn't until a year later that the true culprit had been caught and identified during another attack. A dozen women stepped forward, including the girl who Memito's father had been accused of assaulting, and identified the man who had escaped from a prison in San Juan a year before and hid from authorities in the southern part of the island.

During that year Memito survived the hardship by learning how to scavenge for food in dumpsters when the merchants refused to offer him scraps from their stalls. He slept wherever he found shelter from the rain, but always alone. It was a decision he made after a small bag of his belongings was stolen during the night when he slept under a bridge where other homeless people gathered. He only stole when he had to steal and bartered what he had taken to obtain something else he needed.

Señor Rolando had originally invited Memito to live with him and Isaac, but Memito refused. He felt too ashamed of the accusations against his father and didn't want to burden his friends with rumors, or another mouth to feed.

Occasionally, Uncle Gabriel Aquino provided Memito a meal and a place to sleep, but Memito seldom stayed for more than one night at a time. He didn't want to overstay his welcome. In exchange, Memito would sweep the porch of Uncle Gabriel's boathouse and read from the books of Uncle Gabriel's library at the old man's insistence.

"If you won't accept my invitation to stay then you had better remain literate until you figure out what you're going to do." Uncle Gabriel had said. "It's one thing to be homeless. That can be remedied over time. But you can't fix stupid, and if you're an idiot someone will always find a way to cheat you out of your money and your home."

Memito agreed. He wandered throughout the city in search for food and shelter. He enjoyed his freedom and picked up a few survival tips along the way. It was during that year when he mastered the art of hiding in plain sight and overhearing conversations intended to be kept secret. He sold the information for currency and insisted on anonymity to remain in business. The self-proclaimed procurer of information prided himself on his newfound skill and when Isaac asked him about the Labyrinth he was more than up for the task.

"Yes, I've heard of the Labyrinth, but I thought it was just a local legend," Memito said. He walked with Isaac to the malt shop down the street. "Why the sudden interest in this place?"

Isaac proceeded to tell Memito about his dream. He hoped he sounded convincing enough with the details he provided that his friend would not pry further. Memito promised to find out as much as he could and would be in touch soon.

Relieved with Isaac's explanation, Olivia told him about her father's outburst the previous night. She described the destruction of their furniture, the fear among the servants, and the worry in Tia Katarina's eyes.

"After I got Tia Katarina to calm down I took her to her cousin's house in the shanty district with two male servants as escorts."

"Why did you take her there?"

"She was deathly afraid of my father last night," Olivia said. "You didn't see the rage in his eyes. He looked as though he was going to kill someone."

"Do you think he was searching for the letter?" Isaac wondered.

"I don't know." Olivia lowered her eyes. "If he was, then this letter is far more valuable than we thought."

"What next?" Isaac scanned the plaza.

"We have a few hours before we need to be at the governor's mansion. I promised Tia Katarina I would visit her today. Will you join me?"

Isaac nodded and together they navigated through the bustling crowd in the plaza. Olivia held his hand and led the way. Isaac glanced over his shoulder and caught a glimpse of a man wearing a long trench coat and fedora beneath a tree. A moment later someone passed between them and the mysterious figure had vanished. Isaac searched the sea of unfamiliar faces but did not see him again.

14

They spotted the stranger in the distance when they arrived at the shanty district on the outskirts of Old Sienna. He stood on the corner leaning against a lamppost with a cigarette in hand. He watched them with keen interest, but his hat cast a shadow over his face and obscured his features.

"Who do you think it is?" Isaac asked.

"I don't know, but he kind of looks like Chief Inspector Sedeño." Olivia shielded her eyes from the sun.

Isaac cursed under his breath.

"Don't worry," Olivia assured him. "We haven't done anything wrong."

"Not today, we haven't," Isaac muttered.

They arrived at the home of Tia Katarina's cousin. It rested on the slope to the east of Old Sienna that provided a magnificent view of the ocean. From the water the shantytown resembled a heaping pile of colorful boxes stacked haphazardly along the mountainside like trash.

Within the town's boundaries lie a maze of slender streets and alleyways where the locals shout the drug of choice they have for sale. There are also small plazas and stores to buy alcohol and groceries. The houses are crammed so close together that a conversation in one home can easily be heard by neighbors on all sides. It is known all over the world that there are no secrets in the ghetto and as long as you keep those secrets you may keep your life.

They knocked on the door of the small one room dwelling. When Tia Katarina opened the door, she invited them inside. A mattress lay in the far corner and a couch sat against a near wall. Judging by the pillows stacked on the folded blankets and sheets, the couch is where Tia Katarina had slept.

As they crossed the threshold Isaac wrinkled his nose when a musty odor filled his nostrils. He looked around the darkened dwelling and observed a small two-drawer dresser with chipped paint beside the mattress. The only light within fell through the two square windows above the couch.

After Tia Katarina closed the door behind them her cousin, Cecilia Perez, beckoned Olivia to come closer. "Let me get a good look at you," she squinted and smiled. "You look just like your mother, except for your eyes and your brow. You get those from your father."

Tia Katarina cleared her throat as she walked between them and offered some refreshment. Olivia and Isaac declined. Though they were parched after the long walk beneath the midday sun they didn't feel comfortable accepting what little she had to offer.

"We merely came to see how you are feeling after last night." Olivia said.

Tia Katarina sat beside her cousin. She said she felt better as she smoothed out her dress. "How's your father?" She finally asked.

"I don't know," Olivia shrugged. "He never returned home after he left last night."

"I wonder what drove him to such madness?" Tia Katarina wondered.

Isaac and Olivia exchange a furtive glance. Cousin Cecilia saw it and called them out on it.

"Don't be coy with me," she waved a finger at them and smiled. "I may be old, but I'm not dead."

Tia Katarina looked at her cousin, and then at her niece. "What are you not telling me?"

"My father was looking for this." Olivia removed the letter from the folds in her dress.

"Olivia!" Tia Katarina gasped. "I told you to return that letter to its rightful place."

"Its rightful place is not with my father."

"That is not your decision to make." Tia Katarina reproached her. "Aye Dios Mio," she crossed herself.

"The letter does not belong to my father. It belongs in the Labyrinth of Love Letters."

"I already told you that place does not exist." It is merely an urban legend."

"May I see the letter?" Cousin Cecilia reached for it. Her interest had been piqued. The brief exchange between her cousin and Olivia had been the most excitement she'd seen in a long time.

Olivia handed it over. Cousin Cecilia studied it with keen interest. She rubbed the paper between her fingertips, read the contents of the letter, and asked about the bloodstains.

"We think it belonged to the man found dead a few weeks ago." Olivia said.

"How do you know this?" Cousin Cecilia gazed into Olivia's brown eyes.

"She doesn't," Tia Katarina interjected. "She's simply jumping to conclusions."

"Let the girl speak." Cousin Cecilia waved off Tia Katarina's remark.

Olivia explained how she found the letter in a hidden compartment of her father's coat. Based on the penmanship and the contents of the letter she concluded it had not been penned by her father's hand. She suspected the letter belonged to someone else. Her suspicion was confirmed when Chief Inspector Guillermo Sedeño arrived at the house the following morning. During their brief conversation, he said he'd been searching for a piece of stolen evidence that would help him identify the man found dead in the alley.

After having already spoken with Tia Katarina about the legend of the Labyrinth, Olivia had set out to find it with Isaac's help. She glanced at Isaac momentarily as she contemplated whether or not to divulge whom they had met at the cemetery and what they had observed.

Cousin Cecilia noticed the furtive glance between them. She sensed they were holding something back, but rather than press them about the matter she invited them to sit.

"The reason the Labyrinth is considered a myth is because it has existed since before Old Sienna was established. It was built in a time when marriage for love was dismissed as a foolish notion."

"A foolish notion?" Olivia cast her an incredulous glance.

"Dear child, you must understand that for centuries the purpose of marriage was to form alliances and secure a family's future."

"What about love?" Olivia asked.

"Love? Ha!" Cousin Cecilia laughed. "Love comes later, like the mortar used to bind stones when laying the foundation while building a home. It strengthens over time."

Olivia stared ahead blankly as she shook her head. "What

about Romeo and Juliet, and the stories of Jane Austen?"

"Stories exist to entertain and inspire us. They're merely veils of hope for when we see the ugliness of the world."

"Then what purpose does the Labyrinth serve?" Isaac asked.

"The Labyrinth exists to grant lovers the illusion of secrecy. But in truth, it is a trap door into hell. For you see passionate love is dangerous, and unrequited love drives people to madness. Those who fall in love are condemned to suffer the purest pain." Cousin Cecilia looked from Olivia to Isaac. "Heed my advice and relent your effort to find the Labyrinth. No good shall come from discovering the truth of it."

"I already told her to let things be, but she doesn't listen. She never listens!" Tia Katarina said.

"But we must find the Labyrinth." Olivia insisted.

"Why?" Tia Katarina said.

"So we can hide this letter for the man who died trying to preserve the honor of the woman he loved." Olivia said. "So she may know her lover's last words to her as was originally intended."

Tia Katarina sighed and shook her head.

Cousin Cecilia looked at all three of her guests before she pursed her lips and finally said, "If you insist on continuing with this endeavor then you must find the Last Valentine."

"Who?" Isaac and Olivia said.

Cousin Cecilia lowered her voice and shared with them a secret she had kept for nearly half a century. A tale of forbidden love that lingered in the shadows of Old Sienna like a memory time tried to forget, but remained a legend no one dared to speak of for fear of retribution from the family shamed by scandal.

Before the turn of the century, during the Spanish-American

war, the locals had created a series of tunnels to transport supplies for the American allies. The tunnels fell into disuse after the war and left to be forgotten in the shadows of time.

Years later a young aristocrat named Lorenzo Valentino fell in love. Given that the young woman was from a different social class theirs was a forbidden love. They met during Carnaval, the weeklong festivities of elaborate costumes and parade the week before Ash Wednesday. The townspeople gathered before the cathedral in what is now the plaza at the center of Old Sienna. Hidden behind masks of demons and horned devils the formalities of social status were cast aside.

It was at the refreshment bar when Lorenzo Valentino first laid eyes on the love of his life. Her long dark hair fell in gentle waves to the small of her back. Her light brown eyes met his gaze. Standing a meter apart they froze. Locked in a trance where time stood still long enough for God to give them His blessing they gazed at each other silently.

Lorenzo approached without knowing what to say and she remained rooted to the spot as she studied his statuesque features. She admired his bronze skin as much as he favored her fair complexion.

"Lorenzo Valentino at your service." He introduced himself.

She gave him her hand and he kissed it. She thanked him for the honor of his formality and disappeared into the crowd. He gave chase amid the dancing and cheers. She glanced over her shoulder and smiled before she turned and fled. Despite the urgings of his friends to leave her be he would not relent. He pursued her through the bustling mob. After a few minutes, he found her among a small group of friends near the stage where the band played.

They gazed at each other momentarily. She froze when he

winked. He approached slowly and fixed his eyes on her the way a lion locks eyes with its prey. When he neared neither seemed to hear the pleas of their friends, and the music faded into silence. They stood a handbreadth apart, but neither said a word. Perhaps they were lost in thought, or perhaps they were caught up in the moment.

As she looked into his eyes she recognized something in him she could not explain. She felt a strange comfort in his presence. As if she had known him all her life, and he knew her, and they shared a connection unlike any they'd ever known.

"Tell me your name." He said in a low voice with the hint of a smile on his lips.

She bit her lower lip and slowly shook her head.

His brow furrowed. She slipped away before he asked for an explanation. He gave chase, but she was quickly lost in the crowd. Lorenzo pushed his way through the bodies that pressed around him shoving him this way and that to the rhythm of the music. He lost her in the frenzy of the celebration, but he did not give up. Lorenzo Valentino pursued his destiny. He searched for her amid the sea of unfamiliar faces and masks.

Eventually he found her lingering alone along the edge of the festivities. He watched her from a distance. Admiring the haughtiness of her step and the swaying of her hips. He was captivated by her smile and her laughter as she interacted with strangers and people whom she seemed to know. Lorenzo shadowed her movement and waited for the perfect opportunity to approach.

After the sun had set and the moon emerged he finally decided to catch her unawares. The crowd seemed to fall away as if their attention had been drawn to something at the center of the plaza. Encouraged by the ardent belief that God acted on his behalf Lorenzo eliminated the distance between them and approached her from behind. He stopped so close to her that he could detect the scent of lavender that intensified his desire. He spoke with a low voice and with the intention to seduce the only woman—he already knew—he would ever love.

"All I ask is that you tell me your name," he said.

Without turning to face him, she replied, "I cannot reveal it without knowing your intentions."

Lorenzo Valentino felt a shiver along his spine at the warmth of her voice, whose hushed tone was like a whisper from an angel sharing the secrets of love.

"Tell me what I must do and I will do it." He said without hesitation.

"If your intentions are pure you will know what to do without my instruction."

Lorenzo watched as she walked away from him and once again disappeared into the crowd. He didn't follow her. He didn't have to. For now, he possessed all the confidence in the world that her heart would be his.

He laid awake that night remembering her smile and laughter. He wondered why he had never seen her before that day. Then it dawned on him that he had never set foot outside the wealthy district except to go to church. Even then, he traveled to and fro by horse-drawn carriage without making any stops.

It was in that moment as he gazed at the moon through his bedroom window that Lorenzo Valentino vowed to change his daily routine. Each day he woke at sunrise inspired to find his way into her heart. Convinced the hand of God guided their meeting, Lorenzo learned as much as he could about the young lady he would love until the day of his death.

Mariana Colón was the youngest of three daughters born to Roberto and his wife Carla. Roberto worked long hours in the sugar cane fields and though his two eldest daughters had already been married, finding a suitor for his youngest proved to be a daunting task. Though he loved his daughters dearly Marianna had been his favorite. That favor afforded her the freedom of declining a marriage proposal presented to her father.

It did not matter if the suitor was handsome, or wealthy, or both. If Mariana did not feel a connection, or if the man was not a romantic then she would not accept a proposal for marriage. Unbetrothed at seventeen years of age she dismissed her mother's urgings to accept a proposal soon lest she end up a spinster aunt to her nieces and nephews and with no children of her own.

Mariana Colón knew the one thing she wanted most out of life was love. She was prepared to wait forever to find it. She was not prepared, however, for the moment when love found her.

The seduction of Mariana began on the empty pages of notebooks where Lorenzo Valentino felt close to her during the silent moments when he penned his secret confession. He wrote poems and love letters by candlelight into the early morning hours while his parents slept.

He enlisted the help of servants, not only those in the employ of his family, but also those who worked for the families of his closest friends. Though his male friends thought him a fool, his female acquaintances found the entire situation to be quite charming. In all the years they had known Lorenzo Valentino they believed him to be impervious to love after he managed to downplay their advances with an astute kindness that spared their feelings. They became the handful of individuals to know the secret of Lorenzo Valentino's heart.

Together the small network of spies searched for Mariana Colón to discreetly deliver the sealed envelopes containing his secret messages. Whether they found her in the market or in the plaza, in the church or in the fields, among her friends or in passing it did not matter. They took every opportunity to deliver the missives of love. Be it with a simple handshake when they introduced themselves, or by bumping into her and slipping the letters between the folds of her dress. Everyone played their part to perfection, which left the unsuspecting target of Lorenzo's affection flattered and impressed that the keepers of his secret belonged to both her world and his.

In the end, that proved to be his undoing. The bitterness of heartbreak among those who allowed their jealousies to dictate their actions led to the unveiling of the secret to those from whom it had originally meant to be kept.

A girl from the noble class, whose name had been omitted for the sake of her honor, discovered Lorenzo's secret. She divulged the truth of it to Lorenzo's father, for she had been unable to bear the thought of a field hand's daughter capturing the heart of the man she loved since childhood. The crushing weight of disgrace severed friendships, cost servants their employment as punishment for their involvement, and created a rift between father and son when the elder Valentino forbade his son from marrying Mariana Colón.

"No son of mine will taint our family blood with an uneducated mugrosa who belongs on her knees or on her back!"

"Then I shall be no son of yours." Lorenzo shot back. "Suffice it to say she is not who you think she is."

The elder Valentino glared at his son. His face reddened and his tone had become threatening. "Don't think for one minute that your defiance will earn you my respect. You will do as you're told and that's the end of it!"

For several weeks Lorenzo remained under the watchful eye of his father and with no means of relaying a message to Mariana. The newly acquired servants were ordered to monitor Lorenzo's activities around the clock. They stood guard at his bedroom door and windows to deter him from attempting to sneak out in the middle of the night. Lorenzo accompanied his father to the municipal building during the day where he learned about property deeds and the business of buying and selling land.

It was then that he met his cousin, Eduardo el abogado. Eduardo's nickname, "el abogado" was attributed to his recent graduation from law school in America. A few years older than Lorenzo he offered to take him under his wing making a promise to his uncle that he would help Lorenzo forget the girl. Prior to his arrival he had heard through relatives about the scandal of forbidden love. Though he understood his uncle's position he sympathized with his younger cousin for no other reason than his ardent belief in romantic love. After speaking with Lorenzo and learning the truth Eduardo vowed to keep his secret and act as his messenger with Mariana.

In the mornings Lorenzo continued to accompany his father to the municipal building where he met with his cousin to begin their day's work. Some days they spent locked in an office combing over city records for vacant properties and expired contracts. Others were spent commuting to empty lots and inspecting deserted buildings to determine the best use for each property. For several months during their time together Lorenzo spoke of Mariana and his plan to make a life with her. He also gave Eduardo the letters he had written to her during the night, which Eduardo would later take to her in the evenings after work. And she would send a letter back each night, which Eduardo had to wait until the following morning to deliver.

It was through their work together in the office of geographical records that Lorenzo Valentino and Eduardo el abogado had discovered the series of abandoned tunnels from the war. Concerned that Eduardo's involvement as messenger might someday be uncovered the young men devised a plan to utilize the network of tunnels to their advantage. Eduardo applied his knowledge of property law to acquire the rights to the tunnels, while Lorenzo appealed to his father for a loan to invest in vacant properties.

Together they initiated a secret project to renovate the tunnels and seal off all the entrances except one. They hired different contractors from various regions of the island to work on separate sections of the tunnels. None were aware of the other's work, but all were interviewed individually and only hired if they believed in true love.

Though it might be difficult to imagine such a requirement could be met, Puerto Rico is home to the romantics of the Caribbean and the poets who inspired Puerto Ricans to form their own social and cultural identity in defiance of foreign occupation. For it is known that since the era of the Taíno culture to the rule of the Spanish Crown the people of the island were first and foremost lovers of love.

After several months of renovations, the tunnels were finally complete by mid-autumn. Lorenzo's vision to provide Mariana a quiet place to read his letters and meet him in secret had finally come to fruition. During the celebration of Día de la Raza, Puerto Rico's local name for Columbus Day, Eduardo slipped away to take Mariana Colón one final letter from Lorenzo Valentino.

"What did the letter say?" Olivia pressed cousin Cecilia.

"Alas, nobody knows." Cousin Cecilia sighed and sat back. "Some say it contained instructions on how to find the entrance to the Labyrinth, but that could merely be a rumor."

"What happened after Eduardo delivered the letter?" Isaac asked.

Cousin Cecilia studied him momentarily before she continued.

According to legend they met in the Labyrinth on a nightly basis. It was there in the shadows of secrecy where they fell in love. By then the elder Valentino believed his son had forgotten Roberto Colón's daughter and permitted Lorenzo the freedom to carry on about his life without supervision. Though Lorenzo continued his work with Eduardo in the office of geographical records, and he made a name for himself as a shrewd businessman during dinners with investors and his father, his thoughts always remained with Mariana Colón.

For several months, they met in the Labyrinth after sunset talking and laughing without looking over their shoulder. Each night they parted with a kiss before Eduardo escorted Mariana home safely and Lorenzo returned home high on love. Until one night he arrived home to find his father in the receiving room with another man discussing the arrangement of marriage.

After the formalities of introduction, the man left. Lorenzo initially protested the decision, but his father would not relent. Though the elder Valentino agreed his son had earned the right to choose his wife, he believed the proposal was an offer they could not refuse.

"She is the niece of the most powerful family in all of

Providencia. She is wealthy and beautiful! What more could you possibly want in a woman?"

"I do not care about power and wealth, father. I want to marry for love."

"You want to marry for love?" The elder Valentino scoffed. "Que mierda. Marrying for love is like adding extra picante to your meal. It may seem like a good idea at the time, but your stomach will curse you for it with ulcers in the end."

Despite Lorenzo's pleas the elder Valentino insisted that his son marry the lovely niece of Doña Adelina Cintrón. Though Lorenzo had no intention of marrying her he feigned complicity to buy time to make other plans. After he met Rosalinda Cintrón his afternoons were relegated to entertaining her and her family along with frequent dinner parties and walks in the park. In the eyes of all of Providencia the courtship of Rosalinda by Lorenzo had officially begun.

He continued to meet Mariana in the evenings, and he kept no secrets from her in the privacy of their labyrinth. The predicament proved equally challenging for them both. She understood his dilemma though it pained her to see him at odds with his father. For her part her faith in love brought her comfort when she waited for him in the evenings while he fulfilled his obligations.

It wasn't easy for Mariana Colón to sit and wonder if the love of her life would be swept away by the beauty and charms of Rosalinda Cintrón. Her radiant beauty was legend and they say she engaged in conversation with grace and intellect beyond her years.

Nevertheless, Lorenzo eased her worries when he returned to her each night. But that comfort was short-lived when the demands of his circumstances required him to spend more time with Rosalinda. His visits with Mariana began later and later, which had gradually shortened their clandestine meetings until they seemed like fleeting moments in the night.

One night Mariana waited for as long as her patience allowed. She finally left the Labyrinth just before the clock struck midnight. Though she wanted to believe she hadn't lost him, there remained the thought in the back of her mind—perpetuated by the few friends who knew her predicament—that he would never chose her over Rosalinda Cintrón.

When Lorenzo arrived at the Labyrinth he only found a letter on the bench where they had sat and talked so often in recent months. It sat inside an envelope with a heart shaped wax seal. He opened it, and read it, and immediately penned a reply. It was on that night the exchange of letters began. Day after day they slipped away from family and friends to write each other love notes. Night after night they snuck out of their homes and returned to the Labyrinth where they found and read each other's letters and reaffirmed their love.

They continued this dance for as long as fate permitted. Filling page after page with professions of eternal fidelity in light of the circumstances that kept them apart. They wrote their love story on the pages of time and chance where even if old age robbed them of the memory of each other destiny would never permit their souls to forget the whispers of each other's hearts.

"In the end that is all that remained for Mariana Colón. For it was on the eve of Día de San Valentín that Lorenzo was found dead in his home. Rumor holds that his father discovered the truth of Lorenzo's affair and when Lorenzo refused to obey his father's command to end his relationship with Mariana he murdered him," Cousin Cecilia said gravely.

"Do you think that's true?" Olivia wondered.

"If it is then Lorenzo Valentino died as a martyr for love like San Valentín." Cousin Celia shrugged and leaned back in her seat. "Some say the Labyrinth never actually existed and it is merely an urban legend. Others believe the Labyrinth still stands as a testament to true love and it is Lorenzo's soul that lingers in the shadows of Old Sienna to guide lovers to the hidden entrance if their love is true."

Isaac thought of the silhouette he saw the night before and the mysterious figure he met in his dream.

"If you hope to prove the Labyrinth's existence then you must find the documents Eduardo and Lorenzo would have needed to claim the tunnels and complete their renovations."

"How do you know so much about this?" Olivia said.

Cousin Cecilia turned to Tia Katarina momentarily. Tia Katarina nodded. She turned back to Olivia and Isaac and sighed. "Mariana Colón was my friend. But when Lorenzo was found dead she pulled away from the world. I don't know whether it was to grieve her loss, or because she believed that one of us had betrayed her trust. All I know is that she never spoke to any of us again."

"What happened to her?" Olivia said.

"She accepted a marriage proposal and moved away for a few years." Cousin Cecilia shrugged.

When Mariana returned, she had assumed the condition of an older woman. The mother of a young boy, she carried herself with a distinct confidence that her role in the world had changed. Though she had never forgotten her first love Mariana had learned the intricacies of a different kind of love. A love fueled, not by passion and desire, but by patience and understanding. Nevertheless, the legacy of her first love concealed a secret that threatened the happiness of her last love.

15

When they left Cousin Cecilia's home the late afternoon sun cast long shadows. A cool breeze came up from the ocean. Several voices blended with the music blaring throughout the shantytown and a bonfire cast dancing shadows in the distance.

Isaac stepped away from the door as Olivia and Tia Katarina exchanged farewells. He heard Olivia assure her aunt they would return before long with word about Javier when he noticed the stranger watching them from a distance.

"What's wrong?" Olivia approached and followed his gaze.

The stranger stood on the same street corner where they last saw him a few hours ago. He wore a long dark coat, left hand buried in the pocket of his jacket, a cigarette in his right hand as he brought it to his lips.

"Come," Olivia said. "We have an hour before sunset. We had better return to our homes now if we are going to be ready by the time the carriage arrives."

They navigated through the winding streets of the shantytown until they neared the outskirts at the top of the hill and turned around. The man had followed them, but remained in the shadows where he watched them from a distance.

"Why are you following us?" Olivia snapped.

Isaac cast her an incredulous glance. The stranger approached. He seemed to walk with a limp. Though when he neared they realized he wasn't limping due to an injury, but rather because he was tired from standing and walking for so long.

"What brings the two of you to the wrong part of town?" Chief Inspector Sedeño said.

"Our business is our own." Olivia said.

"Business in these parts is not fit for a lady, Miss Villalobos."

"Your mistake, Chief Inspector, is assuming we are here for unscrupulous reasons." Olivia replied.

Chief Inspector Sedeño lowered his gaze and smiled. "Ever the defiant one." He muttered.

"You never answered my question. Why are you following us?"

"I observed you leaving the plaza earlier today and I followed you on a hunch for your safety."

"Our safety?" Isaac finally spoke.

"As I said," Guillermo glanced over his shoulder. "This is the wrong part of town. There are dangers here you do not wish to meet."

"Well, as you can see we do not require your protection. We thank you for your concern, Chief Inspector, but we must be going." Olivia took Isaac's hand and began to walk away.

"Funny thing about the darkness, Miss Villalobos." Guillermo said. He approached as Olivia and Isaac stopped and turned to face him. "It conceals the shadows that move around you."

They watched the Chief Inspector as he walked past with a slight limp. They waited until he disappeared into the distance before they proceeded ahead.

"What do you suppose is the real reason he followed us?" Isaac wondered.

"I don't know," Olivia stared ahead pensively.

"Do you think he suspects we have the letter?"

"I hope not." Olivia shook her head. "All the more reason we must speak further with La Señora Carmen about her recent trips to the cemetery."

16

The sun had fallen beyond the horizon when the carriage arrived at the governor's mansion. Isaac's stomach twisted in knots. He had tried to convince Olivia to not bring up the subject of La Señora Carmen's recent visits to the cemetery, but to no avail. Olivia was intent on discovering the truth in light of what they had learned at Cousin Cecilia's home earlier that day.

The governor's mansion was unlike anything they had expected. When they passed through the oak double doors with decorative glass they stood in a luxurious foyer with granite floors and two staircases that curved to meet at an interior balcony above. The elegant design of the railings was the same cherry oak wood as the balustrade. A chandelier cast a luminous glow through the tear-shaped crystals that dangled on thin golden links.

La Señora Carmen approached with open arms and a warm welcome. She donned an elegant blue gown and carried herself gracefully. The servants rushed this way and that under her command for the night's occasion.

"What's going on?" Olivia said as she and La Señora Carmen exchanged kisses on each cheek.

"My husband has commissioned the renown artista, Juan Carlos Trinidad, to paint a portrait of him to hang in the capitol building. He only arrived this morning from Cuba and we are hosting a dinner party with him as the guest of honor."

"Señora Carmen," Isaac cleared his throat. "We are humbled

by your invitation, but we couldn't possibly impose on your—"

"Impose?" She rolled her eyes. "Aye Dios mio. You are not imposing. I invited you because I thought you would find this more interesting than a cemetery."

"About that," Olivia said.

Before she could continue a servant approached and whispered something in Carmen's ear. La Señora Carmen excused herself and instructed another servant to show the guests to the palatial courtyard where refreshments were being served. They passed beneath the indoor balcony and through a spacious corridor lined with doors leading into various rooms and an office.

The governor's laughter bellowed from the courtyard where he stood near the bar beside the guest of honor. A crowd gathered around them and they listened to Juan Carlos Trinidad as he told another joke.

When Olivia and Isaac arrived at the double doors leading out onto the patio and the courtyard the servant motioned for them to continue ahead. They thanked the servant and stepped through the double doors. Guests seated at the tables on the stone balcony acknowledged Olivia and Isaac with a glance. Olivia recognized some, but most were unfamiliar to her. The aristocrats recognized her too, the daughter of a forgotten princess who had gone missing and whose father had fallen from grace in the aftermath of the scandal. After they gave Olivia a once over they resumed their private conversations without giving her a second thought. They continued sipping their mojitos in the cool evening air amid the clinging of glass and several indistinct conversations.

Hanging lanterns provided a soft glow against the night sky. Uniformed servants carried trays with drinks and hor d'oeuvres offering them to the guests with theatrical servility.

Olivia and Isaac sat at an empty table over-looking the courtyard. From their vantage point they had a clear view of the assembly of nobles invited to welcome the artista to Old Sienna.

Juan Carlos Trinidad was no stranger to being the center of attention. A young artist who showed a lot of promise as a child for his oil painting skills studied abroad in France, Italy and Spain. He basked in the attention his talent garnered, first from adults as a child and from women as he matured. At the age of twenty-three, Juan Carlos Trinidad had grown into a handsome young man. After making a name for himself in Europe, where he painted portraits of royal families and dignitaries, he returned to Cuba a favorite son.

He possessed an air of confidence accentuated by his charisma, danced the latest dances and was current on the events of the day. Seduced by his smile and by the way he ran his hand through his long brown hair, women vied for his attention to listen to his intellectual discourse on politics and the arts, or to listen to him play Flamenco on his Spanish guitar. He managed to remain in a state of allure, engaging and reserved, until the moment his gaze met the innocent eyes of Olivia Villalobos.

She watched him from a distance. It was as if the world including her best friend, Isaac Quintero, had fallen away. Olivia exhaled slowly. The handsome artista had a strong jaw and high cheekbones. A lean physique evident beneath a dress shirt that was partially unbuttoned at the top.

His soft brown eyes held Olivia's gaze and an easy smile appeared on his lips. His gaze slid down along the curves of her body and back up again. His pensive eyes were warm, sensual, and inviting. In the crowded courtyard of the governor's mansion Olivia

Villalobos and Juan Carlos Trinidad recognized something in that brief instant. Perhaps it was each other from a lifetime before, or from a fantasy conceived in that realm between sleep and awake where one finds comfort in the quiet before the storm.

When Olivia realized he was smiling at her she turned away embarrassed. Isaac watched her in utter confusion. He felt a tinge of jealousy at the way she stared at the artista, captivated by his good looks and lost in thought. Now she behaved as though she had acted inappropriately and wanted nothing to do with him. Bewildered, Isaac asked her what was wrong.

"Nothing," she said before she cleared her throat. "I'm fine."

He knew that was a lie. He watched her fidget. He noticed her change in posture and the way she stammered a reply to the servant who approached and offered refreshment. What had been most telling was her reaction a moment later when Juan Carlos Trinidad appeared at the table and introduced himself.

It was impossible to tell who was more surprised when they saw him, Olivia or Isaac. After she shook his hand and gave her name she smiled and lowered her eyes. He was quite different from the boy who sat across the table from her, but then again there was a five-year gap between them. His brown eyes seemed to shine, and his smile revealed a dimple on his right cheek.

Juan Carlos turned his attention to Isaac who greeted him coolly. When Olivia heard Juan Carlos speak she could not concentrate. The rich sound of his voice stirred something inside of her. She wondered what he was thinking and guessed at his intentions. She wondered how she looked to him, a girl of seventeen or a young lady?

Then she surprised herself—perhaps because in speaking

with him she had found her courage, or perhaps because there are moments in our lives when we take control of our destiny despite our fears.

"Is this your first visit to Puerto Rico?" She met his gaze.

"Indeed it is." Juan Carlos nodded before he motioned for a servant to approach. He pulled up a chair and sat beside her.

Who does he think he is? Isaac cast Juan Carlos an incredulous glance.

Juan Carlos ignored Isaac. He held Olivia's gaze as he described places he found inspiring for a painter. "I daresay nothing on this island, however, is as inspiring as your smile." He winked at Olivia.

From the corner of her eye she saw Isaac roll his eyes. She smiled and lowered her gaze once more before she cast a quick glance at Isaac. His glare seemed to burn holes through Juan Carlos. She sensed her friend's dislike of the artista, but she could not understand why.

As Isaac listened to Juan Carlos compliment Olivia he got the impression the artista was a smooth talker, who, despite the Di Vincian airs he affected, was nothing more than a gigolo. He pictured him traveling from place to place, seducing young women with false flattery under the guise of refined decorum only to abandon them after having his way with them.

Not that Isaac's suspicion was far from the truth. In fact, Juan Carlos did have a reputation as a Casanova. Years ago when he'd first been cast into the spotlight, the fame and notoriety that came with being a talented artista in Europe bothered him. But over the years he grew accustomed to the unsought attention—especially from women—pressed upon him. He knew it wasn't him personally the people were drawn to; it was his name. People clamored to be seen with him for his celebrity.

He fixed his gaze on Olivia. Her expression peaceful, her almond shaped brown eyes hiding the secrets of her heart. He flirted with her making her laugh with witty commentary while gauging how receptive she would be to an invitation to go for a walk, alone, later that night. Though she seemed to enjoy his company she gave no indication she was willing to abandon her friend.

Isaac sat quietly across the table. He pretended not to listen to the conversation between Olivia and Juan Carlos. Inside, however, he was seething with jealousy. Olivia attempted to include him in the conversation, but he feigned indifference. He scanned the sea of unfamiliar faces. He suddenly felt uncomfortable; the third wheel on a date to which he wasn't invited.

"Nice hat," Juan Carlos said. He saw the sympathetic look Olivia cast the boy and sought to endear him to her by playing nice.

"Thanks," Isaac said. He couldn't gauge Juan Carlos' sincerity because he detected a hint of sarcasm in his tone. "It was a gift from my father."

"Your father?" Juan Carlos looked perplexed. *Is that supposed to mean something?*

"His father is Old Sienna's preeminent hat maker." Olivia answered quickly. "Some say he's the best in all of Puerto Rico."

"Impressive." Juan Carlos nodded. "Tell me, Isaac, are you in the hat-making business with your father?"

"I work with him, but I have no intention of taking over the family business."

"What do you aspire to achieve?" Juan Carlos leaned forward.

Isaac hesitated. He felt slightly embarrassed to speak of his lofty ambitions with a renowned artist.

"He wants to be a novelist." Olivia chimed in.

Juan Carlos glanced at Olivia before he turned back to Isaac and asked if he had been published.

"Not yet," Isaac said.

"Don't be modest." Olivia said. "He's had a few poems featured in the local paper."

Does she always answer for him? Juan Carlos thought to himself as he nodded.

Isaac cast her a sharp glance.

"Keep at it." Juan Carlos said condescendingly. "Persistence is key."

Before Isaac could reply, La Señora Carmen appeared at the table. "I see you all have met." Her eyes shone with enthusiasm. She observed the proximity of Olivia and Juan Carlos seated at the table. Isaac looked as though he felt miles away. Juan Carlos made to stand as a gesture of formality to the governor's wife, but she insisted he remain seated. She turned to Isaac and asked him to accompany her inside. He and Olivia exchanged a furtive glance.

"Don't worry about her. She is in the presence of a gentleman." La Señora Carmen urged him on.

That's what you think. Isaac thought to himself as he stood and walked with her inside.

Olivia watched them disappear through the double doors. She wondered why La Señora Carmen asked Isaac to join her inside. Did she plan to speak with him about her visits to the cemetery? Was she going to ask Isaac about their true reason for being there too? Perhaps she was over-thinking everything and the reason for inviting Isaac inside had nothing to do with the cemetery. It suddenly dawned on her that it was a ploy contrived by La Señora Carmen to give Olivia and Juan Carlos an opportunity to speak alone.

She looked around and noticed the occasional sidelong glance from the aristocrats who appeared to want to approach and converse with the artista, but abided by an unspoken command to grant him and Olivia some privacy. She turned to Juan Carlos. He gave her his most charming smile, the one he used to sway many women his way. She stared at him, and he knew she was considering his request.

"Is that a yes?" He winked.

She leaned toward him, and for a moment, just a brief moment, he thought she was going to kiss him. For some reason, the prospect sent butterflies fluttering in his stomach. He was accustomed to being in control of his emotions during his interactions with women, yet with Olivia he suddenly felt nervous. She leaned back in her seat and crossed her arms over her chest. Her voice soft and melodic as she explained that she wasn't in the habit of accepting such an invitation from a man she had just met.

Juan Carlos swallowed hard when she reached for her drink, a mojito, and took a sip. He tried not to stare at her lips and neck, but she met his gaze with a mischievous grin. He studied her eyes; in the low lighting of the courtyard they were like dark brown veils, shadowed and mysterious, revealing nothing about her experience in love. And he remembered the story of Las Lagrimas Perdidas—the Lost Tears—from a small town in southern Spain.

According to legend tears shed from a broken heart fall into the rivers of emotion. They are the rivers that link our souls with the souls of others who have entered our lives. Each river carrying our tears, our pain, and our longing, joining together and drifting apart until they merge with the sea where our memories are lost in the oceans of time.

If her innocent gaze was any indication of her inexperience with matters of the heart then she could never have shed tears of heartbreak, for it is known that such tears can only fall from eyes that have seen true romantic love.

17

The double doors leading into the governor's mansion closed behind La Señora Carmen and Isaac, pushing the sound of music and conversations back out onto the courtyard and the patio. The light from the chandeliers fell against the white walls and ceiling and set the entire house aglow. Gold drapes flanked the large darkened windows where night had fallen into place.

La Señora Carmen ushered Isaac down an empty corridor lined with several closed doors on each side. The door to a study at the far end of the hallway stood ajar. Isaac could make out a bookshelf in the golden glow of a lamp. Once inside he stared in awe at the floor to ceiling cherry oak wood shelves lined with books. The shelves ran across all four walls, leaving no place for a window and just enough room for the door to swing open.

The décor of the study was so dissimilar from the rest of the house Isaac felt as though he had stepped into another world. *This is the library of my dreams*, he thought to himself as he ran his fingers across the spines of leather bound volumes on the shelves. He recognized the titles of the classics his uncle had introduced him to many years ago.

"I read your poems in the paper." La Señora Carmen interrupted the silence.

"You did?" Isaac turned to her perplexed.

"Your uncle showed them to me. He is quite proud of you and he has every right to be," she smiled. "You write beautifully."

"Thanks," Isaac smiled. He turned his attention back to the bookshelves. "How do you know my uncle?"

"That is a conversation for another day," she said.

"Okay." Isaac shrugged.

"I suppose you are wondering why I brought you here."

Isaac nodded and met her gaze.

"You're in love with her, aren't you?"

"With who?" Isaac's brow furrowed.

"Don't be coy with me young man. I can see it in your eyes. It is evident in the way you look at her."

"How do you mean?" Isaac's curiosity had been piqued.

"There are only three ways men look upon women to whom they are not related: indifference, if there is no interest; lust, which leads to undressing them with their eyes; and longing, the soft as a whisper glance of agonizing over desire and unrequited love." She closed the door to the study and motioned for him to sit on one of the three red leather couches. They surrounded a coffee table the same color as the bookshelves and the desk on the opposite end of the room. "Your poetry is quite profound for someone your age. Upon seeing you with Olivia, it is clear she is your inspiration."

Isaac blushed.

"Do not be embarrassed. Every writer needs a muse."

"There is no place for grief in a house which serves the Muse." Isaac said with a pensive look in his eyes.

"You are familiar with Sappho, the sixth-century B.C. poet of Ancient Greece." La Señora Carmen nodded impressed.

"My uncle—" Isaac shrugged.

"He taught you well." She sat on one of the couches.

"Thanks, but we aren't here to discuss my education, are

we?" Isaac approached and sat on the couch directly across the coffee table.

"Indeed we are not." La Señora Carmen smoothed her hands over her dress.

Then why are we here? Isaac thought to himself as he waited patiently for her to continue.

La Señora Carmen cleared her throat. "What do you know of the Labyrinth of Love Letters?"

"I have heard many things, but truly I know nothing for certain."

She studied him momentarily. The golden glow of the lamp sculpted his features in scarlet and amber hues. "Your father is Rolando Quintero, the one they call the Mad Hatter."

"The one and only." Isaac nodded.

"And your mother was Maricela Aquino."

Isaac flinched. "You knew my mother?"

"Providencia was a small town before the establishment of Old Sienna."

"How well did you know her?"

"I cannot say I knew her all that well, but from our occasional interactions at preliminary school she seemed like a nice girl. By the time we reached secondary school she and your father were inseparable. As far as anyone could tell they were best friends and nothing scandalous had ever been said about either of them." La Señora Carmen sighed before she lowered her gaze. "I was saddened by the news of her passing."

"Thank you," Isaac said. "I wish I could have known her, but I was merely a baby when God took her from us."

"God takes His favorite children first." La Señora Carmen

wiped a tear from her eye.

"Pardon my candor, but what does my mother have to do with the reason you brought me here?"

"Love," La Señora Carmen said.

"Love?" Isaac did not understand.

"Your mother was your father's dulcinea, the only woman he has ever loved and will ever love. It is the reason he will never marry again no matter how lonely he feels."

"How do you know this?"

"They shared a unique bond, the kind of love that is more rare than the most precious gems. It is the kind of love that breaks your heart with joy and tears away a piece of your soul when it is taken from you. Once you have felt it you know that no other love will replace it." She met his gaze. "Their love was perfect for them because it was not a forbidden love, and it is for that reason they did not need the Labyrinth."

Isaac sat quietly and allowed her to continue.

"You say you want to find the Labyrinth to better understand love, but it is as I said before. You must experience love to turn ignorance into wisdom. An alchemist cannot study it, nor can a logician explain it. For the beauty of love is as indescribable as a sunset, and in its truest form it is as profound as God. Perhaps love awakens us if we are asleep, or becomes a dream if we are burdened by reality. That is why we love—to turn longing into passion, and to find the part of ourselves we always knew was missing. And when we reach the end of our lives, we hope our love story will have been written by the flames of passion and extinguished by the tears of joy."

Isaac nodded pensively.

"I can tell by the way you look at Olivia that you have

feelings for her," La Señora Carmen said.

"I love her." Isaac snapped. He surprised himself with his confession. He had never told another soul about his feelings, not even Memito.

"Indeed you do, but unrequited love is not the same as forbidden love."

"Love is love regardless of the circumstances."

"Fair enough," La Señora Carmen nodded. "Though what I am trying to say is that the Labyrinth only reveals itself in the circumstance of forbidden love."

"Then you *have* been there!"

"I did not say that."

"Then how do you know?"

La Señora Carmen hesitated. She inhaled deeply before she continued. "I'll tell you what I *do* know. The Labyrinth is cursed! Though legend holds that it exists as a haven for those enraptured in a forbidden love affair, secret love always comes at a cost."

"What do you mean?"

"The Labyrinth is a hidden library of love letters, which allows people to read missives left hidden for them by their lovers. They are led to the Labyrinth by a mysterious figure who comes to them in a dream with knowledge of their secret love and the promise to keep it."

"How does he know about the affairs?" Isaac wondered.

La Señora Carmen shrugged. "That remains a mystery. Some say it is el Diablo and he grants lovers access into the Labyrinth in exchange for their souls. One lives and one dies. Others claim it is the spirit of Saint Valentine himself."

"What do you believe?" Isaac fixed his eyes on hers.

La Señora Carmen leaned forward and lowered her voice. "What I believe does not matter, but what I am about to tell you must not leave this room."

Isaac nodded.

"Olivia's mother did not simply disappear."

Isaac flinched and cast her a suspicious glance.

"To be more precise she did not just wake up one day and decide to leave her daughter."

"How do you know?" Isaac said.

"That's not important." She dismissed the question with a wave of her hand. "What's important is that Olivia does not find the Labyrinth."

"Why?"

"If she discovers the truth about her mother's disappearance then her life will be in danger!"

"I don't understand—"

A knock on the door interrupted their conversation.

"Come in." La Señora Carmen cleared her throat.

A servant peered inside. She had dark skin with coarse hair as silver as the moon. Her body remained hidden behind the door, but her round face hinted at a short full-figured woman. She glanced at Isaac before she turned to the governor's wife. After she informed La Señora Carmen that the governor was preparing to give his speech and requested her presence, she bowed and closed the door as she backed out of the room.

La Señora Carmen turned back to Isaac. "Remember what I said. Olivia must not find the Labyrinth."

"She's intent on finding it!"

"If you truly love her you will make sure that does not

happen."

Isaac closed his eyes and rubbed the bridge of his nose. He thought about what La Señora Carmen had said. He wanted to know why Olivia's life would be in danger and how the governor's wife knew this to be true. But there was not enough time for her to provide answers.

"Promise me Isaac. Promise me that you'll do everything in your power to prevent Olivia from ever finding the Labyrinth." La Señora Carmen stood and walked toward the door.

"You do realize that you're asking me to betray the woman I love, don't you?" He looked at her as she stood in the doorway.

"That's nothing compared to betraying the woman who is in love with you." She disappeared into the corridor.

The door stood ajar. Isaac sat alone in the study thinking about Olivia. She had never known her mother and now the only link to her mother threatened her life. Olivia couldn't turn to her father for protection because everything she thought she knew about him had forever been lost when she discovered the bloodstained letter in his jacket. Isaac had forgotten about the letter until that moment and he cursed himself for not mentioning it before La Señora Carmen had left the room.

Then again what could he have said to her about the letter? For all Isaac knew she would divulge his secret to the authorities, which would lead Chief Inspector Guillermo Sedeño right to his prime suspect for the theft of the letter. Even if he couldn't prove Javier Villalobos had stolen the letter, the Chief Inspector would most assuredly imprison him on charges of being in possession of stolen evidence. Isaac couldn't bear the thought of seeing Olivia lose both parents before her eighteenth birthday. He was sure she would never forgive him if he played a role in that outcome.

Isaac sat with his head in his hands contemplating the situation. What did La Señora Carmen mean by "the truth about her mother's disappearance?" What did she know? What did she not want to reveal and why? Isaac's mind raced with questions when another knock on the door interrupted his train of thought.

Olivia stood in the doorway with a pensive look in her eye. She didn't say anything at first. She merely gazed at him in silence.

"How did things go with—" Isaac began to say. His words trailed off when Juan Carlos appeared behind Olivia.

"We should return to our seats," Juan Carlos said in a low voice.

Olivia glanced at him over her shoulder and nodded.

Juan Carlos gave Isaac a curt nod before he turned and walked away.

"Are you okay?" Olivia stepped into the study and closed the door behind her.

"Yeah, I'm fine." Isaac stood.

He tried to walk past her, but she placed a hand on his chest and stopped him in his tracks.

"What's wrong?" she said. "What did she say to you?"

That's nothing compared to betraying the woman who is in love with you. La Señora Carmen's words echoed in his mind when he gazed into Olivia's eyes.

"Nothing," he said and looked ahead as he proceeded to walk past her. "We should join the others. It would be rude to not be seated before the governor begins his speech and introduces the guest of honor."

Olivia detected the sarcasm in his voice. "Since when do you care—" Her words trailed off when he walked briskly through the corridor without looking back. *What's his problem?* She rolled her eyes.

She stormed after him and called out his name, but Isaac acted as if he didn't hear her when he disappeared around the corner. She felt the agitation swell within her.

"Isaac!" Olivia said with a clenched jaw.

He reappeared a moment later with a wild look in his eye. He shushed her with a finger on his lips and glanced over his shoulder before he ushered her back down the corridor and into the study.

"What's happening?" She whispered.

"It's your dad!" Isaac said as he closed the door quickly, but quietly. "He's here and he's drunk."

Olivia gasped. She felt the blood rush from her face.

18

When the servant answered the door Javier Villalobos announced his presence in formal capacity as Inspector on important business. He pushed his way past and demanded to speak with the governor.

The servant, a tall black man with a slim build and a receding hairline closed the door and walked around Javier to impede his progress. Javier staggered as he sized him up with bloodshot eyes and reeking of Rum de toilette.

"The governor is unavailable at the moment."

"They can dress you up in a fancy suit and tie and teach you how to speak properly, but you're still a Negro mugroso. Now get out of my way!" Javier spat.

"The governor remains unavailable," the man replied.

"Carajo," Javier stumbled to his right. "Fernando!"

Isaac had turned the corner when additional servants rushed to the commotion. Javier shoved a man as he staggered and shouted obscenities. Isaac immediately turned on his heels and bolted back around the corner. A few minutes after he led Olivia back into the study they heard approaching footsteps. They scrambled behind the desk and hid beneath it just as the door opened. When they heard Javier and Fernando speaking heatedly about the inopportune timing of the visit they exchanged an incredulous glance.

"You've got some balls showing up here half in the bag." Fernando closed the door.

"How else was I going to ensure you would meet my

demands?" Javier leaned against the back of a chair.

"Your demands are absurd!" Fernando placed his hands on his hips.

"It's the cost of doing business." Javier shrugged. The stench of rum on his breath filled the air between them.

"Damn it, Javier. We had a deal."

"Yes, we had a deal, but a man ended up dead—"

"Don't blame me for your incompetence."

Olivia and Isaac stared at each other with wide eyes when they heard a soft knock at the door.

"What is it?" Fernando snapped.

La Señora Carmen peered inside. "Your guests are waiting."

"Have the orchestra entertain them a little while longer," Fernando said without facing her.

"I'm not sure how effective that will be after the commotion—"

"Damn it, Carmen, I'm busy!"

La Señora Carmen lowered her eyes and noticed two sets of feet beneath the desk. She glanced at her husband, who stood with his back to her, and at Javier, who appeared too intoxicated to notice anything except for what was directly in front of him and she concluded that neither man was aware they had company. She simply smiled inwardly and pulled the door closed.

"You were supposed to find the man, rough him up and tell him to stay away from my wife. That was it."

"And I held up my end of the bargain." Javier insisted.

"How did he end up dead?"

"Let Guillermo figure that out. I have enough to deal with now that he suspects me of stealing the letter."

"The letter that you are now using to extort more money from me."

"No," Javier interrupted. "The letter was never a part of the original agreement. You asked me to procure it from police evidence after someone tipped you off about its existence and informed you that Sedeño called in a graphologist to examine it."

Fernando turned away.

"You never did say who it was that told you about the letter."

"That information doesn't concern you."

"It does when you ask me to put my career on the line to obtain the letter."

"A career that went to shit after your wife's mysterious disappearance."

Olivia gasped.

Fernando's brow furrowed.

"Don't you ever mention Angelica again Fernando, or it will end badly for you."

"Are you threatening me, Javier?" The governor tilted his head.

"I don't make threats, only promises." Javier glared at him.

Fernando studied him in silence. He did not want to underestimate Javier Villalobos. Not only did he have a reputation for being a mean drunk, but also he was a man with nothing to lose and there is nothing more dangerous than a dog backed into a corner. *Especially a mangy mutt with no loyalty to his master*, Fernando thought.

"I'm going to need some time to put together that kind of money," Fernando lied. He had no intention of paying Javier the amount of money he demanded. His only hope was to keep Javier on the hook long enough for Guillermo to make his case against him and then have the letter destroyed before its contents see the light of day.

"Time is not a luxury we have, Fernando."

"It is the only luxury the poor can afford."

Javier cast the governor a curious glance.

"My cousin is on the board of directors at Banco Puerto Rico. I know you're broke." Fernando smirked.

"My personal affairs are not your concern."

"Perhaps," Fernando shrugged. "But if you insist on extortion then I have to find out why."

Javier leaned against the chair in silence. He glared at Fernando and contemplated his next move. His head was spinning and his eyelids grew heavy. He couldn't risk waiting until Guillermo discovered the truth. He needed the money to leave town before that happened. Otherwise he'd end up in prison and Guillermo would finally have the opportunity to reveal the truth to Olivia.

"You have two days." Javier finally said. "Or the letter makes the front page."

There was a knock on the door before Fernando replied. When it opened, Guillermo stood behind Carmen. Two uniformed officers flanked him on both sides.

"Chief Inspector Sedeño, I regret dragging you out here at this hour on a Saturday night," Fernando approached.

Olivia and Isaac exchanged a wide-eyed glance beneath the desk.

"It's no trouble governor. I came as soon as I got the call." He shook Fernando's hand before he turned his attention to Javier. He assured the governor that the inspector would be dealt with accordingly.

"Don't be too hard on him, Guillermo." The governor leaned in and lowered his voice. "The man is clearly not in full possession of all his faculties."

"That doesn't excuse his behavior." Guillermo stepped into the study.

"Perhaps some sort of home detention with around the clock supervision is called for here?" Fernando suggested.

"I'll discipline as I see fit governor, but I appreciate your input," Guillermo said without facing Fernando. He motioned for Javier to exit the study. "Let's not make this any worse than it already is."

Javier belched and staggered as he continued to use the back of the chair for support. He straightened himself as best he could and walked deliberately past Guillermo without meeting his gaze. He struggled to maintain his balance but focused on each step to avoid giving Guillermo the satisfaction of seeing him fall flat on his face.

When he collapsed into the back seat of the police car he closed his eyes and passed out. The Chief Inspector turned to the governor and apologized again for the incident before he climbed into the passenger seat.

Fernando watched the automobile pull away and vanish into the night. He instructed his servants to resume their duties and inform the guests he would be returning momentarily. Then he turned to his wife and stared at her without saying a word. *What were you doing when you left the party?* He wanted to ask, but he knew she would lie.

She looked at him, but said nothing. She did not like the way he looked at her, but she did not avert her eyes either. Despite the uneasiness she felt, his silence no longer hurt her. In fact, she preferred it now that she knew she was not in love with him.

"I expect you to be at your place by my side when I give my speech."

Carmen gazed at him, but remained silent. In that moment, she felt nothing. No fear, no anger, no resentment, and least of all love. She felt no obligation or inclination to acquiesce to his request. Her reasons were not driven by wrath, or rage, or vindictiveness, for the idea of vengeance felt beneath her—a byproduct of impulsiveness often found in simpletons and the petty.

"I'll be there," she nodded.

Then she walked past him without any display of emotion. She entered the home and made a beeline for the study where she found Isaac and Olivia speaking in hushed tones.

"What in God's name drove the two of you to hide under the desk?" She closed the door behind her.

"We didn't know where else to go when her father arrived," Isaac said.

He stood beside Olivia. She sat in the chair her father had used for support only moments ago and stared ahead in disbelief.

"He doesn't know you're here tonight?" La Señora Carmen said incredulously.

"That's not all he doesn't know." Isaac shook his head.

La Señora Carmen looked at Isaac, glanced at Olivia and turned her gaze to Isaac again. "What is it that you're not telling me?"

19

Two male servants stood outside the front door when the police car pulled up at the gate to the Villalobos residence. The Chief Inspector exited the vehicle and waved them over. The two men exchanged an uneasy glance before they approached. They were equal in height with slim builds and fair skin beneath their white uniforms. Both had receding hairlines with short black hair and dark brown eyes.

The Chief Inspector opened the rear passenger door of the police car when they pulled the gates open. The servants glanced at each other before they hung their heads and approached the car. The shame they felt was more for their employer than for themselves. Despite Javier's reputation in Old Sienna his servants were loyal to him, for most had raised him under the employ of Javier's parents and others grew up with him as the sons and daughters of those same servants.

"We should take this opportunity to search his home for the letter." An officer suggested while the servants pulled Javier from the back seat of the car.

"Negative," Guillermo said without looking over his shoulder. He stared ahead at the house where Angelica had once lived.

"But, sir, we may never have a chance like—"

"I said no." Guillermo finally turned to face his subordinate. The servants each threw an arm over Javier's shoulders and carried him away. They heard the door to the police car close behind them. One thanked the Chief Inspector over his shoulder. Guillermo bid him a good night and pulled the gates closed. He approached the vehicle and looked his officer in the eye.

"We will find the letter, but we won't compromise our integrity in the process." He climbed into the vehicle. "Now let's get out of here."

The officer nodded and followed suit. They said nothing more to each other on their way back to police headquarters. It was close to midnight when they arrived. Most of the officers had gone home to their families. Save for a few whose status as rookies earned them the undesirable task of working the graveyard shift. They played dominoes at a small table behind the front desk in the main lobby of the police station.

The Chief Inspector normally would not permit them the distraction however, tonight he made an exception because the entire population of the wealthy district attended the party at the governor's mansion. "We know where the worst criminals are tonight, and they'll likely be too drunk to harm anyone when the party is over."

They fell silent and acknowledged the Chief Inspector when he appeared in the doorway. The door had been propped open to let in the cool night air. The light from the light post outside fell across the threshold, which hid his expressionless face in shadow. A small light bulb dangled from the ceiling and cast a soft glow in the otherwise dark lobby. The only other light came from the bulb that hung above the table.

"Carry on," Guillermo said as he walked around the large wooden desk. A stack of papers laid spread out across it as if the wind had blown hard. "And clean that up."

An officer immediately stood and obeyed the command. The game continued and Guillermo heard their conversation as he walked up the short flight of stairs. He pushed through the double doors that led to the cavernous hall where the desks of every inspector were organized in four rows of six. His was located at the far end on an elevated platform overlooking the entire office.

All but a few desk lamps had been shut off and of the three ceiling lamps that remained on one flickered silently in the corner. Guillermo shook his head and walked toward his desk. He placed his fedora on the desk and noticed a folded piece of paper set against his desk lamp. He unfolded it as he took his seat. It was a telegram from the graphologist, Julian Aponte, advising the Chief Inspector he'd be arriving in Puerto Rico a day early.

Shit this only leaves me three days to find the damn letter.

The double doors opened. The officer who had driven Javier home with Guillermo entered and approached the Chief Inspector's desk. He apologized for making the inappropriate suggestion earlier. He clarified that he merely wanted to expedite their objective. Given that the letter was stolen evidence in a murder investigation he assumed the Chief Inspector would not object to finding it at all costs.

"Assumption is the mother of all mistakes." Guillermo leaned forward. "Don't fret. Tomorrow is a new day. Go home and get some rest. I want you here before dawn. You're going to accompany me on a stake out."

The officer nodded and left.

Guillermo waited until the officer passed through the double doors before he unlocked a lower drawer of his desk. When he first had the lock installed the locksmith asked Guillermo why he felt the need to have a locked drawer in a police station. Guillermo had said,

"Because lawyers are allowed in here too."

At the time, he firmly believed his fellow officers to be trustworthy and incapable of stealing from each other. That all changed when Javier Villalobos stole the letter from the evidence locker. Although he had no proof Guillermo knew in his gut that Javier was guilty. He wanted to figure out how he did it, and more importantly he wanted to understand Javier's motives.

What was he doing in a closed-door meeting with the governor in his condition? Guillermo wondered.

The private meeting did not sit well with the Chief Inspector. Especially when the governor should have been entertaining his guests. What did they have to discuss in private that could not wait? Something wasn't adding up and Guillermo Sedeño was intent on figuring it out.

20

The door to the study opened before Isaac, Olivia, or La Señora Carmen could say another word. Fernando stood in the doorway. His brow furrowed as he looked from his wife to her guests. He asked if there was a problem before he recognized Olivia Villalobos.

"You're the inspector's daughter," he spoke softly.

Carmen was taken aback by the gentleness in his voice. She had never heard him speak to anyone with kindness. It dawned on her that perhaps it was a tone he reserved for younger women.

Fernando offered to have a car take her home, but Olivia declined. She stood and exited the room. Isaac apologized to the governor and La Señora Carmen before he raced after Olivia.

He caught up with her at the front door and walked her home. They did not speak, nor did they have to, for their friendship was predicated not on what they shared, but on their understanding of each other.

Olivia walked without watching where she was going. Each step taken at a steady pace along a path she knew by memory. It was dark outside. The moon and the stars had assumed their place in the sky, but it was the street lamps that lit her way.

She could not believe what she had heard. Her father had stolen evidence for the governor, and a man had died after her father—under the governor's orders—beat him. Whoever the dead man was he had to have been La Señora Carmen's lover. The scandal was sure to rock Old Sienna to its foundations.

But she would not dare speak of it, least of all with La Señora Carmen. Lest she'd have to explain how she came into possession of the letter and the arrangement she overheard between Fernando and Javier.

What has my father gotten himself into? She thought to herself as she replayed the governor's words in her mind. "I know you're broke."

Broke, how? Olivia wondered.

Her entire life she had lived without wanting for anything. She had a roof over her head, clothes on her back, food in her stomach, and a formal education at one of the best schools on the island. She'd had luxuries even her best friend would have envied, though he didn't. And it wasn't because of an unspoken resentment for the privilege Olivia had been born into. For despite being raised by a hat shop owner who barely earned enough money to keep them from being homeless Isaac had a loving father, which was one thing Olivia wished she'd had for herself.

The only thing they'd had in common was that neither had known their mother and perhaps that was the only detail that mattered until now. The inconsolable truth that both had lost their mothers in a time when all they knew was love even if they didn't understand it.

She missed her mother in that moment and the sudden revelation perplexed her. She did not think it was possible to miss someone she had never known. Though the revelation of her father's secrets—secrets he probably kept from Tia Katarina—had irrevocably changed her life.

When they arrived at her house she thanked Isaac for seeing her home safely and told him she'd come by the shop in the morning.

Once inside the servants approached her. They inquired about where she'd been and told her about her father being brought home by the Chief Inspector in a police car. She assured them she was fine and instructed them to go to their sleeping quarters. They obliged her request, all except for Clara Ruiz. Clara escorted Olivia to her room and sat beside her on the bed. They remained silent for a long while before Olivia finally spoke.

"Life as we know it is over."

21

Isaac waited until she stepped inside before he turned away. He had wandered aimlessly through the streets, asking himself what he could do for his friend. The wealthy district of Old Sienna was quiet. It had been so because most of the residents attended the governor's mansion. The breeze was soft and the stars of the Caribbean watched him from their places.

In the silence of the night Isaac felt like what he had become a sad soul condemned to oblivion. Any hope he had of tasting love on Olivia's lips vanished when her eyes found Juan Carlos Trinidad at the governor's mansion. He knew without knowing by the way she looked at the artista with a gaze she had never given Isaac in all the years of their friendship.

He needed his mother then, as he never had before. He needed her presence and her embrace. Perhaps she would have provided him with perspective had God not picked the flower that was Maricela Quintero-Aquino from the garden of Rolando's heart. Isaac had finally arrived at that inevitable moment in a young man's life when only a mother's love can heal the wound of his first heartbreak.

The streets were dark. He was barely visible in his black suit with his black fedora like a shadow among shadows, a freshly minted phantom of unrequited love. He arrived at the corner of Avenida Dos and Calle Santa Ana where a mysterious stranger stood beneath the light post across the street. It was the same mysterious figure he saw the night before, and also in his dream. The stranger leaned against the pole with a hand in his pocket. He wore a long coat and wide brim hat. He brought a cigarette up to his lips, the orange glow reflected in the black marbles of his eyes as he stared at Isaac in silence.

Isaac stood motionless for a moment. His eyes darted back and forth before he decided to cross the street and approach the stranger. When he arrived beneath the light post he looked up at the man. He was much taller than he appeared from a distance. The stranger's face remained hidden under the shadow cast by his fedora. He offered Isaac a cigarette, but Isaac declined.

"You look as if you have just come from a funeral," said the man.

"Perhaps it was my own." Isaac shrugged.

"Heartbreak has a way of making us feel that way." The man stuffed the box of cigarettes back into his pocket.

Isaac cast the stranger a suspicious glance. "Who are you?"

"You have already asked me that question."

"A question you never answered." Isaac remembered his dream.

"You already know the answer." The stranger turned and walked away.

"I want to hear it from you." Isaac insisted.

"My name is Armando de Maria y Delores-Dios, at your service," he said over his shoulder and tipping his hat.

"But I thought you were—"

"Do you wish to waste time discussing what you already know, or would you prefer to find out why I'm here?" Armando cut him off.

"Why *are* you here?" Isaac followed.

"I've wanted to come for a long time, but you know how destiny is, everything must be precise." His arm moved in a sweeping motion across the sky.

"Destiny?" Isaac asked. "What destiny?"

"Your destiny," the stranger said over his shoulder. His features remained hidden by the shadows. "Matters of the heart are my specialty."

"Are you some kind of charlatan matchmaker?"

"That's a bit harsh, Isaac. Wouldn't you agree?"

"I suppose." Isaac shrugged. "Though your cryptic answers offer little in terms of logic," Isaac said.

"Man and his need for logic," Armando mused.

"Logic is what separates us from the animals," Isaac replied.

"Something else distinguished you from them long before the ancient philosophers studied valid reasoning."

"I don't understand." Isaac's brow furrowed.

Armando turned a corner. Isaac followed. He lagged a few steps behind him. Isaac tried to keep up, but Armando seemed to glide. His black trench coat billowed as he moved ahead.

A series of two-story brick buildings lined both sides of the street. The walls were dark and the windows even darker. The light from the lamp posts on each corner cast a soft glow against the night.

A drunk stumbled beneath a light post at the end of the block. The man turned down a dark alley. A trash can fell over and a cat screeched. Aside from a dog barking in the distance this quarter of Old Sienna slept beneath the full moon and the stars.

"Have you ever known a woman, Isaac?"

"I've met plenty of women."

"I meant in the biblical sense."

"I'm familiar with the wives of Abraham—"

"That's not what I mean." Armando cut him off.

"What did you mean, then?"

"I mean, have you ever made love to a woman?"

Isaac hesitated.

"Do not feel ashamed if you are still in possession of your virginity. In time, it will be a precious gift too often relented to the unworthy."

"I don't understand." Isaac tilted his head.

"In the search for love people will frequently mistake the act of making love with sex. They will rush in and out of relationships, leaping from one bed to the next and become so lost in the frenzy they will forget what they had originally set out to find." Armando continued ahead.

"What does this have to do with me?"

"It has everything to do with you."

"How do you mean?"

"It begins with your writing, which reveals your feelings for Olivia. Olivia Villalobos, the girl in possession of a love letter that belongs in the Labyrinth. The Labyrinth she is not permitted to find."

"Why not?"

"Her amor for Juan Carlos is not a forbidden love."

"It's not?" Isaac felt the jealousy surge in his gut. He hoped his reaction did not reveal his feelings.

"She is destined to fall in love with Juan Carlos Trinidad, and he is destined to fall in love with her. No one, not even Javier Villalobos will prevent this." Armando continued. "Your love for her, however, despite its sincerity is forbidden."

"According to who?" Isaac looked at him in astonishment.

"According to the Fates," Armando said matter-of-factly.

"The Fates?!" Isaac repeated. He remembered them from his lessons with Uncle Gabriel. In Greek mythology, the Moirai—commonly known in English as the Fates—controlled the metaphorical thread of life of every mortal from birth to death. They spun a thread of yarn that determined each person's life, and into the thread they wove sorrow, wealth, travel and love.

"If my love for Olivia is forbidden then why are you here?"

"I am here to reveal to you the location of the Labyrinth."

"What?" Isaac stopped dead in his tracks.

Armando stopped and looked over his shoulder. The darkness continued to conceal his face. "Don't get too excited just yet," Armando said, "there is something you must do first."

"Name it," Isaac said without hesitation.

"You must endure the curse of every man. You must experience the pain of unrequited love." Armando turned away and continued ahead.

"Unrequited love?" Isaac muttered under his breath before he proceeded after Armando.

"I don't understand."

"You are going to witness the whirlwind romance of Olivia Villalobos and Juan Carlos Trinidad. You will feel the agony of jealousy and longing when you see them in each other's embrace. You will be ridden with guilt over your cynical thoughts when she expresses her feelings for him. You will die in silence and cry in the shadows of existence where only God will witness your pain."

They arrived at the end of the street where it t-boned along the high cliffs overlooking the ocean. A cool breeze that smelled of salt swept up from where the water crashed against the stone shore. Lights from the docks swayed in the distance. Isaac estimated the location of Uncle Gabriel's boathouse to be somewhere in the void of night where the heartbroken go to be forgotten and their secrets are taken with the wind.

"What if I refuse?"

"You can't," Armando said.

"Why not?"

"The heart wants what the heart wants." Armando shrugged. "Your only alternative is to leap from these cliffs and surrender yourself to the finality of death." Armando stared ahead. "Which, of course, you won't do."

"How do you know?" Isaac cast him a sidelong glance.

"Destiny, remember."

Isaac nodded pensively. *Destiny*, he thought to himself. What is destiny but some contrived notion we use to convince ourselves that our circumstances will improve? Based on the conversation Isaac and Armando were having it seemed to Isaac that destiny played a cruel joke at his expense. The girl he loved was the girl who knew him best and she was about to fall in love with another man. If destiny was something other than a falsity, then any hope Isaac had of being with the girl he loved was going to be lost to oblivion.

"You will not utter a word of this conversation to Olivia." Armando interrupted Isaac's train of thought. "Instead, you will write love letters to her as you experience heartbreak in the shadows of secret love."

A path of love and ruin, Isaac remembered.

"You will not give her these love letters; nor will you divulge the contents to her."

"What am I supposed to do with them?"

"You will take them to the Labyrinth. You will hide them there, and they will remain hidden until the moment they are meant to be read."

"When will that be?"

"You will know when the time is right."

A long silence lingered between them. The ocean roared and the waves crashed against the stone shore again. Isaac turned to the sound in the darkness. He closed his eyes momentarily and felt the mist spray him in the breeze.

"How will I find the Labyrinth?" Isaac turned to face Armando.

The man was gone. Isaac scanned the empty streets to no avail. Armando had disappeared.

22

The following day Guillermo sat in the driver's seat of a dark sedan with the officer from the previous night. He only knew him by name, Emiliano Robles, a young man in his second year on the police force. As with all the other beat cops Guillermo's interactions with Emiliano had been limited since his tenure as inspector began seven years ago. The demands of his new position required him to spend more time in the field than at police headquarters. As was the case at present when they conducted a stake out at the Villalobos estate.

The sun had not yet peered over the horizon. The predawn shadows allowed them to avoid raising suspicion while they waited for Javier to emerge. Emiliano prepared to light a cigarette when the Chief Inspector knocked the cigarette out of his hand. He looked at Guillermo in astonishment.

"Good God, son. Don't you realize we are sitting in a 1928 Hispano-Suiza H6C?" Guillermo reproached.

The luxury sedan had been confiscated from wealthy Spanish sympathizers during the war. It had been kept safely hidden for such circumstances as this when it would blend in among other elegant automobiles in the wealthy district. The iconic cosmopolitan marque led Rolls Royce to purchase the Hispano-Suiza patent for its own vehicles that have become synonymous with their distinctive body design. The interior leather looked as new as the day the vehicle came off the assembly line in Barcelona nearly a decade ago.

Emiliano apologized as he retrieved his cigarette from between his legs. He stepped out of the vehicle to smoke outside. Daybreak approached amid the chirping of birds in the trees and the coquí frog.

For a moment, Guillermo felt bad for the way he reproached the young officer. His interactions with the beat cops had been limited since his tenure as an inspector began seven years ago. The demands of his new position required him to spend more time in the field than at police headquarters. A follow-up investigation often led to a trail of clues, a winding path weaved by lies, overlapping evidence and misinformation. It was certainly not a life suitable for a family man and seldom afforded one the opportunity to make friends.

Guillermo saw Javier emerge from the house when Emiliano entered the vehicle. Inspector Villalobos appeared to have all his bearings about him as he marched toward the front gate.

"How does he not have a hangover?" Guillermo muttered to himself.

A taxi arrived at the front gate. It pulled away when Javier climbed into the back seat. Guillermo started the inline six-cylinder engine—among the first of its kind—and proceeded after the taxi.

Dawn broke as they arrived at Calle de Las Flores. It was one of the first roads in the oldest section of town that remained from Providencia. Emiliano gaped at the few mansions scattered atop the green rolling hills like castles towering over the land.

"Where are we?" Emiliano stared in awe.

"This is the Forgotten Quarter," Guillermo said. "Nobles lived here once, but enemies of the state seldom live to see old age."

A series of abandoned mansions rested on hilltops for the mile-long stretch of road that became known as the Forgotten

Quarter. Calle de Las Flores weaved like a silent river in the valley. It was flanked on both sides by a myriad of flowers, most notably Flor de maga, a red cup-shaped hibiscus known as the national flower of Puerto Rico. The colorful array of flowers was how the road had earned its name. It was also the only semblance of life that remained along the stretch of road leading to the wealthy district.

The verdant scenery provided a pleasant backdrop to the variety of architectural styles depicted in the gracious old-world mansions towering over the landscape. Along with the homes it was all that remained in the wealthy district of the barrio once known as Providencia. The smaller houses built over the previous one hundred and fifty years were stomped out of existence in less than a generation.

The taxi pulled up to a red Victorian-era styled home. The sharp angles of its towers stood in silhouette against a blue sky. The homes' large dark windows hinted at secrets trapped inside.

"Whose house is that?" Emiliano looked on curiously.

"That is the home of the Elder Valentino. The first of his name and the last of his line."

Javier exited the taxi, climbed the stairs and approached the door. He waited only a moment for someone to let him into the home. The shadows within the home swallowed him when he crossed the threshold. The door slowly closed behind him. No one in Old Sienna ever saw him again.

23

When the door closed behind him, Javier scanned the gloomy interior. At first glance the home appeared to remain trapped in the previous century. The furnishings and décor reminiscent of a forgotten era left in place to preserve the memory of happier times. Despite the angular shadows and somewhat melodramatic appearance the house appeared spotless.

The servant, Diego Muniz, studied Javier with a keen eye. He did not like Javier Villalobos, and he trusted him even less. Though he had not seen the inspector in close to two decades he could not shake his suspicions of Javier's unscrupulous disposition. He had been in the employ of the Valentino family all his life as both his father and grandfather before him. The Elder Valentino had often said the striking resemblance Diego shared with his forbearers would have convinced people an immortal lived among them. He was a tall, slim man with wide shoulders and large hands. A heavy brow and deep-set droopy eyes reminded Javier of the sentient creation of Victor Frankenstein.

He led the inspector through the arched entryway of a long corridor lined with pillars. Their footsteps echoed off the polished hardwood floors as they made their way to the rear of the home. They arrived at a winding staircase that led to the bowels of the mansion. The base was hidden in shadows. The thin steps and black wire railing gave Javier the uneasy feeling that with one misstep he'd tumble to his death.

Though Diego descended confidently, Javier moved deliberately with his hand against the wall. The wooden steps creaked as if no one had set foot on them in a generation. The corridor at the foot of the staircase reminded Javier of ancient tombs he'd read about in his youth. He could barely make out the layered brick walls and cobblestone path when Diego lifted a lantern from a hook and stepped into the darkness.

"I see a lot has changed since my last visit." Javier followed Diego.

The servant did not reply. He continued ahead without looking back. He held the lamp high and stared ahead.

"I hope there aren't any rats down here." Javier muttered.

Diego pretended he did not hear him. They arrived at a large wooden door that belonged in a medieval cellar more than in the basement of a Victorian era mansion. Metal grinded against metal when Diego turned a heavy latch. The door swung upon and the metal hinges groaned. After Diego crossed the threshold he stood with his back to the door to prop it open and motioned for Javier to enter.

The Elder Valentino sat in a high back leather chair behind his desk, enjoying an imported Cuban Cigar and a glass of scotch. A fire burned in the hearth and warmed the luxuriously decorated room with furniture and carpets brought from Europe and the Middle East. The Spanish flag hung on a pole behind him with a portrait of the Elder Valentino and his late wife high on the wall.

"It has been years since you last came to visit. Come have a seat inspector. What brings you here today?" The Elder Valentino invited.

Javier cast Diego a sidelong glance before he approached.

The Elder Valentino thanked Diego and sent him on his way. The servant nodded and pulled the heavy door closed as he backed out of the room. It closed with a thunderous boom before the metal latch grinded to a lock. Javier looked at the door with an uneasy feeling in his gut. When he turned back toward his host, the Elder Valentino held out a Cuban Cigar over the desk.

Javier took hold of it and rolled it between his fingers and his thumb.

"You have not answered my question. To what do I owe the honor of this visit?" The Elder Valentino walked around to the front of his desk.

"I need your help." Javier said.

"Again?" Valentino leaned against the edge of his desk and crossed his arms. His grey hair with streaks of white was slicked back and the same color as his heavy brow and thick mustache. He watched Javier with a cold stare as he puffed his cigar. "What is it this time?"

Javier Villalobos retrieved a lighter from the inner pocket of his jacket. The memory of his last visit remained fresh in his mind despite the years. He had only been married a year, but it had been a year filled with silence and doubt, two things that inspired jealousy and suspicion.

For his part Javier wanted to believe his wife's claims of fidelity. He loved and admired Angelica too much to think her capable of the ultimate betrayal, but he couldn't shake the nagging feeling that she was still in love with someone else. He knew about her relationship with Guillermo and that she had cared for him deeply, but Javier would not allow the circumstance to stand in his way. He had asked his father to arrange the marriage with the aristocrat's daughter and his father obliged.

God alone knows what the authority of men cost Angelica de las Fuentes in not having any control over her own destiny. In a time when women still acquiesced to the laws of God and man she surrendered her fate without question lest she disgrace her father and her family name.

Ever the obedient daughter she agreed to the arrangement, but not without first meeting with Guillermo in secret to tell him the news in person. Javier never knew how much she cried, or how desperately Guillermo wanted to whisk her away that night. He knew only that the forbidden affair had ended, and Angelica had now become his, and his alone. He wasted no time with a long engagement, for he wished to seal their fate immediately and they were wed within a month. Though for her the wedding, the honeymoon, and the marriage had been chapters in a novel that belonged to someone else.

She felt like a prisoner in a house with a man who claimed he loved her, but who had not truly been in love. For despite his claims of eternal fidelity and his efforts to make her happy he was nothing more than the warden of her life.

Javier had sensed the absence of love in her eyes. He recognized the distance between them when they consummated their marriage. He felt the weight of her depression when she wandered throughout the house in silence. When she left for the market or to walk in the plaza he worried she might never return. He wondered if she ever snuck off to see Guillermo, and ordered the servants to accompany her wherever she went.

Angelica seemed to only be happy in the presence of her newborn daughter. She looked upon her with tears in her eyes and a smile on her lips. When Javier looked at Olivia he knew she was not his child, but he had no proof of infidelity. He had only his intuition, which served him well in his capacity as a police officer, and the daily reminder of the features she inherited from her father.

Javier had no one to turn to, or confide in, for he knew of no one who had shared his plight. That is until he remembered when he overheard his grandfather tell the tale of his friend, the Elder Valentino, and the disgrace the family endured when Lorenzo had an affair with a woman from a lower class.

He endeavored to speak with the Elder Valentino and ask him for advice. Perhaps he possessed insight on how to handle the situation without attracting unwanted attention. The Elder Valentino granted Javier an audience out of respect for his lifelong friend, Javier's grandfather, Jorge Villalobos, and when he heard Javier's dilemma he was only too willing to assist.

"We nobles must stick together to preserve our way of life. We mustn't permit these inferiors to infiltrate our ranks lest they taint our noble pedigree with their filthy half-breed blood!" The Elder Valentino had declared. "May God have mercy on my son, for I will never forgive him for his indiscretions."

"Why not?" Javier had asked. "Doesn't the Bible teach forgiveness?"

"Indeed it does, but the Bible also says in Luke 11:17 'Every kingdom divided against itself is laid waste, and a divided household falls.'"

"I see," Javier sank in his seat and felt the uncertainty grow in his heart.

"Either we die on our feet, or we live on our knees!" The Elder Valentino had said. "In exchange for my assistance I will require something of you."

Javier nodded in agreement and asked him what he wanted.

"I'll let you know in due time. For now, we agree as gentlemen to stand by our word."

"You have my word. What do you propose we do now?" Javier had asked.

"We must set an example." The Elder Valentino asserted. He asked for the name of the man responsible for Javier's unhappiness. He vowed to have him dead by the end of the week. Javier flinched. He hadn't expected such an extreme measure. When Javier informed him that Guillermo was an officer of the law the Elder Valentino dismissed the concern with a wave of his hand. "Men of that sort are easily replaced. Trust me, it isn't difficult to find a man with a small cock and a need to be in a position of power."

Again, as before, Guillermo Sedeño was at the core of his problems.

"I see he was recently named Chief Inspector." The Elder Valentino stood and walked around to his chair behind the desk. Despite his age he still had his bearings about him and remained as large as an ox with broad shoulders and a thick neck. "How was he selected for the promotion over you?"

"I don't know, politics." Javier shrugged.

"Politics?" The Elder Valentino scoffed. "Since when is a Taíno descendent permitted to outrank the son of a Spaniard? My great grandfather would be spinning in his grave over the injustice."

The Elder Valentino inhaled deeply when he sat in his chair. He had always regretted the missed opportunity to eliminate Guillermo Sedeño. He had despised him from the first for reasons that went beyond Javier's personal troubles. The truth Javier remained ignorant to; Guillermo's connection to the Valentino name's fall from grace.

"He seeks to ruin my career?" Javier muttered.

"How?"

"He suspects my involvement in a murder and in the theft of evidence."

"Well?" The Elder Valentino asked before he puffed on his cigar.

"Well what?"

"Are you involved?"

"In the murder, no." Javier said.

The Elder Valentino studied him momentarily. *What are you not telling me?* He thought.

Javier met his intense gaze.

"And the theft?" The Elder Valentino finally said.

"That's inconsequential." Javier waved off the question.

"Inconsequential?" The Elder Valentino coughed. "Guillermo is Chief Inspector, which practically makes him untouchable. If I'm going to help you I will need to know everything. There can be no surprises."

Javier puffed on his cigar before he leaned forward in his chair. "Only two other people know what I'm about to tell you." He prepared to divulge the affair the governor's wife had with the unidentified man.

24

That morning, thin clouds spread across the sky like long white fingers. The temperature rose into the nineties as Isaac and Olivia set off toward Calle Margarita in search of the law offices of Eduardo el abogado. The Parque Industrial had become the one section of Old Sienna that represented progress with its innovated architecture, two-lane streets and the plethora of automobiles. Isaac wiped the beads of sweat off his forehead with the back of his hand.

"This heat's killing me," Isaac said. "Doesn't it bother you?"

"Eh, not so much," Olivia shrugged.

They crossed the street and walked along the sidewalk reading the numbers above the doors. After passing several buildings and a couple of blocks they turned down a desolate street. A newspaper tumbled along the sidewalk. Isaac spotted a stray cat at the far end of the dead-end street. The cat's cold stare made him feel uneasy. They followed the numeric of each building until they found the address they had been searching for, which stood in between two abandoned buildings on the east side of the street.

When they arrived at the front door it was sealed with rusted chains and locks. The ground level windows were boarded up. The second-story windows hadn't been boarded, but no glass remained either save for the few shards along the damaged windowsills. The brick surrounding the window frames was charred, indicative of a fire that consumed the building from within.

"How do you suppose we get inside?" Olivia turned to Isaac.

"We find a way in," Isaac pulled on the padlocks and chains. "Even death has an entrance life tries to hide."

"Sounds like something your uncle would say."

"He did say it." Isaac said.

When the locks and chains wouldn't relent, he walked around to the alley. He spotted another entryway halfway down the alley and headed straight for it. Olivia followed and they arrived at a wooden door that stood ajar. The door was blacked and appeared ready to crumble. Isaac gave the door a slight push and the hinges groaned when it swung open.

Once inside they peered through the darkness but could only make out the sharp angles of shadows and slanting light. The floorboards creaked with each step. A hole in the ceiling revealed a glimpse of the second level where sunlight filtered in through the broken windows. When their eyes adjusted to the darkness Isaac and Olivia could make out what remained of the office furniture that survived the fire. They navigated through the debris and kicked things aside as they walked towards a wooden staircase to the rear of the long office.

"How is it that a wooden staircase survived the fire?" Olivia wondered.

"It looks like the fire didn't burn this far back." Isaac observed where the scorched markings halted a few meters before reaching the back corner of the ground level. Though some of the wallpaper remained on the wall its design had mostly been covered by a thin layer of soot.

They heard a drawer slam shut above them and cast each other an incredulous glance. Footsteps shuffled before they heard another drawer slide open.

Isaac crept up the staircase and Olivia shadowed him. The fourth step moaned under his weight and he froze. Olivia held her breath as they listed for any movement on the second floor.

A drawer slowly clicked shut, and deliberate steps withdrew in the opposite direction. Isaac turned to Olivia and mouthed the words: Maybe we should leave.

Olivia's brow furrowed as she shook her head in protest and urged him to continue climbing the staircase. Isaac relented and crouched as he prowled from one step to the next. Each step seemed to creak louder than the last. Isaac had the uneasy feeling that if whoever was on the second floor was armed he'd have no trouble taking aim at them.

When they arrived at the top of the staircase Isaac tried to peer around what remained of the railing, but a pile of burn wood obstructed his few. Light filtered in through the windows and through a hole in the ceiling, which made it easier to see and move through the rubble on the second floor. Isaac and Olivia stood and scanned the office. Most of the furniture and walls was covered in soot and ash. The frame of the building was exposed in various places where the walls and ceiling collapse, or burned. A fire had consumed any evidence of a successful business long ago.

The floor creaked when Isaac and Olivia stepped onto the landing. Everything appeared undisturbed save for where dust and ash was moved out of place by the stranger in their midst.

"Who's there?" Olivia demanded.

Isaac cast her an incredulous glance.

"Olivia?" Memito peered out from behind another cabinet. "What are you two doing here?"

"What are *we* doing here?" Isaac said. "What are *you* doing here?"

"You asked me to find out as much as I could about the Labyrinth. I gathered some information and came here to confirm the validity of what I've learned before coming to you."

"What did you find?" Olivia said hastily.

"Well, let's just say family secrets aren't really secrets at all." Memito brandished a folder from beneath the dirty old coat he purchased from a homeless man. He proceeded to tell them what he had learned about Eduardo el abogado, the first cousin of Lorenzo Valentino, who facilitated Lorenzo's deception of his father.

"Yes, we already know about that." Olivia said.

"Ah, well, as you know, Eduardo was a hopeless romantic. He helped Lorenzo, not only because he sympathized with his plight, but also because he had a secret love of his own. A love so forbidden that when the truth of it was revealed along with his involvement in the Elder Valentino's deception it led to his untimely death." Memito wore a mischievous grin.

Isaac and Olivia cast him a curious glance before they turned to each other confused.

"What secret love?" Olivia said.

"And what made it forbidden?" Isaac asked.

"What little I know is what I've been told by parties close to the situation."

"Who?" Olivia and Isaac said.

"I'm sorry, but I cannot reveal my sources. It's the anonymity and trust that keeps me in business."

"Fine." Olivia shook her head. "Go on."

"Every night after Eduardo escorted Mariana home safely he

slipped away to the home of his lover. A man he had met a few years before while passing through Mexico during a break in his studies from law school."

"Are you sure?" Isaac said.

"I'm as sure as my source, and my source was as sure as the sun rises in the east when I asked him the same."

"What else did he say?" Olivia pressed him.

Memito crossed his arms and studied her momentarily. *Why are you so eager for this information?* He wondered before he proceeded.

"They met in a small town known as Santa Lucia somewhere on the outskirts of Monterrey and at the foothills of the Sierra Madre mountain range. The two had volunteered to assist the townspeople after a hurricane had struck the region a week before their arrival. It was love at first sight for them both and they came to understand that their meeting was not merely a chance encounter, but a destiny found in the service of God."

"What makes you say that?" Isaac wondered.

"Well, according to my source, both Eduardo and his lover were born and raised in Providencia. Each had traveled to the Americas in the interest of higher learning for their chosen professions. Eduardo was a law student, and his lover had been studying to become a mortician, which also required him to serve as an apprentice for two years. After their brief time together in Santa Lucia they parted ways, but not before agreeing to find each other once they returned home."

They had indeed found each other in the shadows of society. Each possessed the secrecy required of his profession, which allowed them to protect each other's reputation from the prying eyes of those who spent more time snooping around in the business of others than minding their own.

It was far from easy. Eduardo belonged to one of the most powerful families in what had now become Old Sienna, and he risked the wrath of the family's patriarch on two fronts. The first was with his involvement in the deception of the Elder Valentino, and the second with his own affair that defied the laws of God and man.

"How did his connection to Lorenzo and Mariana put his life in danger?" Olivia wondered.

"Beyond the betrayal the Elder Valentino felt after trusting Eduardo with keeping Lorenzo on the path of familial obligation, it was the secret that even Lorenzo never knew which cost Eduardo his life."

"What secret was that?" Olivia asked.

"Lorenzo had fathered a child with Mariana before his death."

"What?!" Olivia and Isaac said.

"The thing is, no one knew about the lovechild until years later." Memito continued. "After the Elder Valentino discovered his son's continued involvement with Mariana Colón, Lorenzo was murdered. The culprit was never caught, and the case remains unsolved. When Mariana confessed the truth of her pregnancy to Eduardo he advised her to leave Old Sienna and to never return."

"Which is exactly what she did." Olivia turned to Isaac.

"She accepted a marriage proposal and moved away for a few years." Isaac recounted the details Cousin Cecilia had shared with them.

"And she returned with a son." Olivia remembered.

"This is where it gets interesting." Memito waved a finger.

"According to one of my sources, Lorenzo had set aside money for his elopement with Mariana. He did this in the event his father did not come around to the idea of them being married. Additionally, Lorenzo was entitled to a portion of the family fortune as had been dictated by his great-great grandfather in Spain. The first son of each generation of the Valentino family is set to inherit the portion left for his father regardless of the circumstances of birth."

"That's rather unconventional given our Catholic beliefs." Isaac said.

"It is, but then again, Eduardo had confided in his lover that their great-great grandfather was a rather unconventional man. He believed in charity and goodwill, and that the progeny of a man was his responsibility to the child and to the world."

"Wow!" Olivia mouthed.

"In any case, Eduardo reached out to Mariana when she returned to Old Sienna and invited her to his office. When she arrived, he greeted kindly and revealed to her the fortune Lorenzo had left for her, and subsequently for their child. She refused it, however, and left never to return to claim it or discuss it."

"Well, what happened next?" Olivia said.

"Eduardo believed that someone who was working here that day had overheard the conversation and divulged the details of it to the Elder Valentino."

"Why?" Isaac asked.

"You know how people are, Isaac. No one ever minds his or her own business. The minute someone thinks they know a secret, they can't wait to tell someone else." Memito said.

"True enough," Isaac shrugged.

"Anyhow," Memito continued. "The Elder Valentino

confronted Eduardo about the revelation and Eduardo denied any knowledge of it. The law offices endured a couple break-ins after their meeting and Eduardo was certain his uncle had hired thugs to procure the documents pertaining to the inheritance. Ultimately they never found what they were searching for, but Eduardo feared that the Elder Valentino did acquire the documents pertaining to the Labyrinth Lorenzo and Eduardo had built before Lorenzo's death."

"See, I told you it existed!" Olivia turned to Isaac.

"The Labyrinth isn't what matters." Memito said.

Olivia and Isaac turned to Memito and cast him a curious glance.

"What matters is finding the documents about the inheritance."

"Why?" Isaac tilted his head.

"According to my source, Eduardo used his legal know-how to ensure Lorenzo's son received his inheritance. When we find those documents, we can fulfill a dead man's wish."

"Why would we want to do that?" Olivia wondered.

"It would be one way to stick it to the Elder Valentino, who many believe has insisted on living past his date of expiration just to satiate his greed and prevent his bastard grandson from receiving what is rightfully his."

"That's a good point." Isaac nodded.

"Why didn't you come to Isaac with this information before coming here?" Olivia asked.

"I pride myself on my efficiency and accuracy. I wanted to confirm the validity of my information before presenting it to him. Otherwise, how do I expect to stay in business?" Memito shrugged.

"Fair enough." Olivia said. "How do you suggest we find the

rightful heir of the Valentino fortune?"

"We'll have to access birth records from the time frame when these events occurred and cross reference them with a woman named Mariana." Memito suggested. "They keep those at City Hall."

"That wouldn't work." Isaac said.

"Why not?" Olivia turned to him.

"Mariana did not give birth to her son in Old Sienna. She moved away with her new husband and returned several years later, remember?"

"Then how else do you suggest we uncover the child's identity?" Olivia asked.

"I think Memito had the right idea by sifting through whatever paperwork survived the fire."

"I'm not quite sure that will do us any good." Memito said. He met their inquisitive gaze before he continued. "After the break-ins proved unsuccessful, the Elder Valentino ordered his henchmen to burn down the law office with Eduardo inside."

They glanced around at what remained of the law offices of Eduardo el abogado. All that remained was the legacy of the dangers of secret love.

25

The Elder Valentino leaned back in his seat as he listened to Javier divulge what he knew about Carmen de la Vega's affair. He puffed on his cigar and nodded from time to time, but his eyes never looked away from the inspector.

Javier leaned back in his seat too and puffed from his cigar with lesser frequency than his host as he revealed a secret he vowed to protect. He knew only that her lover's identity remained a mystery, and he speculated it was most likely because he was an outsider. They had never been seen together in public, but the governor's wife had fallen into a routine of leaving the house every morning after the governor had left the mansion.

"Until recently she had taken her carriage to the foothills of mountains not far from here." Javier said before he coughed.

"Is that a fact?" The Elder Valentino nodded.

Javier Villalobos nodded and continued coughing.

"What else do you know?"

"According to one of the servants she frequently wrote letters late into the night. She always had a letter when she left the mansion, but never had one on her person when she returned." Javier continued to cough again.

"Where did she take this letter?" The Elder Valentino feigned ignorance.

The inspector held up a finger as he continued coughing and

felt his chest tighten.

"Have a drink." The Elder Valentino handed his glass of scotch over to Javier.

The inspector took a sip and cleared his throat.

"Rumor has it she visited the Labyrinth of Love Letters hidden beneath the city." Javier finally spoke.

"Surely you don't believe in such nonsense, inspector."

"I like to think I don't believe in anything I can't see, but that wouldn't explain my faith in God."

"For all the faith a man places in God it doesn't do him any good." The Elder Valentino scoffed. "Tell me more about the letters."

"There's nothing more to tell." Javier rubbed his chest and blinked slowly. "Except that her lover too had a letter on his person when he was murdered."

"Really?" The Elder Valentino feigned shock. "How did you discover this?"

"The governor had asked me to follow the man for several days. Each day the man took a different route into the same foothills of the mountains. Each day I lost him in the alleyways of Old Sienna. So, I never actually saw where he ended up."

"I see. Go on," The Elder Valentino rubbed his chin.

"The last day I followed him was the day Fernando had asked me to rough him up and warn him to never see Carmen again."

"And did you?"

"Yes." Javier nodded before he started coughing again.

"What about the letter? You said something earlier about a letter you stole."

"That was the letter Fernando asked me to steal from police evidence. It was the letter the man had written to Carmen de la Vega."

Javier said after he sipped from the scotch to settle his coughing.

"Did you read it?"

"Not at first. No." Javier shook his head. "But when Fernando failed to show for our first meeting I decided to see what he wanted so badly that the man ended up dead for it."

"That's when you resorted to blackmail. Isn't it?" The Elder Valentino said.

Javier nodded before he caught himself. *Wait. I never said anything about—*

The Elder Valentino flashed a wicked smile. "Where is the letter now?"

Javier felt his head spin before he felt shortness of breath.

"Where is the letter?" The Elder Valentino demanded. He stood and walked around his desk.

"I don't know. I don't have it." Javier felt his head begin to ache.

"What do you mean you don't have it?" Valentino towered over him.

"I-I-I don't know." Javier stammered his reply. "I-I-I must have lost it."

"You must have lost it?" The Elder Valentino knew Javier was telling the truth. *Everything is going according to plan.*

"I've looked everywhere. I don't know where it is, I swear!" Javier felt tired and struggled to keep his eyes open. His chest tightened and he grasped his throat.

"It is a shame you no longer have the letter in your possession Javier, for it means you have outlived your usefulness."

Javier collapsed to the floor.

"That took longer than expected." The Elder Valentino said.

He summoned Diego to remove the body. After Diego left the room the Elder Valentino placed a phone call to the governor's mansion.

"It's taken care of," he spoke into the receiver. "Next time I suggest you be more careful of who you choose to trust with such matters. The man told me everything about your situation and I didn't even need to coax it out of him."

"What about the letter?" Fernando asked.

"He claimed he lost it." The Elder Valentino said before he sipped from his scotch and puffed on his cigar. "I'll have Diego check his clothes, but I'm certain he was telling the truth."

"How do you know?"

"Men tend to be honest when they're on death's doorstep."

"You killed him?"

"I said I'd take care of it, didn't I?" The Elder Valentino snapped.

"How?"

"I laced a cigar with cyanide. He never knew what hit him."

"But he was the prime suspect in the Chief Inspector's investigation. Guillermo will look into Javier's death to see if there is a connection between both murders."

"Relax, Fernando." The Elder Valentino cut him off. "Dead men tell no tales. We'll merely plant the right evidence that points to Javier and the case will be closed."

"How can you be sure?"

"No one cares for a drunkard, especially one who was already a suspect in his wife's disappearance. We use the fact that he was broke, combine it with a recent murder and stolen evidence, and use it to stage suicide by guilt. We'll make it look like he drank himself to death and that will be the end of it. Besides, I have another man on the inside to help with these matters."

"What about the letter?" Fernando said. "That letter cannot remain in the wind."

"Indeed it cannot." The Elder Valentino pursed his lips. "Javier has a daughter, correct?"

"Yes. Her name is Olivia."

"I'm certain she is in possession of the letter."

"You think that is possible?"

"You fail to realize something I learned long ago, Fernando. Anything is possible when fools fall in love."

26

When Isaac walked Olivia home they arrived at the gates and saw Juan Carlos sitting on the front steps near the door speaking with the servants. Olivia turned to Isaac. She sensed his displeasure with seeing the artista waiting for her.

"Isaac," she hesitated. She debated with herself about whether she should ask the artista to return later, or wait for Isaac to make the decision for her. She didn't want to be rude to her friend, but she wanted to speak with Juan Carlos in private.

"I just remembered I promised my father I would help him with this month's accounting for the hat shop." Isaac lied. He too sensed Olivia's silent desire and excused himself with a promise to catch up with her later. He waved at Juan Carlos and turned back the way they came.

Olivia watched him momentarily. She knew how Isaac felt about her, but she wasn't sure she felt the same towards him.

"Good afternoon," Juan Carlos approached the gate and pulled it open.

Olivia turned and greeted him with a smile before she asked him about the unexpected visit.

"You left so unexpectedly last night I didn't get a chance to thank you for the pleasant conversation," Juan Carlos said.

"I apologize. Something came up." She moved strands of hair behind her ear.

"I hope everything is alright." He tried to meet her lowered gaze. He was certain her sudden departure the night before had something to do with the commotion at the governor's mansion, but he decided not to pry.

"Yes, yes, everything is fine," Olivia lied. She waved at the servants who stood near the front door of the home. They nodded and waved in return. She turned to the artista. "Want to go for a walk?"

"Lead the way." Juan Carlos gave a slight bow. His long strands of hair blew across his face, and his white shirt billowed as well.

They walked together alone and followed the winding road up the mountain to the north of Old Sienna. They spoke of her father and how Tia Katarina said he had changed when her mother passed away. She tried to ignore the rumors surrounding her disappearance, but it became increasingly difficult when Javier exploded in drunken tirades without regard for his personal dignity. Though she and her father hadn't been as close as she would have liked, she forgave him his trespasses and was grateful for Tia Katarina's presence because she filled the need of mother as best she could, given the circumstances.

"I imagine that a girl who doesn't have a close relationship with her father must feel alone in the world," Juan Carlos said.

"Yes that is true." Olivia nodded. He surprised her with his profound insight.

"The same could be said about a boy and his mother." Juan Carlos continued. He spoke of his solitude while traveling through Europe with his uncle. He'd often felt his uncle was more of a father to him than his own dad, but the absence of his mother had saddened him even more. "Sometimes I wonder if they ever missed me, or if they felt relieved of their responsibility to me by sending me away."

In that moment Olivia felt connected to Juan Carlos in a way she never thought possible. She had only felt a bond with one other person in the world based on circumstance and that had been her best friend, Isaac Quintero. This, however, felt different because with the artista she felt something stir in her heart.

"How is it that we hardly know each other yet we're revealing things about ourselves that those close to us may not even know?" Olivia wondered.

"We share more of our deepest fears with strangers," Juan Carlos said.

"Where's your uncle now?" Olivia said.

Juan Carlos hesitated before he answered. Though he liked Olivia Villalobos, he wasn't sure he should confide in her the truth about his uncle, for his uncle insisted on maintaining his anonymity while in Old Sienna.

"He came to Puerto Rico several months ago. He said he wanted to experience something special in La Isla Del Encanto," Juan Carlos finally said.

"The Island of Enchantment," Olivia whispered. She stopped mid step and gazed ahead pensively.

"As far as I can tell, your island lives up to its reputation." Juan Carlos gave her a once over.

"You still haven't answered my question." Olivia crossed her arms.

"That's because I don't know." Juan Carlos shrugged. "I haven't heard from him in weeks—"

"In weeks?" Olivia cut him off.

"Yes, weeks, which isn't normal for him because he wrote

me frequently while I was in Europe." Juan Carlos admired the landscape from their vantage point before he continued. "In his last letter to me he said he had found his purpose, but feared it would cost him his life."

"What do you suppose he meant by that?" Olivia shielded her eyes from the sun.

"I don't know, but knowing him it had to pertain to love."

"Was he a romantic?" She wondered if perhaps he was the unidentified man found dead in the alley.

"A hopeless one, to say the least."

"Do you have his mailing address?" Her mind raced with ideas about discovering whom his uncle was, for at least with solid proof of his identification she could approach La Señora Carmen about her recent visits to the cemetery and eventually inquire about the Labyrinth.

"As a matter of fact I do." Juan Carlos said. He rummaged through his pockets and brandished a folded piece of paper. "I kept this from his final correspondence because he's the true reason I came to Puerto Rico. After I hadn't heard from him for several weeks I tried making travel arrangements, but it is more difficult than one would imagine. So, when the governor commissioned me for a painting, I jumped at the chance."

"I see," Olivia nodded.

"You know, it's odd that the governor of Puerto Rico is not in the capital," Juan Carlos noted.

"Well, he wasn't actually elected." Olivia rolled her eyes.

"He wasn't?"

"Nope." Olivia shook her head. She remembered overhearing the circumstances behind his rise to power at a dinner party she attended with her father several years ago.

After the United States gained control over Puerto Rico from Spain, President Woodrow Wilson appointed Howard Lewis Kern to be the Attorney General. When the acting governor fell ill to Malaria in 1914, Kern acted as governor for a decade when President Wilson appointed Kern for several terms until 1924. It was Kern's initiatives that authored the Jones Act of 1917, which allowed Don Enrique de Las Fuentes to capitalize on his investments and bring his money to Providencia. Don Enrique used his influence to appoint a governor of his choosing and they gave him the mansion of a Spanish sympathizer who had been caught playing both sides during the war.

"So it is as my uncle said, corruption is everywhere." Juan Carlos mused.

"I don't know if I would call it corruption," Olivia said.

"When the right to choose a leader is taken from the people and placed in the hands of those whose wealth has more sway than the vote then it undermines the ideals of democracy. Trust me it is corruption."

Olivia studied him momentarily. In that moment, she realized there was more to the artista than his charm, his talent, and his appearance. He handed her the small piece of paper. She unfolded it and read the address written in tight cursive script.

"This isn't far from here." She finally said after a long silence.

"It isn't?"

"This address is in the Forgotten Quarter." Olivia turned and faced east.

"The Forgotten Quarter?" Juan Carlos followed her gaze perplexed.

"It used to be a part of the wealthy district. The homes there are much larger than those in the Noble Quarter, but something happened there about ten years ago. Something that nobody speaks of, and the houses along the main road have been vacant ever since."

"What happened?" Juan Carlos pressed on.

"I don't know. I was just a child when it happened, but I remember the rumors and the screams. Parents told their children that El Cucuy had finally come for the children who disobeyed their elders, but as we grew older we knew not to believe it. Others claimed El Diablo had come for the greedy, but I honestly don't know the truth. All I remember is that one night the lights never turned on again and the people who lived there had vanished. No one dared move into the area again, which is why it is called the Forgotten Quarter."

"Let's go and see what remains," Juan Carlos said. "Surely my uncle wasn't the only person to have lived there recently."

But is that the real reason he died? Olivia wondered.

27

The sun was high in the sky and the breeze from the sea felt refreshing when Isaac arrived at Uncle Gabriel's boathouse. From the beach, he could hear the Caribbean tunes on the radio. Isaac immediately recognized the sounds of Pérez Prado, the Cuban-born composer who would go on to become the King of the Mambo in Havana, Cuba years later. When Isaac stepped onto the platform of the boat his nose wrinkled at the stench emitting through the windows.

What is that smell?

He arrived at the door and as he prepared to knock it opened and both he and Uncle Gabriel were startled by each other's presence.

"Isaac, my boy!" Uncle Gabriel greeted him with a smile.

"What's that?" Isaac pointed at the joint his uncle held between his thumb and index finger. "And what's that smell?"

"Did you come to visit, or did you come to interrogate me?" Uncle Gabriel snapped. He shouldered his way past Isaac holding a bottle of rum and a small glass in his other hand.

Isaac stared aghast at the sight of his uncle stumbling past before he plopped himself on his patio chair.

"Well, don't just stand there come join me." Uncle Gabriel filled the glass with rum and handed it to Isaac.

"What will you drink from?" Isaac accepted the glass as he sat in the second chair.

Uncle Gabriel took a swig directly from the bottle and slammed it down on the small wooden table. He then took a drag from his join and held his breath while he passed it over to his nephew. Isaac cast him an incredulous glare, but his uncle urged him to take it. When Isaac refused, Uncle Gabriel exhaled and reproached him for declining the invitation.

"But that's Cannabis!" Isaac said.

"Just another word for God's medicine." Uncle Gabriel countered.

"What about my dad?"

"You let me worry about him." Uncle Gabriel's eyes were red and glossy.

"He won't be pleased to discover I have engaged in recreational drug use."

"It has been used for recreational purposes since ancient times!" Uncle Gabriel laughed. "Even before Herodotus first documented its use by the Classical Greeks and Romans, while concurrently being used throughout the Islamic empire, archaeological evidence shows it was used in prehistoric societies in Euro-Asia and Africa."

"You really think my father will buy that?"

Uncle Gabriel took another swig from his bottle. He wiped his mouth with the back of his arm and cleared his throat. "He needs to get laid."

"Uncle!" Isaac was taken aback.

"In fact, you need to get laid too."

Isaac sat speechless for a moment. Uncle Gabriel took another hit from his joint.

"Are you high, drunk, or both?" Isaac finally said.

"Those are synonyms for happy, and I'm happier than a pig in shit!" Uncle Gabriel took another hit and leaned back in his seat.

"Oh. My. God." Isaac stared at his uncle in disbelief. He had never seen him in this condition. Not even during the celebration of Navidad—Christmas—and Dia de Reyes—Three Kings Day—the most important religious holidays in Puerto Rico.

"Where is your lady love, anyway?" Uncle Gabriel finally said after he exhaled.

"She's not my lady love," Isaac snapped.

"Uh oh, what happened?" Uncle Gabriel took on a more reserved tone.

"Nothing happened," Isaac sighed, "perhaps I should return another day."

Isaac placed the glass of rum on the small wooden table between them. He stood and apologized for the intrusion. Uncle Gabriel quickly leapt to his feet and placed a hand on Isaac's shoulder. Though he swayed slightly he had a serious look in his eyes and appeared to have his bearings about him.

"Mira, nene, your presence is never an intrusion. You are always welcome here. Now come, sit, and tell me about what's weighing on your mind."

Isaac contemplated his uncle's offer momentarily. He nodded and agreed to stay on one condition. "Do you mind if I finish that drink?" He pointed at the small glass filled with rum.

"My boy, when it comes to heartbreak the only remedy is alcohol."

"I thought that was chocolate?"

"That's for women," Uncle Gabriel said with a wave of his hand. "Come, sit."

Isaac took hold of the small glass of rum. He'd only consumed alcohol on religious holidays when his father permitted. And even then, it had been in small doses.

"Now tell me what happened." Uncle Gabriel sat in his chair.

"Are you sure you want to hear this?"

"I may be half in the bag, but I'm all ears."

Isaac explained his predicament regarding his feelings for Olivia and her new-found interest in the artista. Despite the many years of their friendship and the closeness of their bond he felt he had been cast aside for a stranger who barely knew her and might never love her as deeply as Isaac had.

"Don't count yourself out just yet," Uncle Gabriel said. "You're a creative in your own right with admirable talent and skill."

"Yeah, but he's known across Europe *and* in the Caribbean. How am I supposed to compete with that?"

"First, you must understand that pursuing a woman's heart is not a competition. She is not an object to be won, or conquered. She is a gift to be treasured. You know better." Uncle Gabriel pointed a finger at him. "Secondly, I don't give a shit if this Cubano is the second coming of the Florentine, Alessandro Botticelli. A good woman decides with her heart. She never predicates her decision on a man's status, or wealth."

Isaac pondered his uncle's advice. Perhaps he had a point. Then again Uncle Gabriel did not see the look in Olivia's eyes when she first saw Juan Carlos Trinidad. It reminded him of the words of Honoré de Balzac: *A woman knows the face of the man she loves, as a sailor knows the open sea.*

He reflected on his conversation with Armando the night before when the stranger revealed to him his fate. And he wondered, *is our destiny written in the stars, or is our fate what we make of it?*

Was he destined to experience a one-sided love with Olivia, and was she destined to fall in love with Juan Carlos first? Her affair with the artista would ensure she never finds the Labyrinth and consequently would avoid the demise La Señora Carmen predicted. But if, in fact, we control our destiny are we equally capable of finding death despite our love? For if death and love are indeed so deeply intertwined, is it even possible to separate love from fate?

"Something else is on your mind. What is it?"

Isaac met Uncle Gabriel's bloodshot eyes. His uncle leaned forward in his seat and took another hit from the joint. He inhaled deeply and listened. Isaac spoke of the letter Olivia found in her father's jacket, her obsession with finding the Labyrinth, and of the warning he received from La Señora Carmen. Uncle Gabriel coughed as he exhaled when he heard the revelation.

"I'm sorry," Isaac said. "I wasn't supposed to tell anyone about the letter, but after speaking with La Señora Carmen last night I didn't have a choice."

"You did the right thing." Uncle Gabriel assured him.

"It doesn't feel like it." Isaac felt the weight of the secret lift from his shoulders, but it was replaced by the guilt of betraying his best friend's trust.

"I will speak with Carmen—"

"No, please don't." Isaac interrupted him. "I don't want her to think I betrayed her trust too. I simply need to figure out how to prevent Olivia from finding the Labyrinth."

"My boy, once a woman makes up her mind about achieving something even God is powerless to stop her. Though I am curious about what she knows of the Labyrinth that puts Olivia's life in danger."

"Maybe La Señora Carmen merely said that as a means of keeping the location of the Labyrinth a secret." Isaac speculated.

"Perhaps," Uncle Gabriel nodded. "I'd still like to ask her what she knows about the Labyrinth."

"What do you know about it, uncle?"

"Not much, save for what I've heard over the years." Uncle Gabriel shrugged. "Though I never pay much attention to what people say. Most people have no idea what they're talking about anyway."

Even if half of what people believed about the Labyrinth had been true, Uncle Gabriel wouldn't believe any of it. The Labyrinth of Love Letters remained a legend that lingered just beneath the surface of the consciousness of Old Sienna. Like a memory of something that never happened, but one you wished you had experienced.

Isn't that the paradox? We remember loves we never knew, and we forget the moments that broke our hearts. Perhaps it is a fate shared by any who are lured onto the path of love. The heart wants what the heart wants regardless of circumstance, and despite our plea to be loved in return we find ourselves in an affair where we suffer for being the one who loves more deeply.

Few ever choose to walk away from such a love because they cling—not to the hope their love will be reciprocated—but to the idea that to love is to love unconditionally. Therein lies the mark of the romantic, for only the romantic is capable of complete surrender to love.

For his part Uncle Gabriel never wanted anything to do with the Labyrinth. It had not been because of a curse, or the dangers of secret love, nor had it been because his true love was not a forbidden love. In fact, his decision had more to do with the madness of love than with the Labyrinth itself.

In his youth, Uncle Aquino had a friend named Mauricio Rosario. They had been children together. Two boys whose fathers had been childhood friends before them, like brothers, so that when Gabriel and Mauricio grew up together they referred to each other as cousins rather than just friends.

They were complete opposites. Gabriel small and slender was the shier and more reserved between the two and lived in the shadow of his larger friend who possessed the more vocal disposition. Where Gabriel excelled academically Mauricio struggled, and what Gabriel lacked in physical strength Mauricio possessed enough for the both of them.

Closer than most brothers—despite having siblings of their own—they looked after one another. Gabriel assisted Mauricio with his studies and Mauricio ensured no one bullied his smaller acquaintance. Together with Ariana Jimenez as their companion they spent the days of their childhood together until the day of Mauricio's fifteenth birthday.

"You are becoming a man. It is time you cross the threshold and experience a woman's caress." Señor Rosario said when he took Mauricio to San Juan.

Despite the numerous establishments throughout the island, many much closer to Providencia than the capital, Señor Rosario opted for a more distant locale. Not so much for the purposes of secrecy, for it was common practice for men to take their sons to the working girl's establishment when they came of age. Señor Rosario's motives had more to do with avoiding the possibility of having his son fall in love with a whore than anything else.

It wasn't unheard of given that men have a penchant for

falling in love with what they see. And in the case of Mauricio Rosario the experience of feeling the caress of a woman's inner walls drove him mad with desire.

Rather than accept the moment for what his father had intended it to be—a christening of sorts—Mauricio became obsessed with the priestess who baptized him with passion. Her name was Lorena Reyna. They called her the young Queen of the Caribbean, for despite her youth she was well versed in the art of pleasure. Her light brown hair with bronze glints fell past her shoulders in gentle waves. She brushed it daily with coconut oil so that it always appeared wet and possessed an appealing scent for her clients.

Her hazel eyes shone like polished Fire Agate stones that accentuated her perpetual smile and complimented her caramel complexion. She guided him into the dimly lit room were candlelight flickered and cast dancing shadows against wallpaper as red as blood. At first, he could barely see her ageless, naked body as his eyes adjusted to the darkness.

She moved as if she were made of water. Her small hands with black fingernails caressed him with an astute tenderness made him quiver and catch his breath. She lured him to the bed where she undressed him slowly. Between kisses and whispers she traced invisible lines across his body setting his soul ablaze.

Mauricio attempted to caress her, but she moved his hand away. When he cast her a confused glance she smiled, winked and shook her head. "Not yet," Lorena whispered before she kissed him and gently bit his lower lip.

She took hold of his erection and stroked him softly. He inhaled sharply. Then she turned her back to him, pressed her body against his and bent over. She grinded against Mauricio and eyed him over her shoulder.

His eyes burned with desire. He admired the curvature of her hips, which was accentuated by the arch of her back. When she turned to face him she pushed him onto the bed and straddled him. She grinded against his erection and positioned herself to maximize clitoral stimulation while heightening Mauricio's anticipation. Lorena allowed his hands to wander, but when he eagerly groped her breasts she guided his hands across her body.

Finally, she impaled herself on him. Her body soaked in hot perspiration glistened in the candlelight while she moved as if she were riding horseback. Her heavy breathing heightened his excitement and he moaned with pleasure as he felt the wonder of her inner walls. She guided him beyond the realm of inexperience and collapsed on him for a moment, gasping for breath.

In that moment, she stirred something in Mauricio Rosario he never knew existed. And after a few brief moments of feeling her kissing his chest he lifted her off him and stood at the side of the bed. She looked at him and saw the hunger in his eyes. He took hold of her ankles and pulled her towards him. She shrieked. Mauricio grabbed her by the hips and turned her over so that her back was to him. Instinctively she moved to her knees and kept her face buried in a pillow.

He plunged himself inside her and he grunted with each stroke. She felt him drive deeper with each thrust and his pace quickened as he pounded her body mercilessly. He relished the sight of her posterior in all its curved glory and he spanked her repeatedly before he reached forward and pulled her hair. Lorena screamed and cursed and thought she might faint from the confusion of pleasure and pain when she felt him explode inside her.

Together they collapsed on the bed panting. She ran her fingers through his hair, and he recognized something in her that he'd never seen in another woman. But what she recognized as a professional encounter he mistakenly confused it for love. In the weeks that followed he repeatedly returned with his earnings from the fields to relive the moment in her embrace.

She entertained him, as her profession required, but she refused his offer to run away with him and make a life together.

"I already have a life here." She'd smile and kiss him on the cheek.

But Mauricio Rosario would not relent. He continued to visit her with gifts and chocolate and flowers picked from Calle de Las Flores. And she received him as she received all her clients under the cover of night with the promise of anonymity and the fulfillment of their desires.

Afterward she sent him on his way pushing him out the back door as she pushed her thoughts of him to the back of her mind. He'd wander the dark and lonely streets of San Juan and didn't return to Providencia until the early hours of dawn the following day. He began to arrive late in the fields, and then he'd never arrive at all. When his father learned of Mauricio's absenteeism he confronted him, but Mauricio said only that his desire was to be with the woman he loved.

Without employ to fund his secret desire he resorted to thievery first stealing from his family and then breaking into the homes of the wealthy. Soon he resorted to robbing men and women in the towns between Providencia and San Juan hoping he'd gathered enough money prior to his arrival to delight Lorena's embrace once more.

Finally, she denied him entry and implored him to forget

their encounters. For her part, it was an act of mercy. Despite finding him to be a handsome young man with the virility any woman would desire in a partner she could not bring herself to commit her life to a poor field worker. She wanted a life of luxury and ease where she might travel the world and forget the part of her past she believed belonged to someone else.

A few days later he saw her at the port standing beside a wealthy merchant. Dockworkers loaded chests onto the ship. The merchant leaned in and kissed Lorena. It was a long, deep kiss. The kind that led the ancients to believe an exchange of souls occurred. Mauricio felt his heart drop.

Mauricio approached her when the merchant walked away to speak with the ship's captain. He called out to her, but Lorena almost didn't recognize him. His eyes had lost their fire and his face looked as though he hadn't eaten or slept in days. His shoulders sagged and his stride seemed more like a limp than a march. He stood before her and professed his love. He vowed to love her to the end of his days.

She watched him with pity and shook her head. Her silence brought tears to his eyes and he begged her to say something, to say anything so that her voice might caress his soul one last time.

"What you feel is not love, nor is it any semblance of love. What you feel is desire, and that is much different." She turned and walked away from him.

"Who is that?" Her new husband asked when she approached.

"Just some poor beggar."

Mauricio Rosario overheard her comment and watched her leave. He stood there until the sun set hoping she would return. He did not leave until the moon emerged and sauntered over the horizon.

He returned to Providencia the following morning. He stood on the cliffs overlooking the sea. That is where Gabriel Aquino found his best friend, whom he hadn't seen in over a month. Gabriel listened as Mauricio confessed the truth of his dilemma. Mauricio wept inconsolably for several hours while he asked why he had been subjected to such a cruel fate.

Gabriel did not have an answer suitable for his friend. Even Ariana Jimenez, who arrived later that day, had no words to provide solace to her heartbroken friend. She felt a mixture of pity and anger standing beside him, and stayed with him for as long as time permitted. But once again at sun set Mauricio was left alone when Gabriel and Ariana answered the calls of their parents.

Mauricio stood over the cliffs, broken on the shores of memory with no desire to breathe again and threw himself over the ledge. They didn't find his body until it washed ashore a few days later. Though the priest had said he was now at peace Gabriel Aquino knew a soul never rests when it dies with a broken heart.

"Your friend died when he was fifteen?" Isaac said with a pensive look in his eye.

Uncle Gabriel nodded without saying a word.

"Do you think Lorena was correct in her estimation that what Mauricio felt was desire and not love?" Isaac wondered.

"No." Uncle Gabriel shook his head, "Though she was correct in that desire is not love she did not realize that what Mauricio felt for her was passionate love. It is the kind of love that drives people to madness."

"When love is not madness, it is not love." Isaac mused as he repeated the famous quote from the 17th century poet, Pedro Calderón.

"You remembered," Uncle Gabriel nodded impressed.

Isaac shrugged.

"Now you see that one does not need the Labyrinth to define the depth of love."

Isaac pondered his uncle's statement momentarily before he met his gaze and said. "Is that why you left Providencia at such an early age?"

Uncle Gabriel nodded. He admitted to fleeing Providencia to see the world. He was intent on living before falling in love, for if love were to drive him to such madness he did not want any regrets over what he did not achieve before arriving at his deathbed.

"What if Tia Ariana would have met someone else during that time?" Isaac said.

"Then our fate would not have been to be together," Uncle Gabriel said.

"You were willing to take that chance?"

"One must always be willing to take that chance, for life is more than a series of moments strung together by fortune—be it good or bad. In an instant, the future becomes the present and the present becomes the past. So, you must live in that moment, seize it, and define it, because tomorrow is promised to no one. Though love may come in many forms, death comes in but one, yet even death is incapable of extinguishing the flame of amor."

"What do you suggest I do about Olivia?" Isaac said.

"You must continue to be there for her, and you must not cease to love her. True love is unconditional, and if you lose her to the artista in this life then vow to love her in the next."

28

The sun neared the horizon and cast long shadows against the landscape. A yellow blade of light cut through the clouds and cast its hue over the mansions and trees facing west. Guillermo glanced at his watch piece. When he realized the time, he climbed out of the sedan and marched toward the Valentino residence. Caught unawares Emiliano stared at the Chief Inspector momentarily before he followed suit.

A gentle breeze blew past. Guillermo crossed the street and walked up along the curving driveway leading to the front door. It was one of the few stately homes that did not have a wrought-iron gate. Emiliano had never seen homes of such magnitude. As they approached, the house resembled a castle-like mansion that he imagined was filled with pillars and statues along marble floored corridors and cathedral type ceilings. Ivy woven with red roses clung to the walls with leaves as green as the bushes surrounding the base of the home.

Black iron gates guarded the windows with vines curled about like snakes covered with thorns. The Elder Valentino watched Guillermo and Emiliano approach through the darkened windows. He heard the pounding on the door when the Chief Inspector knocked. Diego stood near the door. He turned to his master and met his dark gaze. The Elder Valentino shook his head. Diego nodded and walked away.

Guillermo pounded on the door again.

"Do you have to knock so loud, Chief Inspector?" Emiliano asked.

"It's the only way to ensure they know we're here." Guillermo pounded again, this time using his other hand.

"What if they won't answer?"

"Then we'll have to figure out why." Guillermo tried to peer through the windows. *It's too dark inside.*

"What I'm trying to figure out is why Inspector Villalobos chose to come here?" Emiliano wondered as he too peered through the darkened windows.

Guillermo Sedeño had his suspicions. They originated when Angelica went missing. The pain of her disappearance remained as fresh as if it had only occurred yesterday. Though in Guillermo's case he had lost her before she vanished.

Despite their love for one another circumstances prevented them from being together. After having been promised to another Angelica obliged her father's demand for fear of his wrath and a sense of familial obligation. She severed all ties to Guillermo and bid him farewell in the presence of God.

To Javier Villalobos it was never enough. Regardless of her claims of fidelity she remained under constant suspicion of guilt. Javier knew how much she loved Guillermo. He discovered this when he found a letter she had written him, which had been dated prior to their engagement. In the letter, she confessed her undying love for Guillermo. She vowed to love him no matter what obstacles may come. She spoke of the agony of being apart and of the perils of secrecy, but she knew her father would never understand. Yet, she loved Guillermo anyway.

The aspect of the letter that hurt Javier most, and which had been the source of his mistrust was found in the part of the letter describing the consummation of their love. Her remembrance of his kiss, his caress, and his scent leaving her body in a state of longing and perpetual desire was something Javier knew she never felt with him. He convinced himself of that truth given the absence of such confessions from her during their engagement, and later their marriage.

Unable to ignore the feeling of his stomach twisted in knots Javier attempted to follow her and uncover the truth for himself. Whether it had been when she left her father's home during their engagement, or when she claimed to go for a walk after their wedding day he shadowed her movements without her knowledge. But always he lost her. Be it in the market or the alleyways of Old Sienna somehow she always managed to disappear for a short time.

He questioned her when she returned, but she always maintained that she had gone for a walk and did so alone. Even during her pregnancy, she continued to disappear at various times of the day. When Javier grew tired of losing her, his frustrations came to a head. He confronted her with his feelings of mistrust. He alleged Guillermo was her lover despite not having any proof, but vowed he would attain it and threatened to kill them both when that day came.

It was then that she withdrew even deeper into the shadows of their life together. She did not turn to her father, nor did she seek out Guillermo for help. She would not drag the man she loved into the web of her husband's allegations.

When Javier turned to the Elder Valentino for help he wanted to avoid the embarrassment of a scandal. The Elder Valentino understood and vowed to set things right. "I've grown tired of it," he said.

"Grown tired of what, Señor Valentino?" Javier had asked.

"The foolishness of secret love."

Shortly thereafter Angelica had gone missing. Guillermo suspected Javier's involvement. He speculated that Javier had acted out of jealousy, but he had no proof. He surreptitiously investigated her disappearance, but to no avail. Every lead led to Calle de Las Flores, but they all arrived at the same dead end; to the house on the hill with no wrought-iron gate and windows as dark as the secrets the house concealed.

Guillermo now circled around to the rear of the home. Emiliano shadowed the Chief Inspector's movement. They turned the corner walked along the north wing of the house. From there they had a better view of one of the mansion's towers. The darkened windows stared back at them forebodingly. If the Chief Inspector and his subordinate hadn't seen Javier enter the home, they would have thought it empty and haunted.

They made their way to the rear of the home. Guillermo stared at it perplexed. He turned away and from his vantage point looked over the fences of other back yards. He observed the dichotomy between the Valentino home and the neighboring properties.

"What is it, Chief Inspector?" Emiliano asked.

"Roses," Guillermo muttered.

"What about them?" Emiliano glanced around at the enormous rose garden and the freshly dug soil where none had yet been planted.

"They are often used to mask the scent of death."

Emiliano cast the Chief Inspector a suspicious glance.

"Why are you staring at me like that?" Guillermo snapped.

"You'd think I just asked you to have sex with a dead body."

"My apologies Chief Inspector. It's just that I always thought roses were given at a funeral as an expression of sympathy and respect."

"You thought wrong." Guillermo walked past him.

He led his subordinate back toward the front of the home and explained that flowers had been used for centuries to conceal the offensive odor of body decomposition. Even after embalming had become a common method for preserving the dead, the practice of bringing flowers remained unchanged through the present day.

"Where do you think C. Austin Miles got his inspiration for his famous funeral hymn 'In the Garden?'" Guillermo said as he led Emiliano down the driveway on their way back to the sedan.

"I'm sorry, sir, but I'm not familiar with—"

"I come to the garden alone, while the dew is still on the roses." Guillermo quoted the line from the gospel song.

Emiliano nodded and followed Guillermo down the road. When they arrived at the Hispano-Suiza Emiliano asked why they weren't going to knock on the door again.

"There's no point. They won't answer," Guillermo said as he climbed into the driver's seat.

"What do we do next?" Emiliano said.

"We get a warrant to search the premises." Guillermo turned the engine over.

He couldn't explain it, but for some reason he had a hunch that certain individuals who disappeared over the years ended up in the Valentino garden. Though what perplexed him was how to prove motive. Despite having the means to dispose of a body, the Elder Valentino's motive remained a mystery. Perhaps Javier Villalobo's visit would provide the insight Guillermo needed. To obtain it, however, Guillermo would first need to speak with Javier. Unfortunately, the Chief Inspector would never get the chance.

The Elder Valentino watched the car drive past and disappear down the road. His plan to lure Guillermo to his death was going according to plan. All that remained was to move one final piece across the board, and the stain on the Valentino name would be erased from memory forever.

29

Olivia and Juan Carlos arrived in the Forgotten Quarter just before sun set. They walked all the way up the hill along a gravel driveway. Lion statues flanked the steps leading up to the front porch like sentinels with dark eyes amid deepening shadows. They stood at the front door of a home that resembled a ruined fortress more than a vacant mansion. When the sound of a car approaching broke the silence, they turned and saw headlights weaving through Calle de las Flores. Juan Carlos pulled Olivia close and they ducked behind one of the statues.

The Hispano-Suiza slowed as it neared the edge of the driveway, but quickly sped off and disappeared into the night. Olivia and Juan Carlos entered the home through the front door, which was unlocked despite being closed. When they entered, they saw a lamp on a table beside the front door and turned it on. They knew from the columns, wide staircase, and high ceiling that the home had been colossal in its day. It was not difficult to image what it had once looked like, for despite the decay of some of the walls it appeared to be in the process of restoration. Though most of the furniture throughout the home remained covered in white sheets a couch, love seat and coffee table in the living room had stacks of paper scattered about with sheets, blankets and a pillow folded neatly on one end of the couch.

There were pages and pages of half-written letters. Some left on the table and others crumpled on the floor. Olivia lifted one of the sheets of paper off the table. She recognized the handwriting and turned to Juan Carlos. He leafed through one of myriad of folders stacked on the opposite end of the coffee table. His brow furrowed as he gazed at the contents perplexed.

"What's wrong?" She asked.

He lifted another folder off the table and flipped through it before he answered. Each folder contained personal records of different individuals. From birth records, title deeds, marriage certificates, and political affiliations to photographs and copies of police reports.

"What need would my uncle have for this stuff?" He replaced the folders on the table.

"How well did you know your uncle?" Olivia said.

"I thought I knew him pretty well." Juan Carlos shrugged. "But seeing all this…I don't know. I mean he was an educated man who had been accepted into medical school in the United States. Thanks to my grandfather's extensive library, he was exposed to literature at an early age. He read everything from Horacio Quiroga, Nietzsche, Jack London, Anatole France and H.G. Wells to Robert Frost, John Keats, Antonio Machado, and Walt Whitman. He studied the teachings of Buddha and Aristotle as diligently as he studied the teachings of Christ, Moses and The Prophet Muhammad."

"Wow!" Olivia mouthed.

"My understanding is he left the medical profession after traveling throughout Latin America and discovering the rampant poverty across the land. He grew enraged by the working conditions of the poor. He once said humanity's heart would break upon becoming privy to the suffering endured by the lonely people of our lands at the hands of imperialistic agendas supported by corporate conglomerates that promoted capitalist exploitation."

During their time in Europe Juan Carlos devoted one hour a day to reading—under his uncle's direction—the works of Karl Marx and Friedrich Engels. Despite their wealthy disposition his uncle insisted Juan Carlos understand class relations and the societal conflict inherent in a system that repressed the poor. As a renowned artista, Juan Carlos, along with his uncle—his legal guardian—had often been invited into the homes of nobles to be entertained. His uncle encouraged him to analyze the dialectical methods the wealthy employed at their gatherings, for not all were guilty of social inequalities, and to engage in the discourse to gain perspective.

"Your uncle sure sounds like quite a man," Olivia said.

"Women certainly thought so," Juan Carlos mused.

Antonio Castillo, his uncle on his mother's side, had always been the most eligible of bachelors. An enthusiastic and eclectic reader passionate about poetry and acquainted with the latest dances still possessed the virility of his younger days as a student athlete. The women of his social circles often vied for his attention and devised plans to monopolize his time. And he gambled with them in turn. It did not matter to Antonio that they were married or widowed, engaged or heart broken, conservative or adventurous. When they offered their hearts and their bodies he savored from their lips as a wine connoisseur samples wine.

"Come to think of it," Juan Carlos paused. "I've never known him to be in love. If I were to make an accurate assessment I'd say he was a bit of a womanizer always in search of love, but never truly taken with anyone."

"What about you?" Olivia searched his eyes.

In that instant, it dawned on Juan Carlos that perhaps he had been influenced by his uncle's example. He had mirrored Antonio's behavior without realizing it. In Europe, he was a young boy who did not remember his father's guidance or his mother's love. Under his uncle's supervision he developed the same knack for hiding sadness and solitude and longing behind the veil of desire and passion and love.

Juan Carlos stared into Olivia's almond-shaped brown eyes. Her gaze seemed to possess a secret intended for his heart. He wondered if perhaps, like his uncle, he found love in Old Sienna too. It became the magic moment that changed their lives forever. The rare instance people seldom recognize as the beginning of eternal love. Together they sat and read the unfinished letters Antonio Castillo wrote to Carmen Alicia de la Vega. Page after page of romantic musings revealed that Antonio understood something about how destiny unfolded. He seemed to believe that when the wings of birds and butterflies fluttered they somehow changed the winds of fate and led lovers to find each other in the darkness of a chaotic world.

Antonio's writings inspired something indescribable in Juan Carlos. A feeling he believed was reserved for someone worthy of true happiness. Something he only felt when he painted the memory of his dreams. Yet there was something about Olivia Villalobos that reminded him of his fantasies. She represented the ideal woman he'd seen in that realm between sleep and awake who became his felicity the way a muse inspires a poet.

He had no expectations that night, or any other to be precise. He possessed only the hope that the world ground to a halt and allow him to delight in her company. And it did.

She confided in him her dreams and her fears. She spoke of seeing the world and returning to Old Sienna to have a family. Juan

Carlos stared into her wide, dark eyes and admired her elegant long brown hair. He seemed to be lulled into love by the softness of her voice and the untouchable beauty of her smile. If ever he doubted the existence of God, he found proof in the presence of an angel.

When she apologized for rambling on he grinned and asked her to continue. She looked at him and lost herself in his gaze. She realized then that something had changed since the moment they first met. Although she could not put her finger on it she knew—in the presence of anyone else—she had never felt what she was feeling now.

She felt at ease with Juan Carlos as if she had known him all her life. In every piece of their secret lives they had revealed to one another they recognized a bit of themselves. They shared the same interests, enjoyed the same music, re-read the same books, and disliked the same foods. In addition to everything else, Olivia wondered if this was how the spark of love ignited: a meeting of the minds and a link between souls. This was the happiest she'd ever felt in the presence of a man and she didn't want the moment to end.

Aware of her selfishness she lowered her eyes. Olivia thought of La Señora Carmen just then, and of the tears she shed in the cemetery over the loss of her true love. Even if La Señora Carmen would not admit it, Olivia now knew the truth of it. She considered showing Juan Carlos the bloodstained letter, but decided against it. For despite her desire to find the Labyrinth she couldn't bring herself to break the news to him of his uncle's demise. Especially without knowing the circumstances surrounding his death and her father's potential involvement.

Now that Olivia knew La Señora Carmen had been Antonio's lover she understood the need for secrecy, but there remained too many unanswered questions. For instance, why did her father have the letter in his possession? Why was Antonio occupying an abandoned home? What was he searching for in the files Juan Carlos had found?

"What's on your mind?" Juan Carlos observed the pensive look in her eyes.

She turned to the stack of folders on the table. *Property deeds, marriage licenses and political affiliations*, she thought to herself. Olivia lifted the folders off the table and placed them on her lap. After sifting through a few of the files she spread them out across the table. She recognized the names of most of the individuals as nobles who had been arrested, or went missing in recent years. All of them had resided in the Forgotten Quarter, but now their homes were vacant. She continued to ignore Juan Carlos when he asked her what she was looking for, and upon closer inspection she noticed a peculiar detail they all had in common. The property deeds and titles had been signed over to the same person. When she saw the name, she gasped.

"What is it?" Juan Carlos tilted his head. His eyes shot back and forth between Olivia and the papers.

She pointed at the name of the most powerful man in Old Sienna, Ernesto "The Elder" Valentino.

30

It was nightfall by the time Guillermo secured the Hispano-Suiza in the department garage and returned to his desk at police headquarters. He sat down; poured a glass of rum, loosened his tie and undid the top button of his shirt. He placed a call to the front desk and summoned the five rookie officers who were playing dominoes to report to him immediately. After he replaced the phone on the receiver he instructed Emiliano to pull every case file pertaining to missing persons and unsolved murders going back thirty years.

"And put on a large pot of coffee. We're going to be here a while." Guillermo called out after him.

When the rookies arrived at his desk he instructed them to take a seat at each of the unoccupied desks. He stood and circled the area as he tasked each of them with sorting through the files Emiliano was retrieving. "I want time of death, cause of death, weapon of choice, and location. Get me victimology, methodology, criminology...any type of 'ology' that helps us determine a common denominator of all these crimes. I want to know where these victims lived, where they worked, who they knew, who they loved and who they hated; political affiliations, social status...I want to know which hand they used to wipe their ass with when they took a shit in the morning!"

"If you don't mind me asking, Chief Inspector." Emiliano placed the files on his desk. The pile of folders stood a foot and a half high. "Why so far back?"

"Let's call it a hunch," Guillermo said. "Everyone grab some folders and get to work. No one's going home until we figure this out."

The officers scrambled to retrieve the files and set to work. Emiliano approached Guillermo's desk. He leaned in close, lowered his voice and asked the Chief Inspector if he should look for something in particular.

"I want to find a connection to Ernesto Valentino and the Five Families."

"Why them?" Emiliano looked perplexed.

Knowledge of the Five Families was no secret. Originally, the Cintrón family had been the wealthiest of them all. Headed by their matriarch, Doña Adelina Cintrón, they sought to establish Patillas—and resultantly Providencia—as a major exporter of sugar. With support from the Valentino and Perez families the clans of de la Vega and de las Fuentes brought their money and influence to the region and together laid the foundations for Old Sienna.

"That is when the Elder Valentino pushed to move the capitol to Providencia and when the Five Families rose to prominence," Guillermo said. "Anyone who opposed them was dealt with harshly."

"I see," Emiliano nodded pensively.

"The question remains why did they want to move the capitol to the south?" Guillermo wondered.

"Perhaps the answers are right before us," Emiliano said.

"Let's get to work." Guillermo grabbed a folder from the stack.

"I'm going to double check the cabinet and make sure I didn't forget anything." Emiliano walked away.

Guillermo watched him for a moment. The patrolman

disappeared through the door leading into the Records division. Guillermo resumed his work. Emiliano raced over to a desk in the far corner. Most of the room lay hidden in shadows save for a small beam of light from the lamp on the well-organized desk.

Emiliano spotted the small black telephone on the opposite corner of the desk. The gold rotary dial with letters and numerals gleamed against the light from the lamp. He lifted the phone off the receiver and glanced over his shoulder as he began to dial a number.

"Yes?" Said a deep voice on the other end of the line.

"Uncle, it's me, Emiliano."

"Ah, yes, of all my sister's children you have always been my favorite. Why the call at such a late hour?"

"I wanted to warn you that Chief Inspector Guillermo Sedeño is looking into the Elder Valentino's dealings. Given your association with him and your position as governor—"

"Say no more." Fernando cut him off. "I appreciate the call."

Emiliano carefully placed the phone on the receiver and exited the room. Guillermo eyed him suspiciously when he returned empty handed.

"Where are the rest of the files?" Guillermo asked.

"There weren't any." Emiliano grabbed a few files and walked to a nearby empty desk. He hoped his guilt didn't show as he opened the files. Having never worked with the Chief Inspector he had no idea how perceptive Guillermo was and how stoic he could be.

31

It was well past dawn by the time Isaac woke with a hangover in Uncle Gabriel's boathouse. He had passed out on the small couch and was in the fetal position under a thin blanket. The sun fell through the windows with the sound of gentle waves lapping the shore. He groaned as he yawned and stretched.

"Dear God, my head is killing me," he griped.

"All the more reason to avoid alcohol, my boy." Uncle Gabriel approached. He placed a bowl on the coffee table and handed Isaac a glass of coconut water. "Come, sit up and drink."

"What is it?" Isaac rubbed his temples.

"Agua de coco," Uncle Gabriel said. He explained that coconut water was a commonly used beverage to help with the rehydration process when suffering from a hangover. "I've also prepared you a bowl of asopao. Drink and eat. You will feel much better soon." Uncle Gabriel stood and retrieved his fedora from one of the hooks off the coat rack.

"Where are you going?" Isaac asked as he stirred the bowl of hot soup.

"I have personal business to attend to in Old Sienna. Now eat before your food gets cold." Uncle Gabriel closed the door behind him.

Isaac heard his footsteps fade. He brought the spoon to his lips and was grateful for the meal. The stew consisted of chicken and rice flavored with sofrito—a combination of onion, green pepper, chili peppers, cilantro, garlic and dried oregano—with adobo. Isaac downed the soup and coconut water, which he later discovered were commonly used to remedy the effects of overindulging in alcohol.

He quickly began to feel better and decided to return home. His father was standing in the kitchen when Isaac entered through the back door. Rolando eyed him suspiciously when Isaac stumbled and leaned against the kitchen table.

"Have you been drinking?" He saw the redness in his son's eyes.

"Girl trouble. You wouldn't understand." Isaac blinked.

"You believe drinking is the solution?" Rolando asked.

"Do you think being alone is a better option?"

"Is that what you think?" Rolando's brow furrowed. "That I choose to be alone."

"How else do you explain this reclusive life of yours, dad?" Isaac snapped. "It's unnatural!"

"I admit at first it was a choice." Rolando stepped forward. He cleared his throat. "It was a choice because I grieved the loss of your mother. It was a choice because I wanted to focus on raising you. But when I came to terms with the loss and you had grown up, being alone was no longer a matter of choice. I no longer had room in my heart for anyone else. Your mother is all there ever was for me. I'm convinced she waits for me at the Gates of Saint Peter. I dare not arrive with someone else at my side."

Isaac saw his father in a new light. He apologized and embraced him. It had never occurred to him to see his father, as a man in love, for the notion of romantic love is often deemed exclusive to the young, by the young, and for the young. In their infinite wisdom, they fail to realize that love keeps us young after youth has passed and is the only memory worth remembering when the shadows of forgetfulness linger on the horizon of old age.

In that moment, he thought of Olivia. Would their destiny be to wait a lifetime before finding love with each other? Would her memory of him persist in the winter of her life? He could not risk the arrival of tomorrow without revealing to her the secret in his heart today. Isaac pulled away from his father and raced toward the bathing room.

"Where are you off to in such a hurry?" Rolando looked at him perplexed.

"I have to go see Olivia," Isaac said over his shoulder.

"Aren't you going to help me in the shop?"

"I will when I return."

Isaac washed and dressed quickly combing his hair to one side and using more cologne than necessary, as men are prone to doing. He quickly wrote down the poem formulating in his mind in recent days. It would be the introduction to his first love letter to Olivia and he would hand it to her with a kiss. By the time he stepped out the back door his father had already begun working in the shop. Isaac could hear him speaking with a customer as he pulled the door closed behind him. The sun cast long shadows between the alleys. Isaac made his way along the cobblestone street. It surprised him to see how empty the street was at this hour, but he remembered it was Saturday morning. It was the only day of the week when people slept in, for it remained the day of the Sabbath and no one dared miss mass on the day of worship.

He reached the end of the alleyway and flagged down a taxi that sat idle a few meters away. Though he could have walked the distance to the Villalobos residence he preferred to expedite his arrival. He climbed in to the back seat and provided the driver with the address. The man looked at Isaac over his shoulder. His grey eyes tired, but he still managed a weak smile beneath his bushy mustache.

Isaac opened the window and felt the wind in his face. A storm began to brew in the distance. Clouds gathered and lightning flickered. Despite the change of weather he felt confident and replayed the moment in his mind as he hoped it would unfold. As with all his other daydreams of Olivia that became pleasant memories of what never occurred, he envisioned an outcome favorable for his heart. Her smile would grant him access into her heart and her eyes would invite him to memorize her soul. She would take his hand and permit him to kiss her and the kiss would seal their fate as the paradisiacal moment between yearning lovers.

The storm neared rather quickly. Bolts of lightning lashed out beyond the horizon. It occurred to him just then that perhaps his fate would not be as Armando had predicted. His love for Olivia would not be a secret of repressed passion meant to be contained in the shadows of his heart. Instead it would be a destiny written by God to be seized at the precise moment when heaven and earth collide.

By the time the taxi arrived at the Villalobos residence clouds had blotted out the sun. Isaac paid the fare and the taxi pulled away. He gazed at the house from beyond the gate conscious he stood on the edge of fate.

When the front door to the home opened Isaac knew something was wrong. Instead of Olivia, or one of the male servants, passing through the front door it was Clara Ruiz who approached the gate. She wore a long white nagua style dress common among the Taínos, which contrasted her dark, slow-burning skin. She marched across the yard with a wild look in her eyes. She unlocked the gate and pulled it open. After she let Isaac enter she urged him to enter the home quickly.

"What's wrong?" He asked.

"La Señorita Olivia never returned home last night." Clara closed the door behind her.

Isaac felt his heart drop. She ushered him into the sitting room. It was the same room where Olivia greeted Chief Inspector Sedeño two mornings ago.

"Are you sure?" Isaac asked perplexed.

"I waited up for her." Clara invited him to sit. "I expected her to arrive late after she left here with the artista, but—"

"Wait." Isaac cut her off. "You mean to tell me she's been gone since I walked her home yesterday late in the afternoon?"

Clara nodded.

Isaac's jaw clenched. His blank stare fell to the floor. Lightning flickered through the windows.

"There's more." Clara continued. "Señor Villalobos hasn't returned home either."

Isaac met Clara's gaze. She appeared on the brink of tears. Thunder clapped outside and shook the home. Normally Isaac wouldn't think anything of Javier's absence. The investigator seldom made time for Olivia. In fact, he spent more time at La Cantina than he did at home. But even Javier had sense enough to return home regardless of his level of intoxication.

"We have been worried for them both." Clara interrupted Isaac's train of thought. "Especially after the news La Señorita brought home the night before last about her father's financial troubles."

"Oh, that," Isaac remembered.

"What will we do? How will we live? Where will we go?" Clara's face fell into her hands as she burst into tears.

She expressed the concerns shared by the servants. They had all been in the employ of the Villalobos family for a period spanning five generations when the Villalobos clan first arrived from Spain. The prospect of being homeless and unemployed left them feeling helpless in the absence of Javier, Tia Katarina and Olivia.

"Don't worry about that right now. First we must focus on finding Olivia and Javier." Raindrops tapped the windows.

"What about Tia Katarina?" Clara sniffled. Lightning again flickered through the windows.

"Tia Katarina is alive and well. Olivia left her in the care of a relative after what transpired here a few nights ago." Isaac assured her. Rain drummed against the roof. "Did either Olivia or Javier say where they were headed?"

"No." Clara shook her head. Thunder rumbled across the sky.

Isaac cursed under his breath. He tried to think of where Olivia might have gone with the artista, but his mind drew a blank. He sensed that his anger over her absenteeism compromised his ability to think clearly and he drew a slow deep breath. He knew they wouldn't have spent the night at the governor's mansion. Olivia was far too sensible to leave herself open to that sort of gossip. Besides she resented the governor for the way he treated her father in the aftermath of the missing love letter.

The Labyrinth! Isaac remembered. Perhaps Javier might know something about the location of the Labyrinth and its connection to the letter. If what La Señora Carmen had said about the Labyrinth and Olivia's fate was true, then it was imperative he find the connection.

"Listen to me carefully." Isaac took Clara's face in his hands. He gently wiped away her tears. Lightning continued to flicker sporadically. "I want you to wait here for Olivia. Send word to my uncle's boathouse when she returns. I will see if I can find Javier at La Cantina."

After he confirmed Clara understood his instructions he assured her everything would work out. He stood and stormed out of the Villalobos home. He advanced through the rain toward the gate. He slammed it shut behind him, but did not bother to re-secure it. As he marched to La Cantina he felt conflicted about finding Javier. He would have preferred to find Olivia first, but he had no idea where to begin his search. Even if he did know where to find her, he wasn't sure he was ready to see her with the artista. At present, he was livid over the news that she had spent the night with Juan Carlos, and Isaac needed time to cool off.

As he hurried under the downpour, images of Olivia flashed across his mind. Her pictured her lying on a bed with her eyes closed licking her lips and moaning with pleasure. Jealousy swelled within him and Isaac pictured himself beating the artista to a bloody pulp. When he arrived at the entrance to La Cantina, he was soaked to the bone. Isaac rushed inside to take shelter from the rain and find Javier. Once inside his eyes adjusted to the low lighting. The stench of cigarette smoke filled his nostrils. *It smells like an ashtray in here.*

Silhouettes moved among the haze of smoke and shadows. Isaac felt his pockets for loose change in hopes of purchasing a soda.

"You're the Mad Hatter's boy, aren't you?" The bartender approached after clearing a nearby table.

"Yes," Isaac cast him an uneasy glance. *Talk about looking the part*, Isaac thought as he observed Umberto's dark grey hair with streaks of black and white, which complimented his white dress shirt, black vest and matching bow tie. "How do you know my father?"

"We grew up together in the old barrio of Providencia. I'm Umberto." The bartender gave Isaac a once over. "Aren't you a little young to be in here?"

"I'm looking for someone," Isaac said. "Inspector Javier Villalobos. He's—"

"I know who he is." Umberto cut him off. "He isn't here. In fact, he hasn't been in here for two days."

"The night he arrived drunk at the governor's mansion," Isaac muttered.

"Excuse me?" Umberto raised an eyebrow.

"It's nothing," Isaac stepped back. "I'm just trying to figure something out. I better leave."

"Rolando would kill me if I let you go out in that rain," Umberto said. "Come have a seat and get dry. I'll fix you something to warm you up."

"I'm afraid I don't have a means to pay," Isaac said.

"Your money's no good here." Umberto smiled beneath his thick mustache. He tossed a white towel over his shoulder and returned to the bar.

Isaac scanned the bar. There were no windows and the only light came from the lamps suspended over the booths and tables and the one behind the bar. Most of the men ignored Isaac. A few glanced over their shoulders at him. Some nodded, one or two raised a glass, and the rest simply turned away to resume their conversations.

Isaac spotted a familiar figure in the corner. The light above the booth framed him with slighting light. His face remained hidden beneath the shadow cast by his fedora. He lit a cigarette. Isaac approached, sat opposite the stranger and said nothing. Umberto returned with a glass of Coquito, Puerto Rican coconut eggnog made with rum.

"This is normally reserved for the holidays, but seeing as this isn't a malt shop and I don't want you to catch a cold it's the best I can offer you today." Umberto placed the drink before Isaac.

Isaac thanked Umberto and introduced him to Armando. Umberto cast him a suspicious glance. He did not recall seeing the man enter.

"Armando de Maria y Delores-Dios at your service." Armando tipped his hat before he offered a hand to Umberto. Despite looking up at the bartender his face remained hidden in shadow.

"I've never seen you here before today." Umberto shook his hand.

"Let's just say I'm from out of town." Armando's dark eyes twinkled like onyx briefly reflecting a glimmer of light.

"Indeed." Umberto cleared his throat. "In any case welcome to our humble establishment. Can I get you anything?"

"I'll have what he's having." Armando pointed at the Coquito.

Umberto nodded and promised to return.

"What are you doing here?" Isaac leaned over the table after Umberto stepped away.

"Same as you." Armando brought his cigarette up to his lips.

"Seeking shelter from the rain?" Isaac tilted his head.

"Do not be coy with me young man." Armando exhaled a stream of smoke. "I know the reason you are here."

"What reason is that?" Isaac doubted Armando.

"You are looking for Javier. Perhaps you think he knows the

location of the Labyrinth and he will take you to it. Your hope is that when he does you will find Olivia and profess your love for her."

Isaac leaned back in his seat. Umberto returned with the drink for Armando. They nodded at each other before the bartender returned to the bar.

"No man can defy his fate, Isaac. Regardless of the choices he makes he always ends up where he belongs. Even if it means arriving at the grave sooner than is expected. This is why it is imperative to live in the moment and treasure the gift of *now*, because in order to truly understand the finality of death one must appreciate the infinite possibilities of life."

"It's a little early in the day for a philosophy lesson." Isaac adjusted in his seat. He hated the feeling of his wet clothes clinging to his body. His irritation aggravated by the thought of Olivia spending the night with the artista.

"Do not fret over matters beyond your control. It serves no purpose other than to distract you from finding happiness."

"The woman I love spent the night with another man. Her father is missing and broke, and their household is worried sick about them both," Isaac said.

"All matters beyond your control." Armando sipped from his drink. When he took a drag from his cigarette the orange glow reflected in his dark eyes.

"Olivia and I have been a part of each other's lives for ten years! Now this guy just waltzes into the picture and I'm supposed to accept it?"

"If you lose someone to someone else then they were never really yours in the first place." Armando shrugged.

"Then why do I feel in my heart that we are meant to be

together?"

"I never said you weren't meant to be together," Armando said. "I merely said you aren't meant to be together right now."

Isaac stared at Armando confused. *Why can't I see his face?*

"Why, indeed?" Armando said.

Isaac flinched.

"Do you remember the legend of Cupid and Psyche?" Armando sipped from his drink as Isaac nodded. "Do you recall what Cupid said to her when he fled?"

"Love cannot live where there is no trust." Isaac whispered.

"You must learn to trust your destiny in love, for in doing so you will remove all doubt in life." Armando pressed his cigarette into the ashtray. "Do you have the love letter you wrote for Olivia?"

"Yes." Isaac placed his hand over his ribs and felt the folded letter tucked safely in the pocket of his vest.

"Good." Armando downed the remainder of his drink. Then he pointed at the glass of Coquito Umberto had brought Isaac. "Aren't you going to finish that?"

"Oh." Isaac had forgotten about the drink. "I'm really not that thirsty."

"It is rude not to finish a drink when someone treats you."

Isaac took a sip from his glass. The rich, creamy flavor blended well with the rum. He swirled the drink in his hand and surprised himself when he consumed it in one hard, fast swallow. He wiped his mouth with the back of his hand.

"I don't know if that was such a good idea." Armando stood.

"I'm a little hung-over and pissed. You let me worry about the consequences." Isaac followed suit.

"Fair enough." Armando placed a few coins on the table to

pay for his drink. "Are you ready?"

"Ready as I'll ever be," Isaac said. "Just to be clear. Where are we going?"

"I think you know the answer to that question." Armando headed toward the front door.

Isaac followed. He stopped at the door before he stepped into the rain and he glanced at the bartender over his shoulder. Umberto nodded and resumed wiping down the bar. Armando waited just outside holding an umbrella. Together they walked in silence as the rain wrapped Old Sienna in its shroud.

32

When the storm roused them from their sleep, Olivia and Juan Carlos were lying side by side on the floor amid a mess of papers. They had moved the coffee table to spread the files out for closer examination.

"What time did we fall asleep?" Olivia rubbed her eyes. Lightning flickered through the windows followed by low rumbling in the sky.

"You dozed off just before dawn." Juan Carlos yawned. He had remained awake for a little while and covered her with a blanket as he sat and watched her sleep. He knew she was exhausted after the hours they spent piecing together the mystery of the Forgotten Quarter. He considered waking her and taking her home, for he was certain her absence would not sit well with anyone who waited for her. "I would have taken you home, but you appeared too peaceful to disturb."

"Thanks," she rolled up on one elbow, glancing around at the scattered pages. Raindrops tapped against the roof and windows. *Everything led back to the Elder Valentino*, she remembered. The question that remained was *why*.

"I wish I knew what my uncle was looking for in all of this?" Juan Carlos scratched his head. "And where the hell is he?"

He stood and walked over to the window. He peered through the curtain, but there was no movement outside. A bolt of lightning cut across the sky in the distance. Nothing made sense. From his uncle's abrupt trip to Puerto Rico to his absence and later occupation of a vacant home with a collection of files that led to a man Juan Carlos had never known.

Olivia cleared her throat. She pulled herself up off the floor and asked Juan Carlos to sit with her on the coach. He glanced over his shoulder and observed the sad look in her eyes.

"What's wrong?" Juan Carlos approached.

"I have something to tell you." Her eyes welled with tears. She revealed the bloodstained letter and handed it to him.

"What's this?" His brow furrowed.

"You have to understand," she began as she handed him the letter. "I didn't know at first."

"Didn't know what?" He looked at it suspiciously. *Is that blood?* He wondered as he took hold of the letter.

"I didn't know that it was your uncle who wrote this letter."

Juan Carlos unfolded the letter deliberately. He read it in silence. His eyes widened in disbelief. "How long have you had this? Where did you find it?"

Olivia stammered her reply. She did not know where to begin. Knowing her father's involvement, but not the extent of it filled her with shame. He stood and marched across the room.

"When did you plan on telling me about this letter?"

"I-I—" Olivia's face fell into her hands.

Juan Carlos studied her momentarily. It was clear she was upset but he couldn't understand why given that it was *his* uncle who was missing. He sat beside her and wrapped an arm around her shoulder. She buried her face in his chest and sobbed. She attempted to speak between breaths but her words were unintelligible.

He held her close, rubbed her arm and tried to comfort her

despite the myriad of questions running through his mind. He placed the letter on the coffee table and inhaled deeply.

Knowing he deserved an explanation Olivia regained her composure and steadied her breathing. She apologized as she wiped the tears from her face and pulled away. She lifted the letter off the table and proceeded to explain the series of events that had transpired since the night her father arrived home drunk. She admitted to not knowing his uncle was the unidentified man found in the alley, until she recognized the handwriting on the piece of paper Juan Carlos handed her with the address.

"I've been trying to find the Labyrinth, but it's been practically impossible to find it. So, when you had an address of where he was staying I hoped that maybe we would have found a clue. I didn't expect to see all this." Olivia waved her hand at the collection of files. "I don't even know how any of this is connected to the Labyrinth, or if there even is a connection. But I swear to you that I didn't want to keep this from you. I merely wanted to fulfill his dying wish, which was to deliver his letter to the love of his life."

"The governor's wife!" Juan Carlos said. The realization dawned on him and he fell back against the cushions of the couch. "Son of a bitch."

"We mustn't be too quick to judge," Olivia quickly said. "La Señora Carmen is one of the kindest women I've ever known."

"I'm sure she's a saint," Juan Carlos said. "I wouldn't dare fault her for any of this. My uncle however, has always been a bit of a scoundrel. Not that I mean to speak ill of the dead, but when you mess around with another man's woman you get what's coming to you."

"That's the thing though," Olivia interjected. "I'm not entirely sure his death had anything to do with the affair."

Juan Carlos cast her an incredulous glance. "You must not have a good understanding of the pride and passion inherent in Latin men."

Olivia scoffed before she explained that Fernando had originally instructed Javier to merely rough Antonio up as a means of sending the message to stay away from his wife. "Fernando only wanted the letter. *This* letter." She held the bloodstained page between them.

"Then who killed him?" Juan Carlos wondered.

"That remains unknown," Olivia said. "My father insisted that Antonio was still alive when he left him in the alley."

"And you believe him?"

"My father may be a lot of things, but I know he's not a murderer."

Juan Carlos nodded and accepted her reply. "If my uncle wasn't murdered because of the affair then the clue to his demise is here in this house."

"It has to do with the Elder Valentino," Olivia insisted.

"How can you be sure?"

"Every piece of property in the Forgotten Quarter was signed over to him before the homeowners went missing or ended up dead. That's no coincidence."

"But we've gone through every sheet of paper in these files. There's something that we've missed." Juan Carlos glanced over the array of pages.

Olivia's eyes fell on the files too. She hadn't seen the Elder Valentino since she was a child. A moment in time when she and her father crossed paths with Ernesto, who was in the company of his butler Diego, but that, was many years ago. The memory of that encounter was nothing more than a silent memory. Now she held the bloodstained letter in her lap. Juan Carlos glanced at the letter briefly before he did a double take.

"Wait a minute." He reached for the letter and held it up.

"What is it?" She leaned in close.

"When I was a kid my uncle used to write me letters with codes embedded in plain sight. It was nothing too elaborate. They were mainly instructions on chores I had to complete, or a heads up if he planned to return home late. I thought it was merely a game between us. When I got older he explained that given the shaky political climate in Spain, and other parts of Europe, it would prove useful if something ever happened to him. His plan would be to employ this method to get a message to me without raising suspicion."

Olivia studied the letter carefully. Nothing stood out to her, but she admitted she had no idea where to begin searching for a clue.

"Here it is!" Juan Carlos blurted it. He scrambled to find a pen and paper.

"What did you find?" Olivia peered over his shoulder as he began to write.

He explained that the first letter in each sentence was larger than all the rest. Strung together each letter created a separate message from the original correspondence. He jotted down each letter until he reached the end of the page and double-checked his work. Once he was satisfied that he had accounted for every sentence he worked to decipher the message. Given his familiarity with Antonio's encoded missives Juan Carlos made quick work of the cipher.

Carmen, my love, meet me at the western corridor of the Labyrinth.

"A code hidden in plain sight!" Olivia realized.

"Western corridor of the Labyrinth," Juan Carlos muttered. "Where do you suppose that is?"

"We'd have to find the Labyrinth to figure that out but at least now we have more proof of the Labyrinth's existence." Olivia's eyes once again fell on the bloodstained letter.

"The question is where do we begin to look?" Juan Carlos wondered.

A floorboard creaked behind them. Olivia and Juan Carlos turned to discover they were not alone. A large man stood before them with broad shoulders, a long face and deep-set droopy eyes. Two smaller men intimidating, in their own right, flanked him on each side. They wore dark clothing but only the large man in the center wore a suit.

"You should not be here," the large man said.

After a moment Olivia recognized him as the Elder Valentino's butler, Diego. She stood and took a step back. Diego smirked. It was evident to Juan Carlos that Diego had come for Olivia.

"Who are you and how did you get in?" Juan Carlos demanded.

"My employer owns this property. So, the real question is who are *you* and what right do you think you have to be here?" Diego said.

"I am Juan Carlos Trinidad. I have been commissioned by the governor, Fernando Gonzalo de la Vega, for a portrait."

"You'd have a better chance of finding the governor in his mansion," Diego said. The two men at his side snickered. Diego glanced around at the pages on the floor. It was as his employer had predicted. Carmen's lover had indeed pried into the Elder Valentino's business dealings.

"What are you doing here?" Olivia demanded.

"We heard voices," Diego said.

Juan Carlos and Olivia glanced at each other disappointed. In their eagerness to uncover Antonio's secret they failed to check the rest of the house for other occupants.

"Perhaps it is time you come with us," Diego said.

"Not until you tell us what you're—" Olivia began to say until she saw one of the men brandish a gun.

"The matter is not up for debate," Diego added. "Bind their hands and blindfold them."

"What? No!" Olivia protested.

She fell silent when the man with the gun approached. Juan Carlos stepped between them and stood in front of Olivia. The gunman pressed the muzzle against Juan Carlos' forehead and ordered him to place his hands behind his back.

"Just don't hurt her." Juan Carlos did as he was told.

The other man walked around the couch and slapped a set of handcuffs on Juan Carlos. When he turned to Olivia she shoved him away and punched him square on the nose. The gunman struck Juan Carlos in the head with the butt of his weapon knocking him to the ground. He advanced on Olivia but tripped when he tried to step over Juan Carlos. He fell forward and dropped his gun. A quick *pop* followed a flash of light when the gun hit the floor.

Olivia lifted it off the ground but by the time she set her sights on Diego he had already taken cover. He knelt behind Juan Carlos propping him up in a seated position with his forearm around his neck and a gun to his head.

"Drop the weapon," Diego said. He pressed the muzzle behind Juan Carlos' ear. "I won't ask a second time."

The gunman recovered from his fall. He approached Olivia who sat frozen with fear and snatched the gun from her grip. The third man dusted himself off as he stood. Together they blindfolded Olivia after placing her in handcuffs, and then they blindfolded Juan Carlos who now had a trickle of blood run down his face from the gash on his forehead.

"Take them to the basement," Diego ordered.

They're going to kill us! Olivia thought.

"What about this mess?" The gunman pointed at the scattered papers.

"Leave it," Diego said. "It'll be of no consequence once we burn this house to the ground."

They led Olivia and Juan Carlos down a winding staircase. When they reached the base of the steps they walked down a quiet corridor. The air was damp and smelled of mold. No one said anything at first. Olivia and Juan Carlos stepped forward tentatively as they were guided along in the darkness. Juan Carlos's mind raced with questions, but rather than press his luck he decided not to say a word. He figured the men he was with were not in any position to provide answers anyway and hoped they were taking him to whoever was in charge.

They came to a halt. Olivia and Juan Carlos were pushed up against a wall. A metal latch was unhitched and grinded as it turned. Metal hinges groaned when a door swung open. Olivia and Juan Carlos were pulled across the threshold. The air was cooler in this new passageway. A moment later the door slammed shut and the sound echoed off the walls.

"Where are we?" Olivia wondered.

Her inquiry went ignored. They walked along the uneven terrain, blindfolded and unaware they were in the Labyrinth of Love Letters.

33

Uncle Gabriel quietly entered the Cathedral of Santa Maria. He looked around at the grand structure of the building with its high arched ceiling, stained glass windows and life size statues of saints and Biblical figures. He shook the rain from his jacket and removed his fedora. Movement among the pews drew his attention and he saw a handful of homeless people seeking shelter from the rain. They looked at him over their shoulders. Some offered a smile and others merely turned away to face the altar.

"A pillar of the earth should provide comfort to those in need," Gabriel mused. He nodded and smiled in turn.

He hadn't set foot in a church since his beloved Ariana passed away twenty-three years earlier. Though it wasn't because he had lost his faith. In fact, his relationship with God had grown stronger as a result. For it was his faith in the God of Abraham and Moses that gave him comfort in the knowledge that Ariana waited for him in heaven.

Gabriel crossed himself when he arrived at the center aisle and kneeled. He proceeded to walk toward the alter admiring the prodigious crucifix suspended above. He stopped at the alter and whispered, "Let her know I'll be there soon."

After he crossed himself again he walked toward the door leading to the atrium where he waited on a bench and watched the rain. Carmen entered from the Alley of the Angels carrying an umbrella. Finding shelter from the rain she closed her umbrella and approached the bench. She continued to mourn the loss of her lover by wearing a long black dress and wide brim hat that had a veil to shield her face and hide her tears. Only today she hadn't been crying, for she had yet to visit the unmarked grave.

"I received your missive." She held up the tiny folded piece of paper. It had arrived attached to a string tied around pigeon's leg.

"Thank you for meeting me." Gabriel rose to his feet.

"It sounded urgent." Carmen lifted her veil and smiled. She complimented Gabriel's cryptic method for requesting a private audience. He had merely scribbled *The Mystery of Edwin Drood* on a small piece of paper, which would have been dismissed by anyone else had it ended up in the wrong hands. She immediately recognized Gabriel's handwriting when she saw the title of Charles Dickens' final novel. It was an unfinished murder mystery with elements of forbidden love, a mysterious stranger, a cathedral crypt, and an uncle at the center of the story. It did not escape her that the elements paralleled his nephew's fate.

"Isaac came to me about what you told him."

"I figured he would." Carmen shrugged. "The boy is in love. I imagine he will do anything to protect her."

"Why would Olivia's life be in danger if she found the Labyrinth?"

"Her fate is tied to its origins," Carmen said.

"How so?" Gabriel cast her a suspicious glance.

Carmen paused and pursed her lips. "The very foundations of Old Sienna were laid by men who wish to reclaim Puerto Rico for Spain. The wealthiest and most powerful of those men stands to suffer a great loss if she remains beyond his grasp, but if her anonymity is compromised she's as good as dead."

"Her anonymity?" Gabriel wondered.

"Gabriel, Olivia is not Javier's daughter. Not by birth or blood." Carmen met his gaze. "If her true parentage comes to light the Elder Valentino will stop at nothing to kill her."

"How do you know this?"

"I learned the truth of it from Antonio. He uncovered many secrets during his time in Old Sienna. Mostly concerning corruption that involved Fernando and his relationship with Ernesto Valentino."

"What? How? Why?" Gabriel sat upright with an incredulous look on his face.

"Antonio came here as an operative for the American Popular Revolutionary Alliance," Carmen confessed.

"The APRA," Gabriel whispered. "I've heard of them."

The APRA was founded in Mexico City in 1924 as a political movement to defend against anti-imperialism and promote international solidarity among Latin American countries.

"What role did Antonio play in this deception?" Gabriel asked.

Antonio was an educated man who traveled throughout Europe for nearly a decade as an agent of the alliance to gather information about the imperialistic agenda. He arrived in Spain during the First Biennium of the Second Spanish Republic. His nephew's status as a child prodigy protected his cover. His presence in Spain during the tumultuous period of the Second Spanish Republic allowed him to take a pulse of the political climate during the uprisings in the fall of 1934. It was then that he had been summoned to Puerto Rico to confirm rumors of a clandestine operation to help Spain reclaim the island.

"Reclaim the island?" Gabriel wondered. "Why?"

"It centered around the civil unrest in Spain. With the threat of war looming, there were those who felt they needed money from Puerto Rico for support against the rebels," Carmen said.

"The income generated from the sugar cane fields," Gabriel muttered.

"Some say it's the reason the United States refuses to relent its hold over Puerto Rico."

"What does this have to do with Fernando and Ernesto?" Gabriel looked her in the eye. "And how is Olivia's fate tied to all of this?"

"The Labyrinth of Love Letters is no myth, Gabriel. It spans for miles beneath Old Sienna and the countryside. Even beneath our homes in the noble quarter, the wealthy district and the Forgotten Quarter. I know this because I've seen it."

Gabriel leaned back in his seat. "How?"

"That's not important." She dismissed his question. "What you need to understand is Ernesto Valentino plans to let the Spanish forces use those tunnels for an invasion. He secured all the land surrounding Old Sienna to execute this plan. He turned to Fernando to circumvent legal channels in acquiring those lands."

"In exchange for what?" Gabriel said.

"He promised Fernando the presidency of Puerto Rico when it gains its independence from America."

"But the Spanish—"

"The Spanish have no interest in keeping Puerto Rico as a colony. They'd prefer to have it be an independent state like Cuba, but as an ally."

"And you know this how?" Gabriel wondered.

"I overheard the conversations in the mansion," Carmen said.

"Now that Antonio is dead, why haven't the Spanish arrived at our shores?" Gabriel asked.

"Ernesto's pride is preventing the operation from moving forward. Not only does he wish to secure the land for himself." Carmen continued. "He wants to ensure the property; its value and all his financial holdings don't fall into the hands of its rightful heir."

"Olivia?" Gabriel cast Carmen an incredulous glance.

Carmen nodded.

"How?" He insisted.

"Lorenzo Valentino fathered a child with Mariana Colón before his death. Knowing the Elder Valentino's wrath she quickly married a man who worked in the fields with her father for two reasons. The first was to protect her child, and the second was to grant her dying father his request to see her married before he passed."

"Who did she marry?"

"Efrain Sedeño."

"Efrain Sedeño," Gabriel muttered. "You mean to tell me that Chief Inspector Guillermo Sedeño is Lorenzo Valentino's son?"

"Yes," Carmen said. "but wait, there's more."

Gabriel remained silent and listened.

"Seventeen years later, Guillermo met Angelica de las Fuentes, daughter of the wealthy Don Enrique de las Fuentes and they fell in love. But like his father before him, Guillermo was doomed to endure the affliction of forbidden love."

"Yes, I remember the wedding between Angelica and Javier. It was all anyone could discuss until she went missing."

"And do you know *why* she went missing?" Carmen asked.

"Nobody knows the answer to that." Gabriel looked at her. "But I'm guessing you do."

"What I know is mere conjecture, but I believe her motives were the same as Mariana, which was to protect her child."

The realization dawned on Gabriel's face. *Guillermo Sedeño is Olivia's biological father.*

Carmen nodded solemnly. She gazed at Gabriel in silence and watched him take it all in.

"How did you discover all this?" Gabriel finally spoke.

"Some of it I knew because of my friendship with Angelica. Our servants talked amongst themselves and they revealed to me the source of her unhappiness. I learned the rest from Antonio when he told me of his research and his original purpose for being here."

"I see." Gabriel nodded.

"I felt betrayed though," Carmen confessed.

"Why?"

"Until the moment he revealed the truth to me I believed our meeting was kismet. So to discover his true purpose for being here had more to do with secrecy and the secret dealings of my husband—" Carmen's words trailed off.

"Don't you see that regardless of his original reason for being here your paths crossed as an act of destiny?" Gabriel said. "We never know our journey before it begins, but in hindsight we discover that every experience we have is meant to be ours and ours alone."

"I know that now." Carmen agreed. Her voice broke. "I only wish I had the chance to see him and apologize for running away angry at him when all he did was tell me the truth."

Tears welled in her eyes. Gabriel wrapped an arm around her shoulder when she leaned in.

"I miss him so much that it hurts to breathe." Carmen sobbed.

"I know how you feel." Gabriel thought of Ariana.

"I've gone to the cemetery every day to mourn him. That's when I found Olivia and Isaac spying on me."

"Olivia!" Gabriel remembered. "Do you know where she is?"

"No." Carmen shook her head and wiped away her tears. "I haven't seen her since the night she came to the mansion for dinner."

"Which means your husband now knows what she looks like," Gabriel said.

Carmen cursed under her breath. "How could I have been so foolish?"

"What?" Gabriel said.

"It was Fernando who suggested I invite her since she was the daughter of a noble."

"Javier Villalobos," Gabriel muttered.

"I naturally assumed she would come with her father, but Fernando said he didn't invite the town drunk to the party." Carmen remembered. "He said there was no sense in excluding her given her pedigree and that it would be good for her to meet the artista since they were similar in age."

"We need to find her." Gabriel stood up.

"Hopefully she's with your nephew." Carmen rose from the bench. "You find Isaac. I'll see if I can locate Olivia and we'll meet you at the cemetery in an hour."

34

Guillermo's eyes were red with fatigue as he hovered over his desk. All the other officers were passed out across the desks except for Emiliano who had left the room to make another pot of coffee. He and Guillermo had stayed up the entire night piecing together the string of unsolved murders and missing person's reports that began with Lorenzo Valentino at the turn of the century. At first it seemed odd that there were no other unsolved cases until five years later, but when Guillermo looked at the name more closely it began to make sense.

"Eduardo el abogado deceased in 1905." Guillermo muttered to himself. He remembered the fire at the law office of Ernesto Valentino's nephew. It had occurred when Guillermo was just a boy.

Years later after he joined the police force Guillermo recalled a conversation between a senior investigator and an arson specialist about the mysterious origin of a fire that led to the death of an entire family. They agreed the evidence was consistent with findings in a fire that killed Eduardo, but without a suspect that investigation went cold. Two weeks later the senior investigator and arson specialist were found dead in a nearby ravine.

Their murders also went unsolved.

In the years that followed a string of murders and kidnappings were added to the list of cold cases, but they were forgotten in the shadows of time. Guillermo and his team compiled all the details from the files. Initial background checks on each of the missing persons and murder victims found no link between them. Cross referencing the names of the victims with police records revealed numerous reports of damage to property, theft, assault, burglary, harassment and threats. The only common denominator had been their political affiliations, *Leftists who supported independence from Spain.*

"Wait a minute." Guillermo paused.

Instead of looking at the names of the victims he began to look at the names of suspects and the accused. The list was short but familiar. Each guy had a criminal history report spanning into their adolescence and all of them had come from various parts of the island. *Crime was but a way of life for these guys*, Guillermo thought.

"Holy shit!" Guillermo smiled. "I got him."

"Who?" Emiliano approached with two cups of coffee.

The phone on Guillermo's desk rang.

"Yes?" He answered. "Ok, send him in."

A moment later the double doors open. The graphologist, Julian Aponte, entered wearing a light grey suit with matching tie, escorted by a tired rookie officer who had returned to his post at sunrise. The graphologist reminded Guillermo of an accountant whose youth remained in the previous century. His grey disheveled hair matched his eyes and accentuated his dark complexion. He stretched out his hand and introduced himself to the Chief Inspector.

"My apologies for the intrusion. I know I sent word that I wouldn't be here until tomorrow," Julian said.

"I appreciate you being here, Señor Aponte, but I'm afraid I have inconvenienced you for the time being.

"Please, call me Julian."

"Yes, well, Julian," Guillermo placed his hands on his hips.

"I am no longer in possession of the letter I wrote to you about. I'm in the middle of an investigation concerning its whereabouts. It was stolen from police evidence and my prime suspect has gone missing."

"How may I be of assistance?" Julian said.

"I couldn't impose—" Guillermo began.

"It would be a pleasure to work with you on this investigation." Julian interrupted. He had served in the Cuban infantry and on the police force before moving into the field of forensics. "With all the strife in Cuba, I'm happy to get away, though it was difficult to arrange travel after Vice President Guiteras was killed. You might as well maximize my talents now that I'm here, Chief Inspector."

"There is much conflict on both our islands." Guillermo mused. The question remains who's more at fault: the Americans, the Spaniards, or us?"

"Guilt lies in the hearts of the greedy and wicked," Emiliano interjected.

"A young revolutionary mind." Julian remarked with a hand on Emiliano's shoulder. "Presidente Ramón Grau San Martín would have favored you."

The graphologist was present when Dr. Ramón Grau San Martín took the oath of office on the balcony of the Presidential Palace. For Julian was loyal to the last president of Cuba to be born under Spanish rule. During his short tenure as president Ramón engineered radical change behind the famous words by his Vice President, Antonio Guiteras, which appeared on the front page of *El País* six days after his inauguration. "In our capitalist system, no government has been so ready to defend the interests of workers and peasants as the present revolutionary government."

Ramón's initiatives included, but were not limited to, setting up an 8-hour work day, establishing a Department of Labor, opened the university to the poor, granted peasants the right to the land they farmed, gave women the right to vote, and reduced electricity rates by forty percent. His Vice President, Antonio Guiteras, had encouraged the public to cooperate with the revolutionary government to meet the needs of the common man and avoid being an instrument of imperialist companies. "The National Confederation of Workers will be responsible before History for the setback that the masses will suffer if we give the Americans a pretext to intervene."

As was the case in Spain there was a political power struggle in Cuba and the threat of Communism loomed on the horizon. Despite their best efforts, Ramón Grau San Martín and Antonio Guiteras would forever be known as the leaders of what was famously referred to as the Government of One Hundred Days.

"It's a shame the United States government never acknowledged the Grau-Guiteras presidency," Guillermo said. "Otherwise you would have had a future in world politics, Emiliano."

"Even from your quiet corner of paradise a man with ideas can change the world," Julian said.

"You never know." Emiliano shrugged.

"Yes, well, for now let's focus on the task at hand," Guillermo said.

He instructed Emiliano to call every officer and have him report for duty. It did not matter if it was a scheduled day off, or not. They were to report to police headquarters immediately.

"Why do we need every officer?" Emiliano wondered.

"Rule number one, rookie. You don't question orders. Now I want everyone here yesterday because we are going to raid the

Valentino residence and execute his arrest."

"On what grounds?" Emiliano cast him an incredulous glance.

"One of our own has gone missing and I have reason to believe his life is in danger."

"Sir," Emiliano stepped forward. "That's speculative at best."

"Is it?" Guillermo moved a sheet of paper across the desk for Emiliano to examine. "Look at the name under suspect."

Diego Muniz! It was the Valentino family's butler.

"His name appears on half a dozen of these unsolved murders and kidnappings." Guillermo added. "Now get on the horn."

Emiliano stepped away to place the phone calls. Guillermo turned to Julian. The graphologist had been studying the documents in silence. He mumbled to himself as he placed sheet after sheet side by side.

"What is it?" Guillermo asked.

"Every one of these reports from the past fifteen years was signed by the same individual," Julian said. "All accept for these two, the ones surrounding the most recent murder and the evidence intake sheet."

"How is that possible? They all have different names."

"Different names, yes, but all signed by the same hand." Julian pointed out the similarity in penmanship.

"The signatures were forged." Guillermo realized. He wondered who would have done such a thing. He read the list of names. "Most of these officers are no longer on the police force."

"That means they weren't around to forge any of the signatures that occurred after their date of resignation." Julian pointed out.

"And some of these guys weren't a part of the police force ten years ago." Guillermo continued the process of elimination. "Which leaves us only one name for all the reports from the past decade and a half. Only one of these guys has been on the police force during this period."

"Who?" Julian asked.

"Javier Villalobos." Guillermo turned to the graphologist. He praised Julian's keen powers of observation. *The Elder Valentino must have kept Javier under his thumb all these years, which means he'd be a loose end once he's outlived his usefulness.* Guillermo knew they had to get to the Valentino residence immediately and asked Julian Aponte if he needed a weapon.

"Let's just say I don't travel light." Julian patted his waist through his light grey suit jacket.

"Excuse me one moment." Guillermo lifted the phone receiver off his desk and placed a call. He notified the Chief of Police about his findings and informed him of the second culprit involved in the corruption. "He'll be here when you arrive."

In the privacy of the still vacant records office Emiliano dialed the number to the governor's mansion, but the line was busy. He hung up and tried again. The line remained busy. He repeated two more times to no avail.

"Robles!" Guillermo shouted.

Emiliano slammed the receiver down and raced to the door.

"How are those calls coming along?" Guillermo asked when he ended his call.

"I'm on it, Chief Inspector."

"Good. The Chief of Police will be here soon. Meet with him before everyone joins us at the Valentino residence. This is the case that will define your career." Guillermo led Julian through the double doors. "Wake up!" The desk officer was startled awake when the Chief Inspector pounded the desk with his fist. "Help Emiliano place those calls to everyone on the police force and instruct them to meet me at the Valentino residence ASAP."

"Yes, Chief Inspector." The rookie fumbled with the phone.

Behind the closed double doors Emiliano raced back to the desk and dialed the governor's mansion again. He demanded to speak with his uncle when the butler answered.

"My apologies, sir, but the governor stepped out only moments ago."

"Where did he go?"

"He did not say."

"Damn it!" Emiliano slammed the phone down on the receiver.

35

The bell hanging on the doorframe chimed when Uncle Gabriel entered the hat shop. He shook the rain off his hat and browsed the shop after Rolando acknowledged him with a nod and turned his attention back to his customer. The rain tapped the window. Lightning flickered and thunder rumbled. Rolando completed the transaction with his customer and bid him farewell. He greeted Gabriel with a smile and offered his hand when Gabriel approached the counter.

"To what do I owe the honor of this visit?" Rolando said. He hadn't seen his brother-in-law in several months, and even before that it had been two years. Rolando knew it was nothing personal. He understood Gabriel's reasons for maintaining his distance from Old Sienna.

"My apologies, cuñado. I know I should visit more often, but you know how it is." Gabriel leaned on the counter. "The time escapes us before we have a chance to enjoy it."

"Indeed it does." Rolando nodded. Lightning continued to flicker outside.

"I'm looking for Isaac. I assume he made it home already."

"He was here, yes." Rolando walked around the counter. "By the way did you have anything to do with him arriving home with a hangover?"

"Guilty as charged." Gabriel held up his hands. The ground shook from the loud clap of thunder. "Truth is, I had been celebrating my wedding anniversary to Ariana and was half in the bag when Isaac arrived."

Rolando pursed his lips. He understood how much Gabriel loved and missed her. For he knew how much his sister loved Gabriel and would grieve him in the same fashion he mourned her had their destiny been reversed.

"The boy arrived at my door heart broken. I wasn't about to turn away my only nephew in his time of need."

"I understand," Rolando said. "Heart break is the only pain for which there is no remedy."

"Indeed you are correct, cuñado. For even time and death are merely veils we place over the hurt, but no one ever forgets heart break."

The doorbell chimed again. Rolando and Gabriel turned and saw Memito enter the hat shop. He patted his wool coat, which had beads of rain clinging to the dark thread. Memito then strutted in his dramatic nature like a soldier. He grinned to conceal the sense of urgency within. "Good morning, good sirs."

Rolando and Gabriel greeted Memito in turn.

"Is Isaac around by any chance?" Memito said. "It is a matter of great import."

"My son sure is popular today." Rolando sighed. "He left a little over an hour ago."

Gabriel cast Memito a suspicious glance from the corner of his eye.

The doorbell chimed again. Rolando excused himself to tend to the potential customer. Gabriel wrapped an arm around Memito's shoulder when Rolando stepped away.

"Does this have to do with Olivia and the Labyrinth?" Gabriel asked him in a hushed tone.

Memito studied Gabriel momentarily. He wasn't sure how much Isaac had divulged to his uncle, but given the potential danger Isaac and Olivia were in he had no choice but to confess what he knew to Gabriel. Memito nodded but said nothing more in Rolando's presence.

"Come let us warm ourselves with café con leche." Gabriel declared as he led Memito toward the door. He waved at Rolando and said over his shoulder. "Let Isaac know we were here when he returns."

Rolando nodded and watched them through the window as they huddled close together in the rain. *Birds of a feather*, he thought and resumed the conversation with the customer.

Gabriel and Memito pulled the collars of their coats close to shield their faces from the rain. Gabriel revealed what he knew and how La Señora Carmen had confirmed the details of what Isaac had shared. When Memito was satisfied with Gabriel's explanation he led him to the funeral home.

The mortician, Luis Alfredo, let them in from the rain. He moved deliberately as he took their coats and placed them on the coat rack. Despite the clarity of his memory his body had become susceptible to the ravages of old age. He was balding and jowly with a bit of a paunch accentuated by his slumped shoulders. He donned a black suit with a white dress shirt that had a collar worn beyond a point that no man should allow. Luis leads them into a sitting room where café con leche waits to be served.

"The circle of secret keepers continues to grow," Luis Alfredo said after he invited them to sit.

"In that regard a secret is like a rubber band," Gabriel added.

"Indeed it is. How may I be of service?" Luis Alfredo said.

Gabriel explained their dilemma and recounted his conversation with Carmen de la Vega.

"It seems you know everything there is to know about the matter. What do you want from me?" Luis Alfredo handed Gabriel a cup.

"Is it all true?" Gabriel said after he thanked him.

"Every bit of it," Luis Alfredo said. "My poor Eduardo died because of it."

Memito saw the sadness in the mortician's eyes. He sat silently as Luis Alfredo poured another cup and handed it to him.

"It still hurts to know that the love of my life was taken from me by a man who does not understand the meaning of love." Luis Alfredo poured himself a cup.

"Fate can be cruel that way," Gabriel said softly.

"You think this was fate?" Luis Alfredo stopped and glared at Gabriel with watery eyes.

"A thousand pardons." Gabriel lowered his gaze. "That was insensitive of me."

"Perhaps we all lose the ones we love before we expect." Memito finally spoke.

Luis Alfredo's gaze softened, and his eyes fell on Memito. "So insightful at such a young age. Perhaps you have suffered more than most."

Memito bowed his head. He thought of his parents every day and fell asleep crying for them every night. Their fate changed by the actions of one man. The man everyone knew as the Elder Valentino, for it was he who had brought criminals from across the island to expand his influence over Old Sienna. One of those men had committed the crime his father was killed for, and the reason his mother committed suicide. Memito had as much incentive as anyone else to exact revenge on the Elder Valentino and now was as good a time as any to carry out that task.

"What do we do?" Luis Alfredo looked at them both.

"We must go to the police," Gabriel suggested. "Tell them what we know and ensure they secure Carmen's safety. Given her husband's involvement I'm certain her life is in as much danger as Olivia and my nephew."

Luis Alfredo agreed. Despite his disdain for Fernando Gonzalo de la Vega he was more concerned for his cousin's well-being. Together the three of them stood, grabbed their coats and prepared to brave the storm on their way to police headquarters.

36

Isaac and Armando walked through the torrential downpour beneath the umbrella. They made their way through the Alley of the Angels as they approached the entrance into the atrium of the cathedral. Once inside they walked along the eastern corridor to a small wooden door that led into the church. It wasn't the same wooden door Isaac was accustomed to using. In fact, it was hidden by the shadows in the corner of the corridor that surrounded the courtyard.

Lightning flickered when Armando pulled the door open. He motioned for Isaac to proceed ahead. Isaac lowered his head beneath the low arch as he crossed the threshold. Thunder clapped when Armando pulled the door shut. They stood in complete darkness for a moment before a torch flared to life. Armando lifted it from its place on the wall and led the way. Isaac followed him down a stone cut staircase that led to a corridor deep beneath the church.

"How do you know about this place?" Isaac wondered.

"You will learn the answer to your question when you are destined to know it," Armando said.

The corridor reminded Isaac of a cave or tunnel within a mountain. They walked deeper into the earth until they arrived at a wooden door. It was large with a metal latch and thick rusted hinges. Isaac equated it with a dungeon door from the middle ages. Armando instructed Isaac to undo the lock. Metal scraped against metal as Isaac struggled to pry it loose. He gripped the circular handle and dragged the heavy door open. The hinges groaned and the door swept the dirt on the ground aside.

"What I am about to show you," Armando began to say. "You must not reveal to anyone else. Promise me that you will take this secret with you to the grave."

"What about Olivia?" Isaac tilted his head.

"When the time is right you may tell her," Armando said. "For when that day arrives there will be no secrets between you. Do you understand?"

Isaac nodded.

Armando motioned for Isaac to enter. The air was much cooler inside. Isaac followed him through the passageway and soon they arrived at a grotto that resembled the catacombs of Europe he had read about in books. Except shelves were carved out of the walls from floor to ceiling, long thin shelves large enough for an envelope to be placed in lengthwise. The orange glow of torches pierced the shadows and Isaac could make out a labyrinth of passageways. The stone shelves ran the length of the corridors on both sides filled with letters like a library of love notes. The torches were situated at three-meter intervals to provide adequate lighting. Elegantly carved stone benches sat beneath the torches where lovers read the secret missives left for them.

"Welcome to the Labyrinth of Love Letters, Isaac."

Isaac stared in awe at the vastness of the Labyrinth. Its grandeur left him breathless. For it was the athenaeum of promises and secrets where the legends of forbidden love were guarded by shadows and time.

"Akin to a cemetery where the memory of the soul is preserved, every letter and the emotions contained therein, finds sanctuary on these shelves," Armando said. "Do you have the first love letter you wrote for Olivia?"

Isaac nodded and retrieved the letter from the inner pocket of his vest.

"Find a place for it and leave it for her," Armando said. "She will find it when she is destined to receive your love."

Isaac wandered through the network of passages. He ran his hand along the shelves feeling the envelopes on the edge of his fingers. He thought he could make out the silhouettes of strangers among the shadows. He swore he thought some of them turned to acknowledge his presence from afar, before he realized they were merely apparitions—the echo of those who once walked these halls.

The place seemed more ancient than its history suggested. Perhaps there was more to the story than anyone knew. Isaac's imagination was lost in the immensity of the Labyrinth. He wondered if it was one of many identical to it around the world. He lost track of time as he wandered within the winding labyrinth. He seemed to be following a path already chosen for him. For he could not simply place the letter on any random shelf to be forgotten by the passage of time, but rather it was as if he was being drawn to a specific place by an unseen force.

He continued through the Labyrinth for a while longer when he came upon an opening among the shelves. The vacant space was the largest he'd seen and that's where Isaac decided to place his letter. It would be the first of many he would write for Olivia and he would leave them all on that specific shelf. He would have faith in God and destiny to help her find them.

A scream broke the silence. It echoed off the walls.

"Who else is down here?" Isaac turned back toward Armando, but he was gone. He called out to him again. Silence.

Where the hell did he go?

"NO!" A woman protested.

Isaac recognized Olivia's voice. He followed the sound through the Labyrinth. *What's she doing down here?* He wondered. *And who is she with?* His mind raced with ideas. He heard her again. *Who's she arguing with?* A man's voice followed. *That's not Juan Carlos.* Isaac quickened his pace. He turned this way and that through the Labyrinth following the sound of Olivia's voice. He stopped. He waited and listened. Then he turned around and ran down another passageway. Olivia's protests grew louder, and the conversation became clearer.

"Just let her go!" Juan Carlos said. "She's done nothing wrong."

"You're going to be in hot water when the governor finds out you've kidnapped the artista," Olivia said.

"Silence!" The Elder Valentino commanded.

Isaac froze. He realized he was close. He inched forward and peered around a corner. The Elder Valentino stood before Olivia and Juan Carlos. They knelt before him with their hands bound behind their back. Two men flanked them. One held a gun to Juan Carlos' head.

The Elder Valentino prepared to speak when he turned to the sound of a heavy door open and close behind him. The sound of footsteps echoed off the wall before Diego emerged from the shadows. Governor Fernando Gonzalo de la Vega appeared behind him in the presence of his wife. La Señora Carmen's red eyes fell on Olivia and Juan Carlos. She immediately ripped her arm from Fernando's grip and raced to Olivia's side.

Fernando reached out to grab her.

"Leave her be," The Elder Valentino said. "Their fate will be hers as well."

"What?" Olivia said.

"Let's get this over with," Fernando said.

"You would stand by and let them kill your wife?" Juan Carlos said.

"She knows too much," Fernando shrugged.

"Knows too much?" Olivia repeated.

"You were right." Fernando turned to the Elder Valentino. "She truly is oblivious to the truth."

"Makes no difference at this point," Ernesto said. "Is this the artista you brought over from Spain?"

Fernando nodded.

"Good." The Elder Valentino turned to his henchmen. "Kill them."

Isaac stepped forward and emerged from the shadows amid the cries of protest from Olivia and Carmen. Ernesto, Fernando and Diego cast him an incredulous glance. The henchmen turned to face Isaac when he spoke.

"You're too late. There's no point to killing them. You're secret's out," Isaac lied.

"What the—" Fernando said.

The Elder Valentino motioned for Fernando to keep quiet.

"The Chief Inspector is already aware of your roll in all this," Isaac said. He hoped to buy some time to figure a way out of their current predicament.

"And what roll is that?" The Elder Valentino said.

"Eduardo died protecting Lorenzo's secret. He also died in the name of love. Suffering *your* wrath for his forbidden affair. Prior to his death however, he stumbled upon your plan to prevent your son from receiving his rightful inheritance. Money you wanted to satiate your own greed," Isaac said. He hoped he had divulged enough to lure Ernesto into the trap easily sprung by pride. Provoking him to reveal more than he originally intended, for he knew a man like Ernesto couldn't help but to display his superiority. He was the type of man who needed to remind everyone that he was cleverer than everyone else.

Unbeknownst to everyone in the Labyrinth, Guillermo and Julian had forced entry into the Valentino home. After searching every room in the house they arrived at the staircase leading into the basement and found Ernesto's underground office. They saw a second door ajar and passed through it. The sound of voices led them to the Labyrinth. They hid in the shadows. They listened. And they waited.

The Elder Valentino smirked. A thunderous silence echoed. All eyes darted back and forth from Isaac to Ernesto. Diego stepped toward Isaac, but the Elder Valentino held out his arm to prevent his progress.

"Is that all you have managed to uncover?" Ernesto finally spoke. "You mugroso half-breeds are dumber than I thought."

"Says the man who only concerns himself with status and wealth." Isaac prodded the sleeping lion. "Personally I don't think you have the mental capacity to execute a more elaborate plan."

"Is that what you think?" The Elder Valentino tilted his head. "Boy, you have no idea the patience and meticulous planning it took to arrive at this point."

"Enlighten me." Isaac crossed his arms.

"I'll concede that Eduardo died protecting Lorenzo's secrets. I had him killed for his ungodly affair as well, but it was his willingness to steal from me that pushed me over the edge."

"Steal?" Isaac said.

"Yes. Steal." The Elder Valentino's jaw clenched. "Did he really think he could hide my money from me and give it to some whore?"

"Marina was no whore!" Isaac protested.

"What else do you call a poor puta who spreads her legs for a wealthy man?" The Elder Valentino replied.

"She loved him, and he loved her, and it pissed you off!"

"You're damn right it did," the Elder Valentino said.

"It is just money!" Isaac argued.

"It wasn't just about the money!" Ernesto's face turned red. Though he needed to secure every cent to fund the invasion he had planned.

"What was it about then?"

Fernando placed an arm on Ernesto's shoulder. Ernesto pushed it away.

"It is about preserving our noble pedigree. It is about maintaining social order. Do you think I would permit having our bloodline tainted by filthy Taíno blood? Do you think I would stand to allow everything my ancestors worked for to be handed over to some…some—" The Elder Valentino cursed something unintelligible. "That is why I plotted with the Five Families to bring the capitol to Providencia. That is why I created Old Sienna. I built it from the ground up. Me! I did this!"

"You brought death!" Isaac shot back.

"I sacrificed the few for the many," the Elder Valentino said. "When I discovered the truth of Eduardo's affair, and his role in Lorenzo's deception, I killed him. I knew I needed to restore order, so

I devised a plan to help Spain reclaim Puerto Rico. Their presence here helped to maintain the division of classes."

"They created a suppressive environment," Isaac countered.

"But it worked. And when I discovered this secret network of tunnels that had previously been used during the Spanish-American war I knew my plan would come to fruition. I realized that the vast network of tunnels ran beneath the city and all the homes of the noble class. I reached out to the other nobles for assistance, but when I found Leftist sympathizers I had them eliminated. Naturally I tried to convince them first. A few intimidation tactics here and there, but they wouldn't budge. So I forged their signatures to seize their properties and I linked every one of their basements—including my own—to this Labyrinth."

Guillermo turned to Julian and nodded.

"I roamed through these catacombs and I spied on the comings and goings of everyone who engaged in secret love. Imagine my surprise when I saw Carmen lurking about."

La Señora Carmen raised her chin. Tears welled in her eyes.

"Now you know how your affair came to such a disastrous end." The Elder Valentino met her gaze. "I notified Fernando immediately. He wanted to confront you, but I advised against it. 'Better to uncover the identity of her lover first,' I said."

Fernando nodded. He glared at Carmen but otherwise remained silent.

"It was a good thing, too," Ernesto continued. "For if your lover had fled prior to what we discovered then we never would have learned that Antonio Castillo had ties to the American Popular Revolutionary Alliance."

"Lies!" Juan Carlos declared.

Ernesto and Fernando turned to the artista and saw the surprised look in his eyes.

"The poor boy didn't know." Fernando said. "Let us educate him, shall we?"

"Be my guest." The Elder Valentino stepped aside.

"Your uncle was called here to thwart the plan of the Five Families. He used my wife to uncover our plan. To his credit he did a good job. He remained a secret to us for a while until Diego followed him to the house where you were discovered. We tracked him for several months to see what he had learned. Thanks to my nephew on the police force we made sure his murder remained unsolved."

"How?" Juan Carlos finally spoke.

"After Javier roughed him up in the alley, Diego caught him unawares and killed him. I only learned this detail in the last few days, but it doesn't matter." Fernando glanced at Ernesto over his shoulder. "Apparently, my nephew had been brought into the fold when Javier refused to turn over the letter."

All eyes fell on Olivia. All except for Juan Carlos, for he refused to believe what they said about his uncle.

"It's true," Carmen looked at Olivia and Juan Carlos. "Your uncle confessed to me his role with the APRA. He took you with him to Europe and left you there to avoid having you suffer your parent's fate."

"My parents?" Juan Carlos' brow furrowed.

"They were staunch supporters of the Latin American political movement that promoted anti-imperialism and international solidarity among Latin American countries. He hid the truth from you to protect you," Carmen said. "I was so angry with him at first that I fled before he had a chance to say anything more. Then he died bringing his last letter to the Labyrinth."

"That was the final piece of the puzzle," the Elder Valentino said. "When Javier refused to turn it over I knew it had found its way into her hands."

"How did you know?" Olivia said.

"Yeah, how *did* you know?" Fernando cast him an incredulous glance.

"Because women have a penchant for letting their curiosities get the better of them."

"Fernando wanted that letter to prevent the affair from coming to light. I used it as a means of luring Olivia to this moment," the Elder Valentino said.

"Why?" Isaac asked.

"After months of wandering through the Labyrinth I eventually found the letters Lorenzo and Mariana had written to each other. Imagine the irony of using this place to prevent such a betrayal from happening again."

"This place was created for love, not war," Isaac argued.

"Love is war, boy. It creates more confusion and conflict than any war has ever done," the Elder Valentino said. "Love led my son to disobey me and turn his back on his family. This place is a product of his love and I will use it to undo his betrayal."

"Your granddaughter *is* a product of his love!" La Señora Carmen interjected.

All eyes turned to the governor's wife before they fell on Olivia.

Olivia wondered why everyone was staring at her.

"You think you came to be here by coincidence?" The Elder Valentino glared at her. "Everything that has led us to this moment has been by my design. Antonio's probing was unexpected, but dealt with accordingly. When I discovered he had a nephew I had Fernando fly him here to avoid any vendetta down the line. Carmen played her role without realizing she was being used to our advantage and I was able to kill two birds with one stone when you and the artista got together."

Carmen cast Olivia an apologetic glance. Isaac looked at Olivia and Juan Carlos, but he held his jealousy at bay.

"It's only fitting that you die here." The Elder Valentino glared at Olivia. He had lured Angelica into a trap fifteen years ago, promising to spare her daughter if she signed over Olivia's inheritance. But when Angelica arrived at the Valentino residence he had her killed for betraying her noble pedigree by procreating with a Taíno descendent."

"I don't understand." Olivia met Ernesto's stare before she turned to La Señora Carmen.

"*You* are the last Valentine, Olivia!" La Señora Carmen said.

"Me? How?" Olivia's eyes darted from La Señora Carmen to Fernando to the Elder Valentino and then Juan Carlos before finding Isaac.

Guillermo cast Julian an incredulous glance in the shadows.

"You are Guillermo's daughter," the Elder Valentino said. "As Guillermo is the son Lorenzo fathered with Mariana."

"What?" Olivia and Isaac said.

Guillermo felt his heart drop. He knew he was Olivia's father, but he did not know the truth of his own patronage. All these years he thought Mauricio was his father. The man raised him and loved him as his own. Either Mariana had deceived him, an unlikely scenario because he believed she was too pure of heart to be capable of such a deception, or Mauricio took the secret with him to his grave. Regardless, the truth had come to light. Ironically it happened in a place intended to preserve the memory of secret love.

"Enough with revelation of family secrets. What's done is done and I'm about to set things right," the Elder Valentino said. He turned to Diego instructed him to kill their guests and dump their bodies in the garden. He led Fernando past the butler. "We'll be in my office celebrating with a glass of rum and a couple of cigars."

"Not so fast." Guillermo emerged from the shadows. He pointed his gun at Ernesto's forehead. "Everyone drop your weapons and place your hands above your head."

"There's only one of you and five of us," Diego said.

"I wouldn't be so sure." Julian stepped forward holding two guns. He pointed one at Diego and another at the gunman standing over Juan Carlos.

Guillermo pulled another weapon from the gun strap around his waist and pointed it at Fernando. He instructed the governor to turn, kneel and lie flat on his stomach.

"You don't actually think you're going to get away with this, do you? I'm the governor." Fernando protested. "You can't make a case against me."

"I have your confession based on everything that's been said here today. Additionally, I have all the paperwork with the forged signatures of police reports and property deeds."

The Elder Valentino and Fernando glanced at each other from the corner of their eyes.

"By the way," Guillermo continued. "As for your nephew, Emiliano Robles, I already arranged for his arrest prior to leaving police headquarters."

Fernando's eyes widened.

"I suspected he called you last night and again this morning. And my suspicions were confirmed when the graphologist here identified his signature on the evidence paperwork that allowed Javier to steal the letter."

"Paperwork? Is that all you've got?" The Elder Valentino scoffed.

"Well, I have that and a garden full of remains you buried beneath your rose bushes," Guillermo said. *I'm sure Javier's body will turn up also*, he thought. Guillermo did not dare mention Javier's fate in Olivia's presence. Despite learning the truth, she still only knew Javier as her father and the matter had to be dealt with delicately.

Within minutes nearly every officer on the police force arrived to assist the Chief Inspector with the arrest of Governor de la Vega, the Elder Valentino and his henchmen. Juan Carlos and Olivia led Guillermo to the house Antonio had occupied before his death where the Chief Inspector gathered all the evidence he needed to solidify his case.

In the weeks that followed Ernesto's secret cemetery had been revealed. The search began behind the Valentino residence. From there they uncovered tightly packed, randomly interlocking human bones scattered throughout the hills surrounding the homes of the noble district. The macabre discovery sealed his fate and he died by suicide while in prison.

His co-conspirators were found and taken into custody. The governor was removed from office and handed over to the federal authorities of the United States. President Roosevelt appointed a series of governors after the capitol was moved back to San Juan, but any historical references for that period were lost amid the turmoil during the Great Depression.

Olivia and Guillermo eventually came to terms with their fate. Together they took tentative steps towards forming a bond between father and daughter. A fate taken from them by those who would rather inflict pain rather than accept the truth. They declined to accept their inheritance and instead divvied up the Valentino fortune among the servants of the Villalobos household. Olivia lived with Guillermo for a time until she married Juan Carlos and moved into his home.

Their romance developed into a lifelong love. After the ordeal in the Labyrinth neither of them dared, nor wanted to return to the tunnels of secret love. They moved forward together, not looking back at what brought them into each other's lives except to say that it was written by fate. In all their years, they loved only each other and cherished every moment between them. Good or bad, come hell or high water Olivia and Juan Carlos made a life together. They had children and grandchildren, planted gardens and trees, and despite the secrets they kept they never betrayed one another. It was as Armando had predicted. Theirs was a love of a lifetime until death did them part.

37

Isaac remained in Old Sienna for a time and helped Olivia transition into her new life. He remained her best friend and watched her blossom into a beautiful young woman. Day after day, week after week, and month after month he listened to her confide in him her feelings for Juan Carlos despite the pain it caused him. For despite the way he felt about Olivia he did not betray her trust, as men are prone to do. When her romance with Juan Carlos grew into a deep affection Isaac remained true to his word and kept the secret of his love for her hidden in his heart.

He wrote love letters for her daily and tucked them away on the shelves of the Labyrinth where he had placed the first. Some were short and others were long, but none had been like anything he had ever written before or after. The agony of unrequited love broke him, destroyed him, and molded him in the intense fires of a kiln of passion.

In the years that followed he eventually left Old Sienna. Not out of spite or pain, but to answer a call to arms when the turmoil in Europe plunged the nations of the world into the Second Great War. He continued to write to Olivia, except instead of mailing her the letters he sent them to Memito. He entrusted in his friend, the procurer of information with the task of hiding each of the letters in the labyrinth on the same shelf as the others.

After his first tour of duty in Europe he returned to Old Sienna, but only to bury his father and Uncle Gabriel who passed within days of each other. So, that for the first time in his life he truly felt alone in the world.

During his return to Old Sienna he discovered that Olivia and Juan Carlos had married and started a family. They invited him for dinner, and he obliged their request before he left to fulfill his military obligation.

A missed flight led him to the city of Chicago where his return to Europe was delayed by two weeks. During his time in the Second City he met Francesca Tolomei. He couldn't explain why she seemed so familiar to him, but it was as if he had seen her in a lifetime before with the same dark brown hair and hazel eyes that accentuated her fair skin. She was a young Italian beauty whose family migrated to America amid the rise and chaos of Benito Mussolini. Her father had been one of many men targeted by Mussolini's secret police after he opposed the dictator's outlawing of labor strikes. All too familiar with government corruption and men driven to obtain absolute power, Isaac provided perspective and insight, which she came to appreciate during their long hours of philosophical discourse.

During those first two weeks of their lives together Francesca and Isaac discovered a bond few ever find in such a short period. From the very beginning they initiated a method of seduction unlike any that resembled past loves of their own, or the past and future loves of others. If theirs was to be a love story unlike all the others it would be distinguished by a lifetime of memories intended to be an extensive meditation on love.

On the day of his departure for Europe Francesca saw him off. Isaac recognized the train station with its high arched ceilings of iron and shadow. She stood in his embrace and when he saw their reflection on the dark glass of one of the trains he remembered his dream. The dream he had when he was just a boy of seventeen and Armando came to him claiming to be Eros, the angel of love.

He never saw Armando again after he led Isaac to the Labyrinth. Nor did he ever write another letter to Olivia after that day. Instead he wrote to Francesca about his experiences around the world. He wrote to her from Germany and France, and he vowed to bring her to Paris to behold the wonder of the Eifel Tower. He wrote to her from England and Spain where he walked among castles long forgotten. He even wrote to her from her hometown of Verona, Italy the setting for Shakespeare's Romeo and Juliet.

After the first month since his departure his letters began to arrive. Every letter picking up where the previous one left off like a series of chapters in a novel written exclusively for her. She fell in love with every page and she fell deeper in love with him during every letter. For she had not only received his letters, but she had written him in turn. And in the process of replying to his correspondence she sought to seduce him too. Over time the letters between Isaac and Francesca grew in frequency and in length as well as in thoughtfulness and emotion. The difficulty of the distance between them seemed to vanish and the time that separated them passed almost without notice.

Isaac arrived in Chicago at the end of the war with nothing but what filled his duffle bag and the hope for a new beginning. He married Francesca in the church her family attended that reminded him of the Cathedral of Santa Maria. They recited their vows before God and family to love each other till death did them part. Together they made a home filled with children, and laughter, and tears. They passed through the stages of life without seeing in each other the changes that come with old age, for as they wrote their love story they fell deeper in love with the turn of every page.

In the winter of their lives they spent every day together. After a modest career as a writer he devoted his time to his wife, and she to him. They followed the same routine they had fallen into in their earlier days. Not only because it gave them comfort and security, but because they genuinely enjoyed each other's company. They recognized each other better than they recognized themselves, and when they didn't find each other in their dreams each took turns waking in the middle of the night to watch the other sleep. More often than not it was Isaac who woke first. He'd lie there and thank God for having been married to her for fifty-two years. Until that morning she didn't wake.

"Give me one more day with you," he whispered.

She did not respond. And he knew that in the end she kept her promise when she had once said, "I will never live without you."

Though he never missed a thing during their lifetime together he missed everything about her now. Her smile and her scent, her laughter and her temper and the way her hair fell over her shoulder when she wore it in a braid. He longed for the days when they read to each other and could sit for hours to talk about nothing. He missed the feel of her hand in his and the way she breathed when he held her in his arms. Now that she was gone he seldom spoke. He sat in silence and watched the sun rise hoping to hear her voice again. He stayed up later and later each night. He never slept well without her. He tossed and turned and yearned for her presence trying in vain to create a dream where he might see her once again. When he finally fell asleep it was for an hour or two at best and he always woke before dawn.

Isaac continued like this until the pain of living without

Francesca became unbearable and he began to lose his mind. He gradually lost touch with the world forgetting simple things he thought he'd always know. Not things like how to walk and how to talk, but he would look at a pencil and paper as if he were seeing them for the first time. The turning point came when his children came to visit, a rarity at best, and he didn't recognize them when they entered his home. They found him alone half naked. He had soiled himself and forgotten how to clean. The pictures frames had been knocked down from the walls. The frames on the hearth and on the tables were turned over because he did not want a stranger watching him.

"But dad, she's no stranger. That's a photo of mom," his daughter had said. "Your wife of fifty-two years, Francesca. Don't you remember?"

He lashed out angrily and frightened. He did not know or remember his wife, nor did he remember his daughter. Doctor's suggested around the clock monitoring, but his children refused to admit him into a retirement community where he had no friends. None could afford to hire a caregiver to live with him or with them and they ultimately decided to take him home.

They returned with him to Old Sienna, or at least what remained of the city he once called home. In the decades after he left for the war, Providencia reemerged as a progressive city linked to Patillas as a sister-city. Old Sienna had become known as the Forgotten District and no one passed through its cobbled streets save for the breeze and the ghosts of the past.

Isaac's family found him a retirement community in Patillas, Puerto Rico where they believed he'd find comfort in familiar surroundings. They bid him farewell though he didn't understand why, and he waved them off as he stared into the distance. Isaac

Quintero was never conscious of the curative journey that led him to his final days. What remained of his heart stayed broken, for it was as his father had once said, *Love is the only memory one never loses, because even if one loses his mind the memory always remains in the heart.*

In the months that followed Isaac crossed paths once again with Memito. He became reacquainted with others and met people he had never known. Some even remembered him as the son of the Mad Hatter. Every few days he'd forget his friends and had to learn their names once more, but on occasion flashes of memory opened the door into the past. Not often, and not for very long, but long enough for Isaac to possess a clear-sightedness of better days. In this way, a familiar Isaac Quintero returned to Old Sienna with the memory of feverish love letters written in his youth. Then, after a short time, he'd fall back into the shadows of memory, in the deepest corners of our hearts where even God allows our secrets to remain undisturbed.

The revelation of Isaac's most guarded secret was revealed to himself when a letter arrived addressed to him in a familiar script. When he unfolded the paper, and read the missive he realized he had not been forgotten by the one that got away. She was there in Old Sienna, or Providencia to be more precise a widow for well over a year with only memories and servants to keep her company. When she had learned of Isaac's return she waited for him to come visit, but when he never arrived she was determined to find out why. She learned of his condition through Memito and the network of servants who remembered the friendship Olivia and Isaac shared sixty-five years ago.

"He seems a wandering soul in search of something he doesn't remember he lost." The doctor told Olivia when she asked about the severity of his condition and inquired about the possibility of Isaac venturing beyond the confines of the retirement home. "In the absence of his faculties I'm afraid it's not possible."

She risked writing another letter hopeful he would read it during the brief window in time when his memory of her returned. Her missive went unanswered. She continued to write him letters. She did this as much for the sake of calming her own mind as for the salvation of his. If he was truly lost to her—or more accurately her to him—she was determined to bring him back from the realm of forgetfulness.

Her resolve remained unchanged even after Olivia went to see him and he looked right through her. Despite the passage of time, the fire in her eyes did not fade. She resisted the ravages of her advancing years as best she could but even her once haughty gait faltered in the steps of old age. She returned on several occasions, and then it became a part of their daily routine. Olivia sat down, holding her breath, searching his eyes for a glimmer of hope but she remained a stranger to Isaac despite being the inspiration of the first love letter he had ever written.

It was there. In the middle of the courtyard at the retirement home—surrounded by a well-kept garden—when the idea came to Olivia. She whispered the words no one had spoken in sixty-five years. "The Labyrinth of Love Letters."

Isaac did not flinch. He did not seem to hear her, or if he did the words no longer held any meaning for him. He remained immovable, statuesque, hearing her but not listening.

She repeated herself and waited, but to no avail. After a long while Olivia stood. She placed a letter on the table beside him. She waited for him to acknowledge her, or to at least acknowledge the letter. Finally, she relented. She moved the letter onto his lap and returned home.

Another hour or so had passed before Isaac emerged from the shadows of memory. He hadn't returned for long, but he had regained his bearings long enough to notice the letter on his lap. He opened it and read it with great interest. He smiled as tears welled in his eyes.

"She remembers me?" Isaac muttered.

"Did you say something?" An attendant approached.

It had been one of the few times Isaac said anything to anyone. He turned to the attendant, Samuel, a thin black man from the Dominican Republic. He had come to Puerto Rico in search of work and found a calling in the aid of the elderly. Isaac had been his favorite, for he had been one of his favorite authors despite the lack of notoriety for Isaac's works. Isaac showed him the letter as Samuel escorted him back to his room. He moved confidently across the courtyard and told the attendant about the Labyrinth of Love Letters.

Samuel nodded and listened without interrupting Isaac or challenging his delusion. He figured Isaac was merely recounting one of his unpublished story ideas that came back to him from time to time. He led Isaac into the building and down the corridor until they arrived at his room. Isaac asked how the letter came to be in his possession and the attendant revealed that Olivia had come to visit him again.

"She did?" Isaac smiled. He knew the handwriting seemed familiar.

The Labyrinth of Love Letters.

"She has been here every day for several weeks. Always at the same time and for the same duration."

Isaac shook his head in disbelief. He had no recollection of her visits, for he remained trapped in the darkness of the mind for most of the day and night. Even his dreams were unrecognizable to him. It was as if they were memories that belonged to someone else. Whenever his memory came back to him it was always when he was alone and only the moon was a familiar friend.

"She told us about your friendship and though she admits she never told you, you were the first boy she had ever loved," said the attendant.

"Who?" Isaac wondered.

"Olivia," Samuel said.

"Olivia who?" Isaac cast the attendant a confused glance. "What are you talking about?"

The attendant recognized the veil that fell behind Isaac's eyes. He had once again slipped into the shadows of darkness and was lost to the world again.

"Nothing." The attendant assured him. "I must have been confused."

He helped Isaac remain calm and he brought him his food. He fed Isaac, and bathed him, and tucked him into bed. Isaac fell into a deep slumber. His breathing slow and steady as he curled up under the blankets. Samuel watched him sleep and felt pity for the romantic who no longer remembered love.

The moon still lingered in the sky when Isaac stepped out of the front door. He left the retirement community before the city began to wake. It would be hours before they knew where to find him, but it was all the time he needed. He ventured through the strange city that resembled nothing of the town he once called home.

His memory came and went as he walked. Akin to slipping between the realms of sleep and awake after a long restless slumber.

Except now as he prepared to finally rise from sleep, for if to live is to dream and to die is to awaken, he continued along the path to meet his fate. The brightness of dawn broke through the clouds and cast its golden glow of slanting light when he arrived at the old stone bridge. A stream ran peacefully beneath it with a stone shore covered in moss.

"I wondered if you would return."

Isaac froze when he saw her. He felt as though he was seeing her for the first time, and he watched as Olivia approached. Time stood still when he gazed into her almond-shaped, dark brown eyes and he wondered about the strange sensation swirling at his core. He didn't recognize her. But he knew he had seen her breath-taking beauty in a lifetime before. Her presence calmed him, and her scent reminded him of why he had come.

"There is something I must show you," Isaac finally spoke.

He led her over the bridge and through a narrow trail among the trees. A canopy of leaves provided a bit of shade and caused the sun to fall in slanting light. She walked with him in silence. For to them both, the moment felt like a dream.

"You cannot reveal to anyone what I am about to show you," Isaac whispered.

"I won't have a chance to anyway," she smiled. It was the first time they were both aware of each other's presence in over six decades and it was as if the time and distance between them had never existed.

They followed the path through the underbrush, more of a scar than a trail, until they arrived at a cave. The entrance lay hidden by a curtain of leaves and branches and vines. He had discovered it in the years after the Elder Valentino's fall. Though all other entrances to the Labyrinth had been sealed, Isaac ensured this one remained untouched.

He led Olivia through the arched entryway. The darkness swallowed them. He held her hand and continued forward. Though Isaac had not set foot in the Labyrinth for over sixty years he knew the way by heart. Despite the caliginosity she trusted Isaac implicitly. Soon they arrived at a chamber where a torch sat on the far wall.

"How—" Olivia pointed at the burning torch. She turned to Isaac as her words trailed off.

"Before I left, I made Memito promise to keep the torches lit," Isaac said. "I imagine he will find a suitable replacement in his own time."

He lifted the torch off the wall and proceeded down one of the many corridors of the Labyrinth. The cool air felt familiar to Olivia and Isaac as they passed. Hundreds of thousands of letters lined the shelves. Small envelopes and large envelopes were situated among folded letters that didn't have envelopes at all. The Labyrinth remained as Isaac remembered it with torches every three-meters on both sides. The same elegantly carved benches also survived the passage of time.

He led her this way and that through the network of tunnels. When they finally arrived at the place where Isaac had left his letters to Olivia he noticed an inscription in the stone above the shelf. He realized the inscription ran the length of the corridor on both sides.

Dio de Amor y Amar as Love-Eros

"Oh my God," Isaac whispered. *God of Love and Love as Love-Eros*, he thought.

"What is it?" Olivia's eyes shot between the look on Isaac's face and the inscription.

"The inscription on the wall is an anagram of Armando's full name." Isaac said.

"Who?" Olivia wondered.

"Armando de Maria y Delores-Dios, the man who revealed the Labyrinth of Love Letters to me. I believe he was Cupid, the god of love."

Olivia studied him momentarily. She had always wondered how Isaac found her in the Labyrinth on that fateful day when the Elder Valentino planned to end her life. But it had slipped her mind in the aftermath of the revelation. She had never returned to the Labyrinth despite thinking of it every day. That is why she left the letter on Isaac's lap. She wanted to see it one more time, but she would only return with him.

Olivia wanted to ask Isaac if he had ever returned, but she feared his reply. She feared he returned for a forbidden love with another and she feared he returned for his forbidden love for her. Neither was a fate she was prepared to accept; yet secretly she prayed for the latter.

He sat her on the bench next to the shelf that belonged to her and he repeated the words she said to him on the eve of his departure. "The only true love is unrequited love." And he handed her the first letter he wrote for her over half a century ago.

She sat on the bench, puzzled, yet secretly thrilled by the knowledge that he had written a love letter for her. It was a four-page letter that began with a poem. A short, sweet, lovely poem that reminded her of the poetry he had published in the local periodical when they were young. Except in this way a different side of Isaac Quintero was revealed to her. One possessed of devotion that in no way correlated with the sentimental poetry of his early years. Instead, she glimpsed the heart of a man who later revealed himself to the world through words inspired by unconditional love.

She not only read his letters, but she felt every word as if she had placed her hand on his chest and experienced the rhythmic beat of his heart. Beyond the affections stirred in her heart she found in each love letter thoughtful and profound reasons to believe in love. Each was a confession of unbridled passion and swallowed pride that they were the emotional equivalent of long slow kisses and seductive gentle strokes.

The letters calmed her and relieved her of the tiniest hint of guilt she felt despite their widowhood, for in them she discovered the profound truth that no two loves are the same. She sat for hours reading and re-reading the letters before she folded them as he folded them, placed them inside their envelopes and returned them to their place on the shelf. When she turned to him and met his soft, familiar gaze she smiled and placed a hand on his cheek.

"The only regret I have is that I did not possess the heart to give you the love you deserved for being so patient and devoted." Olivia's eyes welled with tears.

"There is nothing to regret," Isaac said. "Regardless of our paths we are here now."

"But we've only a little time left." Olivia said knowing they stood face to face with each other and with their mortality.

"To say I have always loved you and I always will that's all the time we need." Isaac smiled.

When the townsfolk finally found them in the Labyrinth seated on the bench in each other's embrace they had already fallen deep into their eternal slumber and inspired the legend of an intrepid love.

PREVIEW OF THE LAST LOVE LETTER

PROLOGUE

What does a woman think about in the absence of love? Does she reflect on what once was and could have been? Perhaps she turns her back on the past and looks to the future. Any many who has studied her behavior and broken her heart will confess that she will forever remain as mysterious as the origins of the universe and as lovely as the idiom of God.

It is in this innocent intrigue that men are inspired to pursue a woman's heart, to kiss her lips, and to taste ambrosia. Aurelio Valentino embarked on this endeavor the moment he saw Arabella. Her light brown hair pulled up in a bun revealed the caramel complexion of her slender neck. She had a smile that could stop time, and the honey in her eyes leveled him. He approached the way one comes to the sea and introduced himself with an extended hand.

She observed him with indifference and turned away. But he persisted with the hope of learning her name, hearing her voice, and memorizing her smile. Her silence intended to dissuade him, but had the opposite effect. For it is known that men want what they cannot have. He knelt before her as she remained seated on the bench and asked her name, but she did not reply. The two girls seated on either side of her watched, amused. It wasn't that they doubted his intentions, because they were familiar with the handsome suitor.

Aurelio Valentino, no stranger to the preambles of love had been popular among the girls in his social circle. A bolero who recited romantic poetry by memory and played match-maker among his friends, because he believed destiny placed soul mates close enough to find each other, but just far enough to require assistance being guided to love.

And she, with her nineteen years behind her recognized the initial raindrops of courtly love. His persistence and his poetry impressed her, but it did not convince her of the genuineness of his intentions. Men, as she had observed both young and old, had a penchant for beginning their pursuits at a sprint without ever learning that they merely needed to proceed with patience. Though they hope to be granted access to their hearts, they innately craved the thrill of the chase.

In the case of Aurelio Valentino, his desire to win Arabella's affections was not an endeavor undertaken in vain. She carried herself with a natural haughtiness, her chin up, her hazel eyes keen, her steps confident as her arms swayed elegantly. Everything about her presence from the form of her full lips, her arched eyebrows, and her high cheekbones that she inherited from her mother and the softness in her voice epitomized what it meant to be a woman.

At her side were two young ladies with whom she had become acquainted after recently arriving on the island. Though they encouraged Arabella to leave herself open to the possibilities of love, she remained apprehensive about the stranger. She stood without revealing her name. Her accomplices followed suit. She led her companions through the crowd, and Aurelio followed. She quickened her pace around the parade, and the tables of the merchants selling trinkets, and the carts carrying fruits, and the sound of sizzling meats—the scent of seasoning intermingled with smoke—and the carnival rides flooded with children, still he followed.

Then as the sun faded to the other side of the world, she joined her companions for the nightly walk during the festivities around the plaza. Women walked in groups of twos and threes, sometimes arm and arm, while men lined the perimeter of the walkway on both sides. Upon establishing eye contact, men waited for another pass to approach. Aside from perpetuating the Old World custom of letting men make the first move, his action became a public declaration of his intentions. For women, it became an opportunity to reveal her receptiveness of her suitor's interest with conversation, or to politely decline with silence.

When Aurelio saw her disappear into the crowd of women circling the plaza with her two companions on either side of her, he formulated a plan to get her attention in a unique fashion. He turned back and raced to the merchants. He found the woman selling flowers and quickly decided on a red Chrysanthemum. *Though it symbolizes fidelity and optimism, the red one conveys love*, he thought to himself as he handed the merchant's wife a few coins. He returned to the plaza hoping to arrive at the same time she circled back around. He searched for her among the crowd of passing and approaching women, but she was nowhere in sight. Guessing that he must have missed her, he turned to the groups of women whose backs were to him, and he recognized her hair, her open shouldered top, and her doe's gait.

Aurelio shouldered past the men beside him to get a clear shot, and like an expert darts man he steadied his aim before launching the flower—stem first—at his target. He threw it past three rows of women as it found its mark in Arabella's hair. The men cheered. It landed just above her ear, nestled like a decorative piece he once described in a poem: *I saw her once when she was standing there; she had the loveliest smile with flowers in her hair.*

She glanced over her shoulder upon retrieving the flower and smiled.

Aurelio waited for her again, his anticipation building with each passing second. His heart skipped a beat when she turned the corner again. This time she stood on the far right side of her companions. She held the flower with both hands and pretended to not see him. He stepped forward into the flow of women, a river of femininity carrying the hopes of men beneath the moon. Aurelio bowed and introduced himself again. She smiled without reply and continued past him. He turned on his heel with the deftness of a dancer and fell instep beside her.

"May I accompany you on your stroll this lovely evening señorita?" Aurelio gazed into her hazel eyes, but she stared straight ahead.

"No one is preventing you." Her heart pounded against her breasts. A gentle breeze played on the loose strands of her hair. It was a peaceful night, the twelfth of December. Aurelio walked beside her, cleared his throat, and began to sing a song. He loved ballads as much as he loved books.

"Are you auditioning for a talent contest?" Arabella asked as she finally turned to meet his gaze.

Beside her, Aurelio saw her companions smiling, a mischievous glint in their eyes.

"I am auditioning for your heart," Aurelio interrupted his singing.

"I assure you I am not a contest." She turned her chin up and followed the procession as it turned a corner.

"Ah, but would you kindly accept the compliment that your beauty is worth the effort of winning over?"

"I am more than just my appearance," Arabella met his gaze.

"Indeed, you are," he agreed, "and I want to learn everything about you before it's too late."

"Too late for what?" She cast him a perplexed glance.

"Before it's too late to begin forever in this lifetime."

He had never felt as nervous and excited as he did that night and would remember it always: his heart raced, his sight clear, his stomach twisted in knots. The moon seemed larger and closer than it did on any other night in the history of the world. And there were more stars in the sky. He believed they emerged from behind the dark veil of distance to witness the love story they wrote centuries ago.

Despite her attempts to elude Aurelio when they first met, Arabella let her mind wander that night with her head against the pillow. Sleep waited for her to stage the events in her dreams. She recognized him in the realm of fantasy reading under the trees, singing in the dark, and writing in his notebook. Then, as if she possessed mysterious magical powers, he appeared before her at various places doing just what she had imagined him doing. He sat on a bench in the plaza on Sundays reading beneath an apple tree, and he serenaded her in the evenings singing from an unseen location in the park so as not to draw the ire of her father, and at random times she spotted him writing in his notebook when she went to the market, or the pharmacy, or anywhere else he was not supposed to be.

Except on Sunday evenings when they met in the plaza during the weekly fiestas that commenced after sunset. Their courtship began like a ballad played on the piano, gentle, slow and inspiring. Her eyes glazed with happiness, and his with love. It was there that he did not belong to the realm of her dreams, but to her and her alone. The promise of eternal fidelity he declared on the night they first met seemed as inevitable as a sunrise and a sunset. A dance to be rehearsed and perfected for the remainder of their natural lives.

Please leave a review telling other readers how much you enjoyed this book at:

THE LAST VALENTINE ON AMAZON

BOOKS BY

FELIX ALEXANDER

THE ROMANTIC: A LOVE STORY

The Romantic is a love story about friendship, passion, and the echo of unrequited love.

Hadriel Alighieri has harbored a secret love in his heart for his entire life. It began in his youth, when he fell in love with his best friend, Sophia Paula. After Sophia leaves for America and is later betrothed to Joshua Abrams, Hadriel is devastated, but he is a hopeless romantic.

In the winter of his life he is haunted by the memory of Sophia Paula. When the Angel of Death comes for Hadriel, the journey begins. From his deathbed, he travels to the day he fell in love. He retraces the steps of his life in search of his unrequited love. For she too harbors a secret love in her heart. But what begins as a journey to fulfill a promise turns into a discovery of the only emotion that defines our lives.

Did she wait for him?

HER AWAKENING

When sex shop employee Marina Varela meets Luciano Garcia, she encounters a man who is handsome, intelligent and intimidating. The guarded Marina wants this man, and Luciano confesses his desire for her as well, but he too is guarded. When the couple endeavors to see where things may lead, they find themselves in the throes of a passionate affair. Their sexual exploration of each other leads them to an awakening of their bodies and their hearts.

HER PUNISHMENT

A dark erotic novelette from Readers' Favorite award-winning novelist, Felix Alexander.

Majica is done.
She has waited five years for Ricardo to marry her.
She will not wait any longer.
After several weeks of being away, she returns home for her belongings.
She thought he would not be home.
She was wrong.
He intends to punish her for leaving him, and for the lie.
Trapped alone with him, she is lured into their private chamber.
He wants her to himself and refuses to believe she doesn't love him anymore.
Ricardo always gets what he wants.

Though Majica resists, she struggles to reconcile is passion with his love, but she remembers their agreement: once inside the private room there is no protesting, only submission.

DEAR LOVE: DIARY OF A MAN'S DESIRE
A COLLECTION OF LOVE LETTERS AND POEMS

What if a man loved a woman with such passion that even if she left him, he would still love her with his broken heart?

From the shadows of unrequited love, and an unlikely romance, rises the intense flame of a passionate profession of undying love, a romantic's musings.

Dear Love: Diary of a Man's Desire is a collection of love letters and poems written to inspire & stir the emotions of the soul.

"I fear that one day I'll lose a tear in the ocean -the day you find love with another- and like that tear, I'll never get to have you back."

THE LAST LOVE LETTER
A LABYRINTH OF LOVE LETTERS NOVEL

"What if you were the one?"

With those words, Arabella España is lured into a tale of forbidden love and forgotten secrets. In the wake of a murder in 1950's Puerto Rico, Nationalists revolt against American colonialism. An amnesiac recluse, married to a man she does not love, Arabella finds solace in the only remaining book in her possession. One of many banned by Puerto Rico's Gag Law.

The mysterious novel entitled THE LAST LOVE LETTER by one Aurelio Valentino leads Arabella on a journey with the main character in search of his lost love. But as she delves deeper into the story, she makes a shocking discovery: the novel contains clues to finding the legendary Labyrinth of Love Letters. A place of love and myth linked to the letter stolen from the corpse of the man who had recently been killed.

As each page draws Aurelio and Arabella closer together, she anxiously searches for the love letter that will reveal the identity of Aurelio's lost love. In her endeavor to find the Labyrinth, she discovers that the murder is a fate tied closely to her own destiny. Soon Arabella's literary journey reveals memories of her forgotten past and she discovers what happens when the main character of the story falls in love with the reader.

THE AFFAIR

Ever since his father left and younger brother died, Carlo Ruiz has immersed himself in his work living the kind of life other men aspire to achieve, but could only dream about: success, wealth, and attractive women willing to subjugate themselves to his sexual appetites. None of it, however, has filled the void left by the absence of his family.

When his estranged mother — on her deathbed — summons him to the childhood home he vowed he would never return, he is forced to confront the personal demons that have haunted him since his youth.

During his stay, he crosses paths with Annabelle Lagrandeur — his first love — who recently discovered her husband's affair. Their time together takes her mind off her heartbreak, and grants Carlo time to reassess his most recent, failed attempt at love with Julia Accardi.

Caught between his unresolved feelings about his mother, Annabelle's charm, and the intense attraction the forbidden courtship has awakened in him, Carlo must make a choice: honor the promise of hope he planted in Annabelle's heart, or embark on the path of love he first found with Julia.

But as his mother's condition worsens and his business dealings are affected by the distraction of his personal affairs, the return of Annabelle's husband forces her to reconsider love in lieu of divorce when she realizes her husband's involvement in undermining Carlo's career.

THE SECRET OF HEAVEN

When investment banker Lazzaro de Medici is found dead, Professor of Biblical Studies at University of Illinois at Chicago Aiden Leonardo is the prime suspect. In possession of an encrypted letter given to him by Lazzaro, Aiden utilizes his extensive knowledge of Scripture to piece together clues that lead to a Lost Bible dating back to the time of Christ.

Hidden within the text is an ancient truth about the most controversial message Jesus left to His disciples. But as Aiden embarks on his quest to unravel the mystery of redemption and faith, a secret organization known only as The Group hunts him down to destroy the Lost Bible and tie up loose ends.

With the help of his fiancé Dr. Miriam Levin—a cultural anthropologist and a professor of historical archaeology in her own right, their friend Nagi, a philologist, religious historian and an eccentric cryptographer, Aiden soon realizes the Lost Bible was written by the only disciple who walked with Jesus and had his gospel omitted from Scripture.

Things are further complicated when a mysterious stranger warns Aiden that possessing the secret of heaven could cost him his life. Pursued by the F.B.I. for the ancient Black market relic and the Chicago PD in connection to the murder of Lazzaro de Medici, Aiden races against the clock to prove his innocence and fulfill his mentor's dying wish.

Expose the secret of heaven...

SHADOWS OF TIME:
THE AMULET OF ALAMIN

The veil between the heavens and the underworld has fallen.

Mesopotamia is a region with kingdoms at war. The desires of gods and men sweep across the Land Between the Two Rivers so frequently that peace is merely a memory of a forgotten time. Demons and shape shifters lurk in the shadows, sorcerers and soothsayers warn of impending danger, and a demigod sits in the eye of the storm.

It has been millennia since the Tablet of Destinies fell from heaven. After the fall of angels and the emergence of the Watchers, the gods set out to destroy the Nephilim and retrieve the Tablet, but a piece of the stone chipped away before it was lost.

Fashioned from that piece of the Tablet, an amulet was gifted to Alamin in his infancy, but when he discovers the gods and angels want him dead he is forced to flee with it and only the Fallen Angel can protect him. Princess Safia is betrothed against her wishes and she flees with Alamin on a perilous quest across the Ancient World that blurs the boundaries of reality with the realm of myth until Alamin surrenders to the Fallen Angel.

Troubled by the prophecy, Inanna crosses oceans and deserts to find her son before she journeys into the underworld to retrieve his soul. The King of Kish names Sargon—the boy general—his Cup Bearer. Zagesi condemns his soul for immortality, but his deal with Mephitsophel is an ominous portent for the fall of kings. The fate of existence hangs perilously in the balance and the realm between the heavens and the underworld collapses into chaos.

PRAISE FOR FELIX ALEXANDER'S
THE ROMANTIC: A LOVE STORY

"An absolute gem! All the spiritual warmth of a Paulo Coelho and all the sweeping majesty of a Gabriel Garcia Marquez."
~Bruce Rodgers, A Beauty Beyond Reach

"Poetic and lyrical, which is both unique and lovely to read." ~Annabel Watkinson, The Year of Us

"Felix is a great story teller. The Romantic is beautiful, evocative, delicate and sparsely written, yet full of feelings and the yearnings of a man who plans to see the love of his life before he dies." ~Sebnem Sanders, The Child of Heaven

"Reminiscent of Garcia-Marquez and Isabella Allende with the magical surrealism." ~Lucy Sanctuary, Reconstruction

"Beautiful!" ~Ceri Beynon, The City of the Broken

"Poetic and melodic, allowing the words to flow across the page. This creates extraordinary images and induces powerful emotion right from the opening." – Lauren Grey, Threads of Time

"The writing is so simple, yet so rich. It's what defines his style." ~Sue Hart, Mystical Journeys: Memories

"The strangeness of the opening lulled me into a trance-like state, like watching a weird art film that you don't quite get, but you don't mind because it's taking you somewhere different." ~Jennie Ensor, Stone Circle

ABOUT THE AUTHOR

Felix Alexander (1976-Present) is a Mexican-born, American-raised novelist, and poet of Mexican and Puerto Rican descent.

Acclaimed by readers for his poetic prose, Felix writes in a myriad of genres with sequels in each forthcoming.

Being third-generation military, after a grandfather and uncle who served in the Korean War and Vietnam War, respectively, Alexander is proud of his service in the U.S. Army, and grateful for his experience.

After his honorable discharge from the U.S. Army, he embarked on the long and arduous journey of a writer. Having made a name for himself during his tenure, serving his country, he vowed to himself and his fellow soldiers that he would answer his true calling.

When not spending time with his children, a son and daughter, he volunteers to promote literacy among youth with Villament Charities and the VM Mag (vmmag.org). Then he journeys through the portals in his extensive, personal library. When he returns, he immerses himself in his writing, and pursues the scent of his muse.

Made in the USA
Middletown, DE
23 August 2021